His Scandalous Viscountess

LUSTFUL LORDS, BOOK THREE

SORCHA MOWBRAY

Published by Amour Press 2022, Second Edition

ISBN Print: 978-1-955615-16-7

ISBN ePub: 978-1-955615-04-4

Cover design from Fiona Jayde Media

Chapter Images from Illustration 13209099 / Victorian Vines © Freeskyblue | Dreamstime.com

This novel is entirely a work of fiction. The names, characters, incidents, and places portrayed in it are the work of the author's imagination and are not to be construed as real except where noted and authorized. Any resemblance to actual persons, living or dead, events or localities is entirely coincidental. Any trademarks, service marks, product names, or names featured are assumed to be the property of their respective owners, and are used only for reference. There is no implied endorsement if any of these terms are used.

Chapter One

February, 1862

"Gather round, ladies and gentlemen. Tonight, we have a most unique entertainment."

Madame de Pompadour's voice quivered with excitement as Grayson Powell, Viscount Wolfington, walked into The Market. He was late, but the unusual announcement grabbed his attention.

Despite the frustration that pulsed beneath his skin—not uncommon after a confrontation with his father—curiosity had Wolf veering away from the stairs and edging into the back of the half-filled salon.

The attractive madame continued her pitch, exciting the men, and a few of the women. "In a rare occurrence for an establishment such as The Market, tonight we shall have...an auction!"

Murmurs ran through the crowd. Moving closer, Wolf couldn't help but find himself intrigued. Auctions occurred all over London, but most of them were of a questionable nature, typically featuring a virgin prize. He found the practice disturbing for multiple reasons, primarily because if the woman being auctioned *was* in fact a virgin, it was doubtful she was participating of her own free will.

Most of the time, the woman in question was not a virgin at all, which meant the buyer was being duped. Toss in the notion that buying and selling human beings smacked of slavery—a practice he could not condone, and England had outlawed in 1833—and all around it made the auctions an objectionable practice.

All of which made The Market holding one entirely outside the norm.

"The woman up for bid this evening is *not* a virgin." Madame paused, drawing out the moment. "In fact, she is a woman of experience, who has been a wife to a peer of the realm and lover to a desert sheik. Tonight, she seeks an enthusiastic lover—or two—for a night of unrestrained passion."

Wolf spotted his friends, Flint, Linc, and Arthur, milling about toward the back of the crowd. He stepped up and greeted them with a quiet nod.

"Interested in the auction, Wolf?" Linc grinned, a clear indication that he was most certainly intrigued by what Madame might have on offer.

"Not particularly. I have my doubts about these spectacles. Honestly, I would have thought The Market above such practices," Wolf said and returned his focus to the front of the room as Madame raised her hands to quiet the murmuring crowd.

"Ladies and gentlemen, I give you Lady Eatifi 'Ahmar."

Wolf's heart suddenly leapt from his chest, only to lodge in his throat. A woman had appeared next to Madame de Pompadour, her hair a deep, fiery red that seemed to ignite in the gaslight. She might call herself Lady Eatifi 'Ahmar now, but Wolf would know Julia Fairchild—or more aptly, Lady Wallthorpe—even if she were covered in robes from head to toe. And covered, she was not.

Next to him, Linc murmured, "Bloody hell, that woman is brazen. Wanton *and* brazen."

And she was. Julia stood before a room full of mostly men wearing a puffy-sleeved chemise that ended far short of where such a garment should. Just below her breasts, the material banded and stopped, leaving her torso uncovered and exposed to all and sundry. The rest of the garment reappeared at her waist, creating a full-skirted look that swished about her ankles, offering suggestive peeks at her lower legs. Around her hips, she had wrapped a brightly colored scarf and a coin-draped belt, which tinkled as she paraded around the makeshift stage in her bare feet.

When she stopped at one end, she turned and flicked her hips, causing the coins to jangle and the material to swirl about her legs. Wolf's mouth felt as though he'd ridden across the dells, only to be rewarded with cotton in lieu of water.

Finally, Lady Eatifi 'Ahmar returned to Madame's side and finished her tempting display with a shimmy of her shoulders that set *everything* to jiggling in the most enticing manner.

And with that, the bidding commenced.

"One hundred pounds from Lord Glennmore," Madame announced.

It took mere moments for the bidding to reach a thousand pounds. With each subsequent raise in price, Wolf's fury swelled.

How could Julia do such a thing? What of the scandal this would mire her in?

Had she no care for her reputation?

He listened to the lascivious men call out ridiculous sums of money for the privilege of slipping between her long legs, all the while watching for the point when the bidding slowed.

Wolf leaned over to Linc and nudged his friend. "How much blunt do you have on you?"

"Not interested?" Linc jabbed an elbow in his ribs. "I've got seven thousand pounds. Hit a run of luck at the tables tonight."

"Can I borrow it? I'll write you a draft on my bank."

Linc grunted and handed him the wad of cash. "I don't want the money. Share her with me."

Wolf's gut churned. *Could he do such a thing?* There was a time when he had been deeply in love with Julia. But he'd long ago closed off that part of himself, and willed it to wither and die. His intervention tonight was nothing more than common decency, a way to ensure she didn't suffer at the hands of some pompous, overblown lord who wouldn't take no for an answer.

"I plan to release her from any obligation to us."

Linc sighed. "I rather figured. Go on, then."

As the offers reached the five-thousand-pound mark, Wolf made his move. "Ten thousand pounds. *Ready.*"

The room grew quiet, except for a few mutters of annoyance from the previous highest bidders. Madame looked fit to burst, she was so pleased. Julia appeared surprised, almost as if she couldn't fathom such a large bid.

Or perchance it was because it had come from him?

"Sold to Lord Wolfington!"

Madame's excitement bubbled over, even as Julia leaned over and whispered in her ear. The enigmatic owner of The Market merely held up her hands, as if to say it was already done, and Julia frowned in response.

A few men grumbled, but it was clear Madame had achieved whatever her goal was, and she would not continue the auction.

Wolf pressed through the now-dispersing crowd until he reached the raised platform. Stepping up, he towered over the petite Madame de Pompadour, as usual, but the statuesque Julia still all but looked him in the eye. Years ago, when they had been young, her height and her refusal to appear of lesser stature was one of the many things he'd loved about her.

Wolf bowed over the proprietress's hand. "Good evening, Madame." And then he turned toward Julia, who automatically lifted her hand. Good manners always won out—even hers, so it seemed. "Ju—Lady 'Ahmar, such a lovely surprise to see you again."

Madame waggled her eyebrows. "Ah-ha! Now I understand. You know each other already."

"Yes, we were acquainted many years ago," Wolf replied. "But alas, she left me behind and gallivanted off to tour the world with her new husband."

The bitterness over that turn of events was hard to squash down again, since it currently felt as though someone had ripped the bandage off the wound, causing it to seep anew.

"Well, that is what one does when they are deserted on a London street corner and left to be married off."

Julia's green eyes flashed sparks he'd never seen from her before. When he'd known her, she had been strong-willed, but soft-spoken

"And I suppose one also stays away from England for nearly ten years after his death?" Wolf let one of his brows rise, his anger refusing to be quelled.

"Such passion between you two, it gives me chills." Madame's eyes appeared glassy, and her cheeks flushed. "Alas, we must conduct business before pleasure."

"Of course, Madame." Wolf looked about and spotted his friend standing nearby. "Linc, can you take Lady...uh, 'Ahmar, upstairs? I'll be along in a moment."

"My pleasure." Linc held out his hand and assisted Julia down from the platform. Leaving Wolf to quickly follow Madame into her office to settle their business.

When he finally headed upstairs to find Julia and Linc, he tried to tamp down his more hedonistic instincts. He'd told Linc he planned to let her leave unmolested, which he fully intended to follow through with. But images of her standing on the dais with her torso exposed kept flashing through his brain. All that smooth, creamy flesh bared, and then the small peeks of her ankles as she'd stood barefoot.

Next his dastardly mind retrieved images that took him up her calves, over her thighs, and presented him with the notion of feasting on her sweet pussy. His cock flexed in his trousers, rising to the occasion, regardless of it being all in his mind.

Determined to be a gentleman, he willed his lusty thoughts to retreat and his shaft to soften as he steeled himself to see the woman he had once wanted more than his next breath.

Julia sat beside the man Grayson—no, Wolf—had called Linc.

Wolf? She tested the name out in her head, and thought about the man who had strode onto the makeshift stage to claim her. There had been a predatory quality to him that had not been part of the young man she had once known and loved. The moniker suited him far more than Grayson.

Linc eyed her speculatively as she sat across from him in the growing quiet. "Lady 'Ahmar, it appears you have already met Lord Wolfington."

Julia tried not to sigh as she thought of the idyllic young man she'd once known. "We were neighbors, many years ago."

The blond man seemed to ponder that notion for a moment. "You must have been quite young."

She couldn't repress the smile that came to her lips as she remembered their youthful romps across the countryside near Marribone Manor, and then later, when they'd met again after he finished school and she had been launched into Society. He had acted the earnest, doting suitor during her first seasons, and made her believe in fate and fairytales.

While not the daughter of a peer, Julia's father had been very successful in his business endeavors, which had afforded them the ability to move amongst the *ton*. Of course, as she later learned, that had all been done with a very *precise* purpose. Specifically, for her to marry into the peerage, thereby making her parents related to that upper echelon of Society versus the fringe dwellers they had been relegated to as nouveau riche upstarts.

"We were young and blissfully ignorant of gender and class expectations at the time." Not to mention naïve about how unreliable love could be. Following her heart again was *not* a mistake she would make anytime soon. Memories of her past tasted bitter on her tongue, even as she waited for the source of all her heartache to reappear.

The door suddenly swung open, and she peered at two men and the ladies that accompanied them. However, Wolf was not among the small party.

"Hello!" One of the men, whose short-cropped hair fell in a soft wave of golden brown across his forehead, lifted a glass of amber liquid in a salute. "Where has Wolf gotten off to? I figured you two would be relishing your spoils by now."

Julia's cheeks heated at the obvious reference to their having won her in the auction. She drew a deep breath. She had known what would occur. Had even arranged for the event downstairs, but that knowledge didn't mitigate the fact she had all but been forced into the event. Nevertheless, she had intended to make the most of an untenable situation.

Why shouldn't I have the opportunity to explore a new sexual experience while holding the jackals of Society at bay?

Linc glared at the friendly man. "Hold your tongue, Dunmere. Lady 'Ahmar is our guest."

Dunmere's eyebrows rose, but he ceased asking uncomfortable questions, which Julia was grateful for.

Then the door of the room swung open once again, and this time Wolf strode through, looking fiercely determined. About what, she had no idea. However, she hoped it had something to do with having hot, sweaty sex with her. And if that happened to include the boyishly handsome Linc, all the better. The man *owed* her a little pleasure after all the pain he'd caused.

"Julia—uh, Lady 'Ahmar."

Wolf seemed unsure for a moment as he pulled up short and stopped.

She rose to her feet. "Please, Julia is fine. My identity is no great secret, despite the nom de guerre."

"Very well." He nodded sharply. "I came to escort you home."

"Home?" She was confused by his words, as images of the two men wrapped around her still teased her brain.

"Yes. Shall we?" He indicted the door, which he held open.

She crossed her arms under her breasts. "I believe we have some business to attend to first."

Wolf's golden-brown brows drew down over his clear blue eyes. "We do not."

Her spine stiffened in indignation. "On the contrary, you won a night of sexual adventure with me, and I have no plans to renege on that promise."

Just then, a group of noisy men and women stampeded past the open door of their room.

She let one brow rise. "Perhaps we could have this argument with less of an audience than the one both currently in the room with us, and the one passing by?"

Wolf grunted and waited until the man called Dunmere and the rest of his party departed. Then he closed the door with an imperious thud. "I bid on you with the full intention of releasing you from your obligation."

Julia drew a deep breath. The man was going to be impossible about this. With no warning, she turned and wiggled onto Linc's lap as he sat in a wing chair. Completely caught off guard, he had no chance to block her maneuver.

"Unfortunately, I have no such good intention on my part," she continued. "You bid on me and won, and I fully intend to extract my night of pleasure from you *and* your friend. I believe you won together, did you not?"

Linc looked distinctly uncomfortable as she wrapped an arm around his shoulders and pressed her breasts closer to his chest and face. He coughed, then answered. "Yes, I provided some blunt."

"Excellent. It was my preference that *two* men would win the night with me. Wolf, will you be joining us, or am I to be disappointed by you once again?"

She winced inside at her reference to their past, but she needed to move him off the mark. She needed to know what having Wolf as a lover might be like, just this once. Because despite her lingering anger with him, her body still responded to his mere presence.

To her excitement, Linc appeared to be game for her plan. His cock grew harder by the moment beneath her thighs. She turned her face so she was close to his ear and could whisper to him. "What will it take to get him to join us, do you think?"

"This secret conversation alone might do the trick," Linc whispered back. "But if not, then maybe you could kiss me. That ought to get him moving...though hopefully not to punch me in the face."

She chuckled and then leaned in and captured Linc's lips with her own. Pushing past his teeth, she swept in to taste the whisky on his tongue and explore his mouth. He met her with a vigorous twist of tongues that reminded her of what it was to have a man touch her again. It had been nearly a year since she'd last felt the touch of a desirable man in his prime. And Linc fully met both requirements.

Though Wolf might easily obliterate the competition if he would remove himself from hovering near the door like a clucking hen.

And then his presence suddenly loomed over them, casting a shadow from the gas lamps along the wall. Rough hands, like those of a laborer, cupped her face and pulled her mouth from Linc's. As she turned to look up at Wolf, their gazes met. His expressive blue eyes had shifted to a more stormy gray, and he slammed his mouth down on hers in a move that was pure declaration.

Julia's senses reeled as Wolf kissed her. He tasted of man, and the faint hint of mint, which triggered the echo of a memory as their tongues tangled and twined. The wet slide was an erotic caress that had her nipples hardening and her pussy dampening in immediate response. Then one big hand slipped around to the back of her neck and hauled her up and off Linc's lap. Once she was standing, Wolf pressed closer to her, deepening the kiss, as though he wanted to crawl inside her.

Behind her, Linc rose and pressed closer to her back, sandwiching her between them. He unfastened her belt, letting it fall to the floor with a muffled tinkle. Then he loosened the scarf at her waist and slipped it free from her hips.

Wolf broke the kiss, finally retreating for a much-needed breath. Julia's head spun as she tried to take in the truth of the matter. The man she'd dreamed about for a decade was here in her arms, if only for one night.

How could she let the opportunity to bring every fantasy she'd had to life pass?

Wolf's tumultuous blue gaze bore into her, demanding the truth. "Do you truly want this, Jules?"

Chapter Two

Her heart hitched as he called her by the name he'd once used, the only person who'd *ever* called her that. "Yes." She hesitated, and then added, "Please."

He merely nodded once, and then behind her, Linc's lips settled at her nape, warm and sensuous as he trailed them down her back until he met the fastenings of the bodice she wore. He released the fabric, and then continued unobstructed, to pepper her spine with kisses and licks that set her skin to tingling.

At the same time, Wolf peeled the bodice from her front and drew it down her arms, his gaze still locked with hers as he exposed her breasts to the cool air. Her nipples tightened, and he slowly let his focus drift downward until his breath strangled in his throat as he took in her breasts. Gently, he reached up and cupped each globe, as though testing their weight, and then scraped the rough pad of his thumbs over each hardened tip.

She shivered in response, her thighs squeezing together while desire thrummed through her.

Linc quickly released her skirt, sending it to the floor with the rest of her clothing, only to emit a loud groan. "Christ, she's not wearing anything beneath that flimsy excuse for a skirt."

Wolf's gaze dipped lower and he growled in response. Her heart skipped a beat, even as her body sang with excitement. It had been hard for her to accept that as independent as she was, she relished relinquishing control in the bedroom. Her last lover, Tariq, had shown her just how much pleasure she could experience at the hands of the right man.

Masculine hands smoothed over her body, front and back. Two sets of hands, two muscular forms bracketing her, and two mouths tormenting her flesh. Linc reached around from behind and cupped her breasts. She spilled over his hands, but he didn't seem to mind as he massaged and kneaded her flesh. Then his lips traced along her shoulder and up her neck, leaving a damp trail in their wake.

Before her, Wolf lowered to his knees and peppered her stomach with kisses. She ached for him to touch her pussy, and was close to demanding he do so when his big warm hands wrapped around the insides of her thighs and nudged one of her legs up. Supported by Linc, she shifted her weight onto one leg and let Wolf place the other on his shoulder. Then he reached up to grip her bum as he drew his tongue along her slit.

She knew how wet she was, how turned on, but she was not prepared for the shock of pleasure that ripped along her limbs, making her tremble. Slowly, Wolf lapped at her lips, delving a little deeper with each stroke of his tongue, until he reached her clitoris. Her hips bucked into his mouth and she flung her head back against Linc's shoulder.

The heat and strength of Linc's body supporting hers as he pinched her nipples allowed her to relax and focus on the amazing things Wolf was doing with his tongue. The long, slow sweeps over her aching flesh sent a quiver through her body, and then he would shift direction and suddenly drive deep into her core. The slow swirls over her soaked opening pushed her to the edge of control. He worked her quim with an expertise that she both enjoyed and—if she were honest—hated. Clearly, he was a man who was familiar with a woman's body.

Unwanted jealousy invaded her thoughts, but the intense pleasure that began to coalesce into a tight ball low in her pelvis distracted her. Her supporting leg shook. The ball grew tighter. Wolf grew more assertive, latching onto her sensitive nub and sucked. *Hard.*

Bliss exploded through her, a rush of ecstasy that made her knees weak as her heart raced. She tingled from head to toe as Wolf continued to suck, while Linc rolled the hard tips of her breasts. For a moment, she swore she was floating, but she quickly realized that the two men were simply holding her up as she regained awareness.

Once she was steady on her feet again, she blinked until the fog cleared and Wolf's satisfied grin came into focus. "The pair of you are dangerous."

His smile grew wider. "We've only begun to show you pleasure, Jules. On the bed."

The command in his voice stirred her to movement, and she crawled onto the bed where she sprawled, waiting for his direction. Wolf and Linc stood a little apart, each taking in her display. If she were honest, she'd never felt more beautiful than in that moment.

"So many lush curves," Linc sighed. "I could spend a week exploring, and still be lost."

Wolf shot a glance at his friend that told Julia he wasn't so enthused about that idea. But in lieu of making a comment, he simply moved toward the bed. Standing over her, he reached out and stroked his fingertips down her cheek, the long column of her throat, and then along her breastbone and stomach, leaving a trail of gooseflesh in his wake. Curious as to what he might do next, she watched the play of muscles under his skin in the low light.

A movement on her other side drew her attention as Linc crawled onto the bed beside her and knelt there, apparently waiting for some sort of signal. She assumed he was looking to Wolf for guidance. The silence stretched out, and it dawned on her that the three of them were the only occupants in the room. She wondered when exactly the others had slipped away, because she honestly couldn't remember. It scared her that she had been so lost in Wolf and Linc's caresses that she'd forgotten they had not been completely alone—at least at the start.

Then the men before her leaned over and each sucked a nipple into their mouths, and all her thoughts flitted away. Her awareness pinpointed down to where their lips were fused to her skin, and the pull from her tips all the way to her toes, which had begun to curl. Wolf released the nipple he'd captured and looked at her as Linc continued to suck on her other breast. He worried one tip with his teeth as he tweaked the other with his fingertips, making it difficult for her to focus on what Wolf was saying.

He stroked her hair with a reverent touch. "...so rich and vibrant, like a living flame." Then he lifted some of her tresses and rubbed them between his fingers. "You've lived a much different life since I saw you last, Jules, but I need to understand your boundaries for tonight. Is there anything you will not allow? Have you ever had two lovers at once? Have you taken a man in your arse while another filled your quim? Is it something you would enjoy?"

The raspy quality of his voice sent shivers down her spine that melded with the lust Linc continued to stir in her with his mouth. Desire winged through her sharply, for all that the two men offered, and possibly something they didn't. Even as Wolf waited for her response, Linc lifted his head and peered at her in interest.

She hesitated, not having expected to discuss things so plainly. She licked her lips and tried to tamp down the heat simmering in her cheeks. "There are no barriers to our pleasure tonight. While I have only ever had one man at a time as a lover, I have heard of a woman taking two at a time, and I am curious about this experience."

Wolf nodded, but then hesitated, his face scrunching as though it disturbed him to ask such personal questions. "And have you ever had a man"—the hand stroking her hair lifted and clenched into a fist before dropping to his side—"take your arse?"

A confusing rush of emotions swept through her. On the one hand, she felt no shame for her sexual explorations, but at the same time, she hated that her past might distress Wolf. Pushing aside her jumbled feelings, she simply replied, "I have."

Linc returned to sucking her nipples at her answer, swirling his tongue over each tip in turn. Then he slowly dropped kisses and nibbles down her softly rounded stomach before reaching her mound. While he shifted between her knees, spreading her legs wide, Wolf hovered over her, stroking his cock as he watched her reaction to Linc's efforts. When the blond man lowered his face to her quim and slid his tongue along her sensitive flesh, she gasped.

A tremor rolled through her body as Linc pushed two fingers into her pussy while he dragged his tongue roughly over her clit. She dug her hands into the covers of the bed and attempted to ground herself, despite the onslaught of pleasure. Then Wolf moved closer to her head. Gently, he lifted it up as he tucked a pillow underneath it, elevating her face until she was in proximity to his erection. Long and hard, his shaft stretched out toward her, and she suddenly wanted to swallow him whole, to gift him with the same pleasure he and Linc were bestowing on her.

Releasing her hold on the covers, she reached up to wrap her fingers around his cock. Her hands were not small, by any measure, and still she could not fully join her fingers.

"That's it, Jules. Suck my cock."

His dirty words spiked through her pleasurable haze to stoke her desire to taste him.

Many nights she had lain in bed alone and wondered what kind of lover Wolf would be. She had always thought he would be a gentle, considerate lover. Certainly, the young man she'd once known would have been. But this man? This bigger, darker version of the young man she'd known was everything she had come to appreciate in a bedmate.

Despite his dark golden hair, nearly brown in places, and the bright blue eyes that were at once familiar and not, he carried shadows within that teased and taunted her mind. She wanted to push at the darkness in him, and see how different the man was from the boy. She liked that he was commanding, vocal in his desires, unashamed by his needs, and still a generous lover.

Hungry to taste him, and to discover what made him cry out, she lapped at the tip of his cock. The moisture that had beaded there was slightly sweet, but still carried the essence of man that she had come to appreciate. Willing to test his resolve, she swirled her tongue around the tip, teasing the crown. As he remained unmoving, she pushed him further. Taking only a few inches into her mouth, she then retreated back to the tip. She repeated the motion, swirling over the head and then sinking down a little more each time.

Finally, he cursed and fisted his hand in her hair. "Take it all, Jules. Cease teasing me."

And then he pushed into her mouth until he struck the back of her throat. He retreated and pushed forward again, but changed his angle a bit so he could sink further into her. Her hands fell away from his shaft and she let him take over, relishing the way he pumped in and out of her mouth as Linc was pushing her higher and higher toward another orgasm.

The two men were working her body, owning it together in a way she had never experienced before. And it was everything she had imagined.

As need crested into climax, she sucked harder on Wolf's cock, while Linc pumped his fingers in and out of her pussy and lapped at her juices. And then Wolf cried out and pushed deep into her throat, spilling his seed. She worked to suck all she could from him until he drew back, dragging the last few drops across her tongue.

Linc had gentled his touch between her thighs, now slowly lapping at her, causing shiver after shiver to cascade through her body.

Wolf lowered himself to the bed, sitting just above her head as Linc eased back from her cunny. The three of them sat there catching their breaths as silence stretched out.

She stretched. "Mmmm. I could sleep for a week."

Wolf chuckled. "Not quite yet, Jules."

Slumber reached out for her, trying to drag her under, but she fought to lift her lids, to see if he was serious. Linc had moved up beside her at some point, his stiff shaft gripped in his hand. Working his hand up and down his length, she realized he had coated it with something. Before she could ponder his intentions, he slung a leg over her torso and laid his cock between her breasts.

"Any objections if I fuck your lovely titties?"

"None at all."

She grinned. It had been a favorite of Tariq's, and she knew a few tricks that might surprise even these two.

As Linc slid his cock between her breasts, his hands pushing them together to create a tunnel, she tipped her head forward and took the tip of him in her mouth each time he pushed forward. The man groaned and thrust more vigorously. Then she turned away for a moment and managed to wet her finger. When she returned to taking him in her mouth, she also reached behind him and found the tight pucker of his anus. As he pumped his cock in her cleavage, she wiggled the tip of her finger inside him. He lost his rhythm for a moment, and hesitated.

"Don't stop, Linc." She wiggled her finger a bit deeper. "I promise, you'll like this."

He continued fucking her tits as she worked her finger deeper into his passage. When she found the spot she was looking for, she stroked over it.

"Bloody hell!" Linc's hips jerked wildly. "Oh, God!"

With a satisfied smile, she focused on stroking over the spot Tariq had taught her would give a man the most explosive orgasm of his life. Linc's face pinched as he continued to shuttle between her breasts. All the while, she stroked the spot she'd accessed, pushing him hard.

Wolf remained sitting above her, watching the two of them. Then he leaned down to whisper in her ear. "Make him come, Jules. I've never seen him so excited. You did this to him. To me, as well. I'm getting hard again just watching you."

She moaned as Linc pushed into her mouth again and then tensed up.

"I'm going to come! Fuck!"

He pulled back from her mouth and stroked his cock as he came, letting his seed land on her breasts. All the while, she continued to work her finger in his arse, and relished watching him fall apart.

The lassitude she'd felt previously had evaporated with the renewed sexual energy Linc gave off. Julia was now wide awake and ready for more of the two men.

Linc moved over and flopped next to her and Wolf, his breathing labored as he lay there recovering. "Christ, woman, where did you learn to do that?"

Wolf handed her a damp rag to clean up with, and then she raised up on one elbow to look at Linc. His blond hair was mussed, a few strands sticking to his sweat-dampened forehead.

"In the Far East, there are texts that provide guidance for maximizing both a man's and a woman's pleasure. I have read some of them, and other things I have learned from lovers I have taken."

Linc grinned. "Oh, it's not a new sensation to me, and I'm not one to quibble about who or what is shoved where when it comes to sex, but it was a wholly unexpected experience when bedding a lady."

Julia couldn't help but laugh. "I can't imagine too many English ladies have discovered the technique. But the few times I've allowed a lover to take me there have proven to be extremely pleasurable in ways I had never expected." She laid back down, letting her hands stroke over her stomach and along her sides. "If you can appreciate the comingling of pain and pleasure, the experience is delicious. Hence, my curiosity about two lovers at one time."

Wolf growled then, drawing her attention. "And tonight, you shall satisfy your curiosity. On your hands and knees, Jules."

Her heart pounded in her chest as she rolled over and lifted up into the requested position. Nervous fluttering in her stomach stirred to life as she waited excitedly to see what would come next.

Wolf rose from the bed, opened a drawer in the nightstand, and then crawled back on the mattress behind her. Linc remained where he was, watching and waiting for further direction.

Behind her, Wolf dragged a finger through her soaked folds. "You are a wanton woman, Jules."

"And would you have me any other way?" She let one brow lift as she looked back at him over her shoulder.

He offered her a wicked, wicked grin. "Not in the least."

And then he used his moisture-coated finger to press against her tight rosette. As he applied pressure, she pushed out against the intrusion, which opened her to him. He groaned as he slipped in a short distance and then withdrew. "So tight."

Linc's shaft was already recovering as he watched Wolf prepare her arse.

Something thick and moist was dropped between her cheeks.

"A salve to ease my way," Wolf said, and pushed two fingers inside her, stretching her. "Suck his cock, Jules. Get him ready to fuck you."

Linc rose to his knees and pressed his semi-erect shaft toward her. She easily took him in her mouth, letting him sink deep into her throat until his balls pressed against her chin. Behind her, Wolf had inserted more fingers inside her, spreading her wide to open her up for his cock.

She moaned around Linc's shaft, appreciating the growing fullness inside her body, the sense of being filled and used by both men.

Linc's cock had quickly become hard again, ready for whatever they wished to do. He withdrew and looked back at Wolf. "I'm ready, if you are."

Wolf must have nodded, because Linc sat down, his back pressed against the headboard of the bed as he donned a French Letter. Then he held out his hand. "Come here, Julia."

She crawled over to him.

"That's it. Now come up here and slide down on my cock."

He helped her rise up and position herself over his erection.

Wolf came up behind her, spreading her cheeks as she slid down on Linc's cock. "Hold still, Jules."

His raspy command in her ear made her nipples pebble again as her channel tightened on Linc's shaft.

And then Wolf was pushing against her sphincter, stretching and invading her already-filled body. She moaned and squirmed on Linc's rod.

He closed his eyes and sucked in a breath through his nose. "Double damn."

Wolf pushed into her arse then, an inexorable motion that drove any thought from her head. All she could do was *feel*. Feel him, feel Linc, and feel stuffed full of cock in the most delicious way.

Linc opened his eyes as Wolf seated inside her. Her gaze locked with his as she continued to wiggle, letting her body adjust.

Wolf leaned in close to her. "Now ride our cocks, Jules."

Her gaze flared wide in surprise, locking with Linc. "I can't. I can't move."

"Yes, you can, and we'll help you," Linc replied, placing his hands on her hips. "Raise up, sweetheart."

And she did, rising up a bit. Strong hands lifted her higher, and then let her slide back down. As their cocks slid out and then back into her, she gasped. With each rise and fall they established a rhythm, slowly increasing their pace until the three of them worked together. Wolf and Linc pumped into her arse and quim, while she lifted up and sank back down.

And then Linc leaned forward and sucked one pebbled nipple into his mouth, and she exploded.

Her orgasm slammed into her like one of those new steam locomotives. She screamed out her pleasure, a litany of Wolf's and Linc's names, as her body gripped and released them over and over. Had they not been holding her up, she was sure she would have melted into the mattress from pure bliss.

The two men continued pumping into her, working their cocks in a delicious rhythm that pushed her towards yet another climax. This time, the two of them were with her as they all crested the peak. The three of them came together, their shouts of pleasure mingled in a melody of satisfaction. Sated and beyond exhausted, she let sleep claim her before she'd even touched the mattress.

Chapter Three

Wolf sat alone, watching Julia sleep. Linc had slipped away after they'd laid her down. Wolf had remained to see that she was cared for and taken home safely. He also wanted a private word with her. His head spun with questions. Too many questions.

Why had she auctioned herself off? Why risk such a scandal for a pleasure that could have been arranged in a much more discreet fashion? What had she been doing since her husband died?

His stomach cramped as yet another thought occurred to him, even as he discarded it. Of course she hadn't remarried. She wasn't the kind of woman who would be at The Market if she had.

He cursed himself for a fool for getting involved with her once more, and then stood. Restlessness drove him to move around the room. Certainly, he had failed her long ago. *But hadn't she failed him as well?* Never had she sought him out or tried to discover what had happened that night. Never had she fought for what he'd believed they'd shared. His gut twisted as he unnecessarily straightened a picture on the wall.

It occurred to him that there was every possibility he had been a fool to believe she'd actually loved him once. His father had always been cold and remote, and had never showed him the least bit of affection—which of course made sense, knowing what he did about his own parentage.

And his mother? Well, she could barely look at him, let alone show love or affection.

Moving on from the picture, he headed toward the ever-present crystal decanters and glassware. His nerves were strung tight. *Too* tight. He needed a drink, and it didn't matter what time of the morning it was, though he was sure it was still dark out.

And in the ten years since he'd walked away from her? He'd avoided debutantes and other marriage-seeking women. His was a life spent sans female companionship, but for his time spent at The Market. He poured a finger of whisky and slugged it in a single swallow. The alcohol burned through his gut, replacing the tightness with a pleasurable warmth that eased his tension, if only for the next little while.

Without question, his bachelorhood was a state of his own design, but even considering that circumstance, no woman ever seemed totally enamored of him. Not one looked at him with softness or desire beyond the physical. It seemed each of his friends, however, had found themselves the object of a female's fancy at one time or another, but never him.

Was he so unworthy?

Julia moved on the bed then, rolling and shifting until the covers slipped down, exposing her breasts. For the hundredth time, he crossed to her and pulled the covers back up to shield her modesty, and then sat back down. Not that she'd been concerned about modesty when she'd paraded before a room full of tongue-wagging lords, or later, when she'd been pressed between him and Linc, with their cocks buried deep inside her body.

She moaned in her sleep, mumbling something.

Wolf stilled.

Then she rolled again, tangling the covers around her legs. She whimpered in her sleep and cried out. "No! Please, don't..."

Wolf was about to cross the room and wake her from whatever nightmare had her in its grip, but she sat up with a gasp. Wide green eyes that a man could get lost in darted about the room. Fear had her face pinched up as she gripped the sheet to her chest.

He sat forward from the shadows so she could see his face. "It's just me."

Her shoulders sagged with what he assumed was relief.

"I thought it was another dream." Her bright green gaze bored into him with surprise and a touch of fear that dissipated the comforting heat in his belly. "But you're truly here."

She dreamed of me?

He rose from his chair again. "I am."

He watched her closely and tried to ignore the knots that had reshaped in his gut.

What would she do next? Would she be embarrassed as her memory returned? Would she claim he'd ruined her? Or perhaps she would merely slink away in embarrassment? Many women did the latter, preferring to pretend that nothing had occurred.

"And Linc?"

She looked around the room for his friend and fellow Lustful Lord.

He waved toward the door. "He left a few hours ago. Was it a dream or a nightmare?"

She sat there a moment, letting her eyes close as she appeared to gather herself. The silence stretched out for four or five heartbeats as he stood there, and then one more before she opened her eyes again. She seemed unsure for a moment, but then she rose from the bed and let the sheet fall from her nudity.

Would she answer him?

"I see. Well, thank you both for a perfectly wonderful evening."

It seemed she was choosing to ignore his question.

Wolf watched in shock as she strode about the room, calmly collecting her clothes. She tugged on her skirt and tied the ribbons. Then she pulled on her bodice, but was unable to refasten it herself. After a brief struggle, she gave up and searched for the next piece of her clothing.

He stood there stunned, ever the unsure one—though he was certain he hid it well most of the time. "That's it? A simple thank you, without so much as a by-your-leave?"

She stopped tying her scarf around her hips and stared at him. "What more did you want?"

Confusion made his head hurt, or conceivably it was the multiple drinks he'd consumed as she slept. "An explanation?"

Her green eyes narrowed. "What kind of explanation?"

Frustration, doubt, and possibly some long-misplaced anger finally broke free in him. "What was this? Why did you auction yourself off tonight? Why put on such a scandalous display?"

Where have you been for the last ten years?

He just managed to hold the last question back.

"This was exactly what it was billed as: one night with me. No more, no less. As for the rest, I do not owe you the least explanation."

She resumed tying her scarf and all but dismissed him.

He stalked across the room, his roiling emotions propelling him toward her. "Jules, I am not just some random lord who won you in an auction. I was your fiancé, your friend, and once upon a time, the man who loved you."

Her emerald eyes grew hard as the jewels they reminded him of. "You were the man who had sworn to protect me, who swore that he loved me, and who ultimately deserted me when I needed you most. You are the man who taught me that love does not, in fact, conquer all. I assure you, I owe you *nothing*, my lord."

Her words were like a spear straight through his heart. The truth often cut deeply, and there was no doubt in his mind she spoke the truth. He drew a deep breath through his nose, letting his eyes close as he steeled himself against the pain. "You're right, of course. But please, let me help you now. Give me a chance to make reparations for our past. I can't help but believe you are in some kind of trouble."

Pain softened the hardness of her gaze, but she remained stubbornly silent. With a shake of her head, she donned her slippers and grabbed her belt from the floor. "I'm sorry, Lord Wolfington. I'm afraid there is nothing more you can do. There is nothing I *need* from you, not even a carriage ride home. Your bidding on me, and following through on the inherent promise of winning me, shall have to suffice."

Helpless to make her do as he wished, he watched as she squared her shoulders and walked to the door of the room. She stopped and turned to look at him. "Goodbye, my lord."

And then she slipped from the room, leaving him utterly alone and lost. His gut screamed that she needed help. That she needed him. But the headstrong woman refused to ask for his help. Of course, considering his history of failing her, he could understand her reluctance. Possibly even accept it, if only he hadn't touched her again. Felt her quiver in pleasure.

If he had never watched her come apart in his arms, then maybe he could have walked away and taken her at her word.

But now? After their night together, even with Linc sharing the experience?

Never.

He would *never* abandon her again, *never* let his own shame be more important than the woman he loved. And the hard, ugly truth was that he had loved Julia Fairchild. For the last ten years, he had continued to love Lady Wallthorpe. And if she had married again, unbeknownst to him, he would continue to love her.

All of which meant he could not stay out of whatever trouble she was dealing with now. He would simply have to take action and dig until he uncovered the darkness that troubled her. Jules deserved a knight in shining armor, and this time, he was determined to be it.

Wolf wearily strode from The Market and headed home, since there was little he could do for her at the moment. However, one thing he *would* do was closely shadow Jules in Society. He was certain something would eventually point him in the right direction. All he needed was a little patience.

Chapter Four

Julia and her sister, Rosalind, stood in the home of Lady Swinton, tucked into a corner of the main salon. Julia wanted to curse as the front door opened again, admitting yet another guest. By her count, her mother's blithe assurance that Lady Swinton was hosting a small, intimate gathering now stood at a total of twenty-five guests.

That did not include herself, Rosalind, or her parents. She sighed.

Ros' brow creased in concern. "Julia? Are you feeling well?"

Julia tried to muster a smile for her sister, but as she stared at the room full of people, she couldn't help but wonder how many of the men might have been in attendance at her auction at The Market. It was, of course, too late to undo what had been done, but she had planned to more or less retire from Society after her little display. After all, she'd needed a scandal to protect herself, but she hadn't actually *wanted* one.

She hadn't wanted to be the subject of wagging tongues throughout London's salons and ballrooms. But she hadn't had another choice. Had she?

Wolf's handsome face came to mind then, his chiseled features which to some would look austere, even forbidding. But to her merely appeared finely honed, if not resolute. He was, by her account, a beautiful man.

"Oh, look!" Ros patted her arm and smiled. "A friendly face I have not seen in ages."

It was as though Julia had conjured the man. The crowd had parted to reveal Wolf in all his evening finery. Her well-intentioned sister immediately lifted her hand and waved from across the room to gain his attention.

Julia's corset—despite being loosely laced, as a private rebellion against Society's strictures—suddenly squeezed like a vise around her ribs. Her breathing felt restricted as sweat trickled down her spine. Somehow, she had been less disturbed facing him in her flimsy outfit of a few nights ago than she was in full London ladies' armor. Her stomach flipped as he presented a rare smile to Ros and strode across the room.

"Mrs. Smith!" he exclaimed, as he took her sister's hand and gallantly bent over to kiss the gloved appendage.

Ros grinned at their one-time playmate. "Lord Wolfington, I wasn't sure you would remember me. It has been many years since last we spoke."

His face took on a pained expression. "You wound me, madam. How could I ever forget such adventures as we three had?" He then turned to Julia, and with an aplomb she could not credit, greeted her as though she had not romped in the bed with him and one of his friends only a few nights earlier. "Lady Wallthorpe, it is a pleasure to see you again as well."

Unable to be rude in such a public place, she allowed him to take her hand. "And you, my lord."

"You must be the loveliest ladies in attendance this evening."

Wolf's smile had taken on a predatory quality that made Julia think of the animal for which he was named.

Ros smiled at him before she shot a small glare at Julia. "Thank you, my lord."

Julia refused to encourage the man, but her sister could do as she liked—mostly because Ros was safe as cotton-packed china when it came to Wolf. He'd always seen her as a friend, and even a little sister. As for Julia, she had crossed into much murkier territory: that of friend, former fiancée, and now lover.

Ros being Ros, she launched into polite conversation with all of the enthusiasm that should have been beaten out of her first by life as a soldier's wife, and now that of a widow. However, her sunny disposition and insatiable curiosity seemed to overcome any such trials and tribulations thrown her way. "I'm afraid we missed the sporting season, having only just returned from being abroad. How was the grouse hunting this year?"

"It was rather tepid, I'd say. Perchance I found it so because the company with which I fell in with was also tepid? I suspect had I had you two for company, traipsing across the fields might have been far more stimulating."

Wolf winked at Ros.

"Do behave, my lord. What would people think should they hear you say such things?" Ros chastised him, laughing all the while.

Julia chose to remain aloof in hopes her erstwhile lover would depart their company. However, she soon realized she had a much bigger issue when she spotted Lord Wallthorpe—her stepson, not her dead husband—waltzing through Lady Swinton's dinner party as though he were the catch of the season. Cringing deeper into the corner in hopes she might remain unseen, she held her breath and waited for him to pass their little trio.

Unfortunately, her attempt to go unnoticed by one man merely drew the attention of the other.

Wolf eyed her quietly, and then glanced about the room. "Is there someone you wish to avoid besides me, Lady Wallthorpe?"

His question drew her sister's inquisitive gaze her way, and had her cursing him under her breath. "Of course not. Don't be ridiculous."

Wolf let one brow lift, silently calling her out for her blatant lie.

She sighed and pressed her fingers to her temple. "I believe I need some air. Please excuse me."

And with that, she slipped away and walked swiftly around the crowd until she made her way to the Swintons' patio and garden. It was a lovely spot, if a trifle cold, with all the snow on the ground. But she needed a moment away from the unexpected crowd, and particularly the men who could not restrain their unwanted attentions.

What with the cold, she could not stand outside all night, so eventually she returned to the main hall of the house, just off the salon. She was about to go in search of her sister when a masculine voice she had hoped to avoid altogether stopped her progress.

"If it isn't my dear sweet stepmother."

She repressed the groan that crept up her throat and turned to face him. "Lord Wallthorpe, I did not realize you were acquainted with the Swintons."

He offered his most charming smile. However, the lack of sincerity was as obvious as his flat brown gaze. She had seen many a man with light brown hair and dark brown eyes who were quite handsome. The problem with her stepson was that he was fouled on the inside, and that ugliness shone through to anyone who bothered to look properly.

"I have come to know Lord Swinton quite well since I took my father's seat in parliament. Had you returned to the bosom of your family after his death, you might be more aware of who I am acquainted with." He sighed softly. "As I told you when we last spoke upon your return, your family has missed you these many years. You are always welcome at Wallthorpe House."

Julia's spine stiffened at the reminder of their previous conversation. "And as I told you, while I appreciate the offer, I have lived as I please these many years. I find keeping my own household suits me."

He closed the short distance between them, leaning in close to her as he sneered. "And am I to assume auctioning off your body for the use of the highest bidder is what pleases you? Possibly I was wrong in offering you my affection when last we spoke. It seems my wallet would have been more welcome."

She inhaled sharply, though clearly, her plan was working. "How I choose to conduct my affairs is none of your concern. If you will excuse me."

She turned to go, but found his hand on her forearm, gripping it tightly. When she made to jerk free, he tightened his hold to the point she was sure he would leave bruises. Then he dragged her into a nearby study off the main hall and pressed her against a wall.

"It is my concern, madam, when your actions bring scandal upon my family. I do not understand why you have rebuffed my generous offer to make you my marchioness. I am at least of your generation, unlike my father, who you happily married when he was forty years your senior."

He paused and drew in a sharp breath through his nose, as though he were trying to calm himself, or maybe he was smelling her perfume. Neither possibility was comforting.

"You *will* marry me, Julia. Simply allow me to offer the protection of my name, and all this nonsense about you auctioning yourself off will go away."

Fear and anger warred within her breast as she considered how she might best extricate herself from such an untenable situation. He still held her arm in his grip, and his fetid breath fanned over her face. Anger overrode any sensible plan she might have conceived of. "Release me at once, you overbearing cad. I have no need of you, your wallet, or your protection. Now unhand me."

"Why, you—"

And then he was jerked away from her, though he still gripped her arm.

"I believe the lady has made her feelings quite clear, Lord Wallthorpe."

Wolf's glowering countenance loomed over her stepson, an ice-cold fury blazing from his deep blue eyes. Wallthorpe's brown eyes bulged from his head as he stared at her rescuer. And while Wolf was the last person she would have wished to overhear her exchange with her stepson, she could not deny the relief she felt at having him step in.

Taking the opportunity to extricate herself from Wallthorpe's hold, and possibly evade any of Wolf's questions, she jerked her arm free and tried to move toward the door of the study. But before she could make good on her escape, Wolf shoved the other man through the doorway and closed it unceremoniously in his face. All of which freed her from Wallthorpe and trapped her in the room alone with *him*.

Wolf eyed Jules as she eased across the space, putting distance between them. He stifled a sigh of frustration. The woman clearly needed assistance with her problem. However, she still seemed reluctant to seek such help from him.

Considering how he'd walked away the last time she'd needed him, he supposed he could understand her reluctance. But this time would be different. This time, he would ensure she *was* protected.

Determination flooded him with a sense of calm as he closed the gap she had opened between them. Her grass-green eyes widened as she noted his movement toward her. He stopped short of invading her immediate space, but close enough he could touch her if he reached out. "Are you well?"

She blinked a few times. "Am I well?"

"Did that bastard injure you?"

Wolf felt like the words were scraped from his throat. Now that he was closer he could see her pulse fluttering in the long column of her throat, and a restlessness emanated from her that reminded him of a skittish colt.

She drew a deep breath. "Of course not. My stepson and I merely had a difference of opinion."

He was stupefied. "You consider that exchange a mere difference of opinion?"

She closed her eyes for a moment, leaving him a few ticks of time to appreciate her beauty. The deep red hair he'd so enjoyed touching the other night was neatly tied back, except for one lone curl that dangled tauntingly over her shoulder. Her skin was no longer the creamy white he remembered from years earlier. Now she had turned a soft, golden tan from her years in the sun, and he was far too aware of just how many of her lovely curves had been kissed in such a fashion. Tonight her dark green velvet gown lovingly hugged each of those lush curves, drawing a man's eye, whether he willed it or not.

Opening her eyes, she seemed to have pulled herself together. "Indeed, we had a difference of opinion about a number of things. However, he has—as have many of my old acquaintances—discovered I am my own woman. I no longer allow others to form my opinions. I certainly will not be directed, told, ordered, or otherwise bullied into doing something I have no desire to do."

The mutinous flash in her eyes should not have turned him on, but oh, how it did. He wanted to hold that defiance in his arms and tame it. To bend her will to his in the most intensely pleasurable ways. His cock stirred, rising to such libidinous thoughts. "You may have every intention of not marrying him, of not capitulating, but men like him have ways of achieving their goals." He shoved his fingers through his hair, disrupting the previous orderliness wrought by his valet. "Christ, woman. You should know this. You were married to his father."

"Be that as it may, I am not the same girl who was cowed by—"

Suddenly she gasped and spun about, giving him her back.

Was she crying? No, he heard no telltale sniffle, though her shoulders sat stiffly.

Wolf cursed again. "Jules, you are still a woman subject to the whims of men. If you do not see that, then you are indubitably courting trouble."

She looked back at him, her gaze narrowed. "I am well aware of the limitations placed on me by Society, solely because I was born a woman." She turned to face him, her cheeks flushed with anger now. "I have no need of you to remind me of the disadvantages my sex bears on a daily basis. But as a widow, I do have some protections under the law. Beyond that, I have other strategies in play to ensure I remain unencumbered by Wallthorpe, or any man, for that matter."

Wolf trembled with the need to take her in his arms and whisk her away. To protect her as he had not done previously. Stymied by her staunch independence and determination to manage the situation herself, the need that had been pounding his self-control since he'd spotted her from across the Swintons' salon finally broke his tight grip.

He reached out and hauled her into his arms. Her sweet mouth opened in surprise as he swooped in and captured her lips with his. Their tongues twined and twirled around each other. Her breasts pressed against his chest as he held her tight and tried to memorize every detail of how she tasted and smelled. He feared he might have to survive on this flimsy memory for years to come. She was truly a stubborn woman.

Drawing back, breath heaving, he allowed his protective instinct to take control. "Jules, marry me. Marry me, and let me protect you."

All the desire in her gaze dissipated as pain filled her shimmering eyes, and he realized the glistening was a result of tears forming. But then she blinked them away with a self-control he could only envy in this tense moment. His heart pounded in his chest, yet he could have sworn it had migrated up into his throat as he waited for her answer.

Her face stilled, all emotion retreating behind a calm mask. "I appreciate the gesture. But, as I said, I have a strategy in place to protect myself from Wallthorpe. I shall not be forced to marry anyone again, not by my parents, and not by circumstances. It wouldn't be fair to myself, and it certainly wouldn't be fair to a man such as yourself."

Wolf stared at her, the sensation of his heart shattering an all too familiar one when it came to Julia. His knees buckled, and it was sheer force of will that held him up as she turned to leave. Once the door closed on her retreat, he stood there, regrouping. Slowly collecting the shattered pieces of himself, he decided he would deal with reassembling them as soon as he had time to lick his wounds in private.

Being no eternal optimist, he knew this had been his last chance to grasp happiness, and now it was gone. So he retreated back behind his own protective shields and reminded himself it was probably for the best. He had too much of his mother in him, with her wandering affections and illicit liaisons. He'd probably have made a terrible husband.

Taking a deep breath, he tugged on his waistcoat, straightened his jacket, and smoothed his hair before he stepped out of the Swintons' salon, intent on departing the fete unnoticed. Unfortunately for him, the dinner chimes rang just then, and with Lady Swinton marshalling her guests, there was no escape. He'd suffered through similar events before, and tonight wouldn't be any different.

What did it matter that he'd just had his heart smashed into a million pieces once again?

Chapter Five

March, 1862

Julia warily watched her sister as she poured tea. It wasn't that they didn't regularly take tea together. In fact, they did it almost every day. But it was more the determined glint in her sister's blue-green gaze as she gripped the teapot that concerned her.

Ros handed her a cup, and then poured her own. "Did you notice that Henrietta Wallace has a new suitor?"

She offered her sister a mischievous grin as she poured cream in her tea.

Julia took a bracing sip of her own black tea, and then shook her head. "I had not noticed, but then, why would I?"

"Because that parade of men across the street has finally ceased." Ros took a sip of her own libation. "For the last week, I have only seen one man coming and going, and he's quite a handsome one, too. Mark my words: We will see a posting of the banns soon."

Julia took another sip and considered the assortment of finger sandwiches their cook had prepared. "Well, then, I suppose we shall have to offer her our felicitations."

Ros huffed. "But that is just it, Julia. We cannot do so just yet, not until the banns. You, my dear sister, are not paying attention at all. In fact, you have been utterly distracted since the night of the Swinton dinner party."

Julia's brows lifted, even as worry insinuated itself into her consciousness. She knew her sister had taken note of her agitation, and it would seem her reprieve from discussing it was finally up. "It is possible I have been a touch preoccupied."

"A touch?" Ros snorted. "You couldn't have been more distracted had a naked man paraded through our parlor.

Now tell me, what is it that has you so out of sorts?" She hesitated for a moment, and then quickly set her tea on the side table. "My goodness. Is it seeing Viscount Wolfington again? Do you still harbor some tender regard for him?"

Julia suppressed the sigh of resignation that welled up from within. Though many mistook her sister for being very sweet, but not that bright, they could not have been more mistaken. Rosalind was as smart as she was sweet, and too perceptive, by half. Though she had never been a very good liar.

However, Julia was not prepared to discuss her feelings with her sister. At least, not yet. "Considering our rather unsatisfactory history, how could you think such a thing?"

Ros laughed. "Oh Julia, how can you be so experienced in living, and yet so naïve about the heart? A woman's heart often works independently of her mind."

Julia sighed. "You are not wrong. Despite what has happened in our past, I am still very fond of Viscount Wolfington. Perhaps too much."

Her sister leaned over and laid a hand on hers. "What happened?"

Julia drew a steadying breath. "You are aware of my difficulties with Wallthorpe, and my plan to dissuade him of his interest."

Ros nodded. "I am. And I still disagree with your solution. Your reputation should not have to be the currency for your freedom."

"Well, Wolf...um, Lord Wolfington, I mean, won me the night of the auction. So, the Swinton dinner was not the first I had seen of him since our return to London."

"Oh, how romantic!" Ros released a delighted breath of air as she sank back into her chair and stared off dreamily into space.

Julia sat forward, a small smile playing about her lips "Less romantic, and more erotic, actually. He is not the same young man I once knew. In fact, he shared me with one of his friends, and I was able to fulfill the fantasy I had harbored for so many years."

Ros sat straight up on a gasp. "Never say you did!"

Feeling very much like the cat that ate the cream, Julia nodded. "Oh, but I did, and I enjoyed every moment of it."

Her sister's cheeks grew to such a violent shade of magenta, Julia was almost certain Ros was having an apoplexy. "Drink some tea and calm down. It was necessary, or at least I thought it was."

"What do you mean? Did something go wrong?"

Ros was instantly distracted from her shock by the notion.

"No, not so much wrong, as not effective. The night of the Swinton dinner Wallthorpe cornered me alone in the study, and informed me that once we married, the stain of my auction would be wiped away. So I'd say the auction wasn't quite enough to tarnish me. I'm thinking I'll have to up the ante there. Would you agree a bit of gambling is in order?"

"Julia! I should think the auction was enough, and if not, then we need to seek another option." Ros crossed her arms in defiance. "Regardless, what has that to do with Wolfington?"

"Wolf found us and promptly dealt with Wallthorpe, sending him on his way. But the real issue came to light when Wolf proposed marriage."

Julia's gut twisted as she once more remembered how the man had stomped all over her heart with his emotionless proposal.

"Why, that's brilliant, of course!" Ros replied, clapping excitedly. "If you are married to Wolfington, you cannot possibly marry Wallthorpe."

Julia raised her hand, palm forward. "Cease. I declined his offer."

Her sister terminated her excited motions. "But I don't understand. Why?"

"Because he offered it as mere protection. He did not do so out of love for me." Julia struggled to rein in an unexpected surge of emotion. "I am quite certain he made the offer out of a sense of duty. Or worse, in an attempt to make reparations for his failure to protect me from my marriage to the elder Wallthorpe."

Restless, she stood and paced across the sitting room. "And having suffered a marriage—however short—to a man I did not love, I shall not do it again."

One furious tear slipped down her cheek despite all her best efforts to staunch the flow.

Instantly, her sister flew to her side and pulled her into a tight embrace. "Of course not. No one would expect you to stay married. I am positive Wolfington would release you as soon as it was possible."

"It makes no difference. I shall not solve my problem by marrying him." Julia looked at her sister, her eyes still watering even as she dashed her tears away. "I'm afraid if I did I wouldn't be strong enough to walk away when it was time to let him go."

Ros leaned back from their embrace. "Oh, poor dear, you've never stopped loving him. Have you?"

Unable to say the words, Julia simply shook her head. "I've tried everything I can to purge him from my heart. But despite the knowledge that he once left me to our parents' mercy, I cannot hate him as I should. And I cannot stop the surfeit of emotion that comes whenever he is near. The night at The Market nearly undid me. I can only imagine what marrying him would do to my heart."

Julia's palms were sweaty within her gloves as she smoothed her skirts down beneath her cloak. She climbed the steps of Lucifer's, hesitating when the door swung open. A burst of laughter rang out through the night, followed by the snarl of angry voices. And then, as she cleared the entry, a big burly man strode by, carrying another man by his belt and the neck of his garments. The doors remained wide open, allowing the intimidating man to hurl his burden out into the street.

"And don't come back. Lucifer's won't abide a cheater."

Then the giant turned and saw her standing in the foyer between the two gambling rooms, her eyes wide.

A slim butler-like man shut the doors and then stepped around the giant. "May I take your cloak, madam?"

Struck speechless, Julia merely nodded and pulled the string holding her cloak closed at her neck. Almost in a daze, she handed off her outer garment to the servant and tracked the giant's stride as he approached the stairs that would carry him to the upper level of the gambling den.

He turned and looked at her, studying her for a moment, as though taking her measure. "Please feel free to make yourself at home."

Then he waved toward the tables that teemed with men and women alike, deep in the throes of gambling.

Julia nodded and turned to walk around one side of the establishment, taking in the commotion. No stranger to gambling, she appreciated the excitement of the activity around her, yet found no pleasure in the abject waste of money. But she was here to both be seen and to play heavily, and more importantly, to *lose heavily*.

Wallthorpe had to be thwarted by the notion of such largesse on her part. After all, no man wanted a spendthrift for a wife. Although she had also thought no man would want a woman steeped in a sexual scandal, and he had proven her wrong on that count. She sighed at her predicament. Her dead husband's son was proving to be more problematic than he had been when she had first come out. At least during that time, he'd merely been content to leer at her from across a ballroom. Even then, he'd made her shudder.

Pushing aside her doubts and worries, she focused on her current goal. She needed to lose and look like she didn't have a care in the world while doing so.

Finding a table that appeared less inhabited than some of the others, she sidled up to the felt-covered surface. Wary of her rather low-cut bodice, she leaned over to lay her money on the table. Then one of the three men tossed a set of dice. Everyone groaned and cursed as the house employee quickly scooped up the cash from the table. Careful to hide her pleasure at an immediate loss, she again laid her money on the table. Another man rolled the dice this time, and they all cheered. To her dismay, the employee added to her pile of money. She left the stack and let the next player roll.

Again, she won.

The process repeated for another half an hour, until her pile had grown inordinately large. Finally, the employee said, "Madam, I'll need to gain house approval if you are going to continue to leave your bet on the table."

Julia bit her lip in indecision. If she left it, feasibly she could lose it all in one roll of the dice. *The table's luck had to change, didn't it?* "Please gain approval from whomever you need to."

"That would be me."

A deep male voice caused the nearby chatter to peter off into silence.

She looked up to see a tall man with dark hair and black-as-sin eyes. His gaze bore into her before dipping down to peruse her display of cleavage. Everyone in the vicinity had turned to see what had occurred. Determined to take advantage of the opportunity, she leaned forward and offered a seductive smile. "My, my. It seems I should have wagered more from the start."

"At the rate you are winning, I doubt I could have afforded such a turn of events."

He smiled deprecatingly, but there was an edge to the gesture that indicated an underlying danger.

Letting her lashes lower, she gazed up at him from beneath the fringe. "Oh, something tells me you'd have no issue covering such a wager. But then, mayhap the house will pull the luck on the next roll and I'll lose it all."

The dark man she assumed was the owner of the gambling hall gave a short nod. "I suppose we shall see. The wager of twenty thousand pounds stands."

A murmur raced through the room, even as Julia felt all the blood drain from her face. She had not realized how much she had accrued so quickly, having started with a mere five hundred pounds on the table. One of the men took up the dice, while the surrounding crowd pressed in closer. The heat grew stifling, and sweat trickled down her back. Silently she prayed for a bad roll of the dice as the man let them fly across the table. Then they fell to the felt, tumbling over each other, and finally landed.

"House wins!" the employee yelled, so everyone would hear.

Julia's knees went weak with relief. The men around her grumbled and walked away. But Mr. Lucifer remained, an unreadable expression on his face.

"Well, I suppose that is quite enough of a loss for one night. Thank you, Mr. Lucifer, for indulging me."

Julia hauled herself to her full height and turned to head to the bar. She'd barely taken a step, and the man was at her side.

"You have me at a disadvantage."

"Do I?" She let one brow rise. "I can't imagine anyone having you in such a position."

He grinned, though it was far more reminiscent of a predator baring its teeth. "You do, though. Whom did I just relieve of such a large sum?"

They arrived at the bar, and she took a moment to inspect the man now that he was no longer half hidden by a dice table. Without a doubt, he was attractive, with his rough and dangerous aura, but with Wolf's touch still so fresh in her mind, Mr. Lucifer merely did not measure up. "I am Lady Wallthorpe."

His gaze gleamed with desire. "My, my. I am delighted to make your acquaintance. As a patron of The Market, I was heartbroken to discover I missed your auction. Could fate be so kind as to offer me a second chance?"

Julia offered a stilted laugh. "I am afraid that was a one-time opportunity. However, I'd be happy to let you buy me a drink before I set about losing a bit more money in your establishment."

He released a dejected sigh. "I suppose sharing a drink with such an infamous woman shall have to be enough." He let his gaze roam seductively over her décolletage and down to the curve of her waist. "Though if you should change your mind, please do let me know." He lifted his gaze to clash with hers, offering both desire and a challenge. "What may I offer you to drink?"

"Red wine. Perhaps a Madeira?"

Lucifer waved the bartender over and requested their drinks. A few moments later, their drinks in hand, they resumed chatting.

He took a sip and cast a speculative look her way. "I am curious about something. For an establishment such as The Market, where anonymity is part of the lure, how is it that nearly all of London seems to know that you were auctioned there?"

In that moment, she found she liked him. He was shrewd, and quite intelligent. But she was not prepared to answer him. "What makes you believe that was anything but an unlucky slip of the tongue?"

"Because I know Madame Celeste too well to believe she or any of her staff would be so careless with your identity." He swirled his drink and seemed to savor the aroma for a moment. "And now you have appeared in my gambling hall, wearing a dress designed to draw attention, and tossing money on the table as though you are made of the stuff. It makes one believe you are seeking a certain amount of notoriety."

Julia considered him again, and decided he might be a useful ally. "And if I were seeking such notice, would that be a concern for you?"

"On the contrary. I find I am both intrigued and entertained by the idea of my establishment being associated with such scandal." He tossed back the last of his drink. "Truly, I couldn't buy such profitable advertising as being associated with an outrageous lady." He set his drink down and stepped closer to her, placing a hand on her waist in too intimate a manner. "Imagine the scandal we could cause if I paraded you upstairs and into my bed?"

"Mr. Lucifer, if you please." She plucked his hand from her person and stepped back. "I made it very clear I have no amorous intentions with regards to you."

He frowned. "With regard to me? That suggests that there is someone you *do* have such intentions with."

Her cheeks heated, and she turned slightly away from him. "That is none of your concern. If you will excuse me, I believe I have a bit more gambling to do before I depart."

He reached out and grazed her arm with his fingertips, halting her exodus. "Please forgive my persistence. I did not achieve all that you see before you by accepting no for an answer. Enjoy the rest of your evening."

Julia smiled. "You are forgiven. But do not think I shall change my mind based on pressure. I have learned the very valuable lesson that giving in to someone else's wishes, when counter to your own, is a path fraught with unhappiness."

With an incline of her head, she sauntered off.

She crossed to the other room, which appeared to be dominated by card tables, and found a rousing game of high stakes *Vingt-Et-Un*. Sitting down, she proceeded to gamble away the remainder of the money she had brought with her for the evening. Still sipping her one drink, she followed the game closely, ensuring she did her best to lose whenever possible, without hurting the table more than was required.

The evening progressed while her funds dwindled and the crowd grew, until she became aware of a particularly disturbing sensation. It was as though someone was boring a hole into the back of her head. Finally unnerved enough to turn and look, her gaze locked with a very angry pair of sapphire blue eyes. Her breath caught as Wolf wedged his way through the crowd and took up a position near her elbow.

What the devil is he doing here?

As the last card fell and she lost all she had left, she stood and excused herself from the table.

Wolf was on her heels, and then he took her arm in a solicitous fashion, with the exception of his firm grip and angry stare. "How much do you owe Lucifer? Do you have any idea what the man is like?"

Wolf was all but frog-marching her toward the door of Lucifer's, when the man himself reappeared.

"Please excuse me, but it appears you are escorting an unwilling woman from my establishment. And I'm afraid I cannot allow such activity."

Again, that predatory smile appeared.

"Stay out of this, Lucifer," Wolf snarled as his eyes darted about the room, as though assessing who else might attempt to stop their progress.

Julia was still reeling from Wolf's suggestion that she had borrowed money to lose. She wanted to smack herself in the forehead for not having realized she could have made the situation much, much worse by doing so. But then she decided to see how much Lucifer might wish to have his establishment linked to her infamy. Pulling out her most winsome smile, she hiccupped and leaned toward the dangerous man. "Do not worry, Mr. Lucifer. I shall pay the blunt I owe you. All thirty thousand pounds of it."

She hiccupped again and winked at him.

"You will, I have no doubt. Because the punishment for non-payment would be a tragic result for a woman of your beauty."

He remained stone-faced as the three of them stood there, and she thanked heaven the man was wily enough to play along with her ruse.

Wolf actually snarled after that exchange, and then dragged her to the exit. Linc stood there already, holding her cloak. With a drunken giggle and a finger wave, she allowed the blond man to help her before they all departed.

Outside, Wolf's carriage stood waiting for them to climb in. As the three of them settled, Julia bit her lip and wondered if she had overplayed her hand. Wolf seemed even more angry than he originally was, but he was causing such a scene, it was an opportunity she could not pass up.

The silence stretched as her worry grew, until she felt compelled to speak. "Wolf, I—"

"Not a word, Julia. Not a single, solitary word." His growl usually proved worse than his bite, but for the first time, she wasn't so sure.

Chapter Six

Wolf sat next to Jules, and it was all he could do to restrain himself from turning her over his knee. She had always been high-spirited, game for whatever adventure he had imagined when they were children. But he would have expected that she'd outgrown such impulsiveness—though, apparently not.

Thank goodness Ros had sent him a note, alerting him to Jules' plans for the evening. He'd been determined to stay away from her, but upon reading that she would be gambling heavily at Lucifer's, he'd nearly tossed up the very fine meal he'd been sharing with Linc. After hearing what the note contained, his friend had insisted on accompanying him to the notorious gambling den to fetch Jules.

Now Linc sat across from them, quietly peering out of the carriage windows. But Wolf realized he needed to sort out this issue with Jules in private. "Linc, where can we drop you?"

"White's will do, as long as you assure me you have no plans to throttle our fair Julia."

Linc grinned at him, his irreverence on display, as always.

She snorted. "He wouldn't dare."

Wolf let his brows rise as he focused on her. "Oh, I would dare a great many things, though causing you harm is not one of them."

He then knocked on the roof of the carriage. When the small door near the driver opened, he provided direction on where to go.

The three of them returned to silence. When the vehicle eventually drew to a halt, Linc opened the door to hop out.

Wolf laid a hand on his arm. "Thank you for accompanying me tonight."

"No trouble at all. I'm happy to help." Linc nodded then looked at Jules. "Until our next meeting, Lady Wallthorpe."

"Always a pleasure, my lord."

She dipped her head regally and then turned back to staring out the window to her right.

With Linc delivered to his destination, the small door opened again.

"Where to, my lord?"

"Just drive," Wolf instructed.

He wasn't quite sure what to do with her yet.

The carriage pulled away from the curb, and they jostled along in silence once more.

After a few minutes, Jules finally looked at him. "We can't drive around all night. Will you please take me home?"

"Sobered up already?" Wolf asked, gritting out the words.

He was angry at her for being so reckless, and furious with himself for not taking control of this situation sooner. He knew when he'd left her in the Swintons' study that no good would come of her handling Wallthorpe on her own.

"Don't be obtuse. I was never drunk to start with."

Though he couldn't see her features in the shadows of the carriage, he could hear the contempt in her voice. "And how would I know such a thing? I only arrived in time to see you lose the last of your money at cards, before you stood up and announced to all and sundry that you owe Lucifer a debt of thirty thousand pounds!"

"Yes, well, it is too bad you didn't stop to consider what you know of my character. But then, people have been underestimating what I am capable of all my life. My parents, my dead husband, his idiot son, and now you." She sounded weary from carrying that burden for so many years. "Only a desert sheik saw me for the woman I truly am."

Wolf flinched. "I see glimmers of the girl I knew and the young woman I loved, but they're buried beneath this woman I've never met. This worldly, scandalous woman, who won't give me a chance to know her. You've behaved in a way that's paved the road to my assumptions. If none of that is true, then please tell me what is. More importantly, let me help you."

"I do not owe Mr. Lucifer a single farthing. Any money I lost tonight was mine to lose. You are well aware of my desire to stir up scandal in order to deter my stepson, and being drunk and discussing obscene amounts of money were merely part of that effort. For heaven's sake, stop thinking with your wee head, and start engaging that rather larger one sitting atop your shoulders."

Wolf sat there blinking for a moment, taking in her rapid monologue. It was a strikingly intelligent way to deal with Wallthorpe, but only if it worked. From what he'd seen, the man was unflinching in his determination to wed her.

Surprising him, Jules then turned on the carriage bench and leaned close to him. "Do you truly wish to help me?"

Wolf nodded, wary of what she might say next. But instead of speaking, she cupped his face, staring into his eyes for an interminable moment before she kissed him. Her lips captured his, her tongue driving past all his barriers and all his worries, until he wrapped his tongue around hers. Eyes closed, he surrendered to the sensuous feel of her licking and tasting him, until his cock grew hard and his anger melted into a molten hot desire that sizzled through his veins.

The one thing he knew about Jules, old or new, was that he always found himself drawn to her like a lodestone. She fired his blood and made him ache with wanting her, needing her. And in ten years, nothing had changed.

They finally broke apart, both of them breathing heavily as they clung to each other.

Wolf managed to gather his wits first. "This is familiar, this driving need to taste you and touch you. It's always been there. Marry me, and let me help you. Give us a chance to explore this connection we share."

She moved her head from side to side slightly, even as their foreheads pressed together. "I'll not deny it, this connection between us. But it is a distraction at the moment. Perhaps later, after I've dispatched Wallthorpe, we can take the time to become reacquainted. For now, though, I have my hands full fending off my dead husband's whelp, and marrying you or anyone else for any reason is simply out of the question."

She drew a deep breath and let it out as she leaned back from him, though her hands still cradled his face. "Please, Wolf. Take me home."

Julia slept late. Whether it was from emotional or physical exhaustion didn't much matter. The result was the same. By the time she woke, dressed for the day, and made her way downstairs, she could hear voices in the front parlor. Ros was one person, and she quickly recognized the other two. Unfortunately, by the time she realized it was her parents, it was too late to retreat upstairs and hide.

They hadn't been horrible parents growing up. Of course, her mother would get upset when Julia and Ros came home with mud and grass all over their pinafores, and they were often scolded for fidgeting at the table, but they were allowed to be children. They were also permitted to run and play, read books and learn, and until Wolf went off to school, they were allowed at least one friend in the neighborhood.

But once he was banished to Eton, Julia and Ros were suddenly thrust into training to become the wives of noblemen, despite the fact that their parents were neither from old money nor part of the peerage. Until Julia was nineteen, she was forced to submit to training in dining etiquette, dancing, piano, singing, de Brett's History, the art of conversation, household management, and of course, needlework.

Even had Wolf come home from school, she would never have had the time to see him.

Pushing thoughts of him aside—she could not entertain old desires while defending against current unwanted advances—she glided into the front parlor and greeted everyone. "Good morning, Father." She pressed a kiss to his cheek. "Mother." Another kiss. "Ros."

One last kiss hello, and she finally made it to a nearby chair.

Patrice Fairchild looked pointedly at the clock. "So good of you to join us, Julia."

"My apologies, Mother. I had something of a late night. But had I known you were going to be visiting at this hour, I certainly would have left instructions to be woken in time to greet you."

She made no attempt to hide the censure in her tone or words. She was no longer a young girl who would be intimidated by her mother.

Her mother sniffed in reply. "It is unseemly to laze about, but I suppose that is a habit you acquired in your travels."

"Well, she is up and about now, dear."

Her father stepped in and quelled the brewing disagreement. He'd always played the pacifier between them. As Julia came of age, the yoke of her mother's expectations had grown burdensome and less wanted. Now those expectations were completely ignored.

"And just in time, too. Lord Wallthorpe is due to arrive shortly."

Her mother nodded at that, pleased with herself.

Ros gasped.

Julia's vision turned red with fury. "What do you mean, Wallthorpe is due to arrive shortly?"

For the first time in Julia's life, her mother looked slightly uncertain about a decision she'd made. "What could possibly be wrong with your stepson joining us for a family luncheon?"

Julia growled as she rose from her seat. "He is *not* family. He was an *adult* when I married his doddering old father. And most importantly, I did not invite him to my home!"

"Julia, he has been nothing but solicitous toward your father and me over the years. The man is far more appropriate in age for you, and he has also indicated an interest in courting you." Her mother looked at her, earnest as ever.

With a huff of frustration, Julia strode away from where her parents sat, looking genuinely baffled by her reaction. "I am well aware of his interest in courting me, but *I* have no interest in marrying him."

Her mother looked annoyed. "I shall not have this conversation with you again. Ten years ago was sufficient. You need a husband to handle your affairs. Someone to support you, to give you children. And think of your sister. Ros needs you to set a good example."

Julia drew to a halt. "Ros is quite capable of determining her own needs and wants without relying on me as a guide. However, she could do worse than to follow my lead. I handle my own affairs, and I am wealthier now than most men who might seek my hand in marriage. As for children? Why, one just needs to stroll near the docks to see that a husband is not required to become pregnant."

Her mother gasped.

"Here now, Julia," her father blustered. "You'll cease such talk this instant."

To her dismay, her mother then turned to her father. "When did she become so vulgar? She was never this way as a girl. She needs a husband to rein in such bad habits."

"I am standing right here, Mother."

She had to tamp down the urge to stomp her foot in frustration. And with yet another mention of a husband, Wolf's words flitted through her mind again.

Could he be of assistance now?

No, she refused to give in to her mother's ridiculous demands.

"Be that as it may, I have still invited Lord Wallthorpe, and you will not be rude to him."

For the first time, Ros entered the fray. "Mother, that is outside of enough. This is not your home."

Mrs. Fairchild blinked in surprise.

"That man has been perfectly horrible to Julia," Ros continued. "All clingy and handsy, each time she runs into him in public. And I am just fine as I am. I shall never love again"—she pressed a hand to her heart and fought back what appeared to be tears—"after the loss of my Archie."

Julia knew how deeply her sister still felt the loss of her beloved husband, even after so many years. Lieutenant Archibald Smith had died during the Sepoy Mutiny, as had many Englishmen.

"Do not upset yourself, Ros. I doubt Lord Wallthorpe will come to visit, anyway. Certainly, last night's escapades will have reached his ears by now."

Her parents looked worried at her latest statement, her mother more so than her father.

"What have you done now?"

Julia was about to deliver the *coup de grâce* when a loud, malevolent rap sounded on the door. Her stomach plummeted, because under the circumstances there was only one person who would be knocking on her door at this hour.

John Johnson, her butler-cum-footman, opened the door. After a brief exchange, he announced their visitor. "Lord Wallthorpe to see Lady Wallthorpe, Mrs. Fairchild, Mrs. Smith, and Mr. Fairchild."

Julia sighed and pinched the bridge of her nose. Either the man had not yet heard of her visit to Lucifer's, or he was so determined to have her that he was blithely ignoring all the scandal she had ignited. Unfortunately, she believed it was the latter and not the former, which meant she was damn near backed into a corner. Short of pointing a gun at him and definitively saying no, she had no real recourse to dissuade him from his suit.

Well, none that she wished to employ.

She dug deep to find some modicum of civility for the wretched man. "Good morning, Lord Wallthorpe."

"Good morning, Lady Wallthorpe. You look particularly ravishing this morning." He took her hand and bent over it gallantly, even as he muttered for her ears only. "Especially considering your evening activities."

And it was then she knew that she was truly stuck. Once more, Wolf's offer came to mind. He was a friend, and he wanted to help her.

Surely he would release me from a fake betrothal, especially one he had not really committed to?

Wallthorpe greeted the rest of her family, then settled into a chair and commenced discussing the latest *on-dits* with her mother, as though he was a regular in the gossip circles. Julia found the whole conversation nauseating.

Her mother tittered at something he had said, as Julia's father sat silently, looking incredibly bored. But then her mother looked at her and said, "I was just telling Julia how wonderful you've been to us while she was abroad."

Her stepson grinned. "Well, one must always have time for family."

Julia gnashed her teeth. "Only if family knows its place."

"I should think that place is close to hand. When you care for someone, it is important to let them know you value them." Then he turned and patted her mother's hand. "As I have tried to do with your parents."

"Yes, well, I am sure they appreciate all the attention."

The droll tone rang through her voice, despite her best efforts to squash it.

Her mother looked increasingly angry, as Julia all but crossed the line into rudeness. And then Julia grew concerned as her mother's familiar eyes lit with a fierceness that could only spell trouble.

Mrs. Fairchild suddenly looked at Julia's stepson and smiled. "You know, my lord, I was just telling both my girls how important it is for them to remarry."

Wallthorpe tut-tutted. "I strongly agree, Mrs. Fairchild."

"Oh, do stop, my lord. I have told you many times to call me Patrice," her mother simpered.

"As I have told you to call me Wallthorpe. I hear 'my lord' enough, everywhere else I go." He proceeded with his previous train of thought. "I know my father would have wanted Julia to be cared for."

With her stomach in knots, Julia smiled and perched on the edge of her seat. "I am so glad to hear you say that, my lord."

Her mother shot her a startled look as her father's head popped up from where he had practically dosed off during the insipid conversation.

"I had hoped to tell my parents in private, but since we are all family..." She shot her mother a pointed look. "Lord Wolfington has requested my hand in marriage."

Her mother paled, even as Wallthorpe grew beet red.

Determined to wring all the drama she could from the moment, Julia waited while the silence thickened. "I was so moved by his eloquent proposal that I agreed."

Chapter Seven

Hours earlier, Wolf had stared at the delicate scrawl on the page. The very first thing he'd noticed was the huge, looping *J* at the bottom of the page. Something akin to satisfaction had welled up inside and permeated his limbs. Finally, she had contacted him. The missive had been short and direct, much like the woman who had penned it. It was hard to imagine that anything could be scandalous about a stroll through Hyde Park at the fashionable hour, but a small voice in the back of his head wouldn't let him fully believe she merely wished to see him without some ulterior motive.

Much later, as he waited for her, the question that still nagged at him was, what was Jules about?

She had always been intelligent and quick on her feet. More times than he could count, she had been the one who'd come up with the most plausible story to avoid trouble with their respective parents, after his adventures had landed them squarely in a tight spot.

He knew in his gut that this would be no simple social call.

He stood by the Queens Gate and scanned the crowd for the fiery redhead who was quickly taking over all his thoughts, much as she had when he was a young man, fresh out of university. Carriages drove by and people strolled, but he saw no sign of her. A few riders walked at a sedate pace amongst the general hubbub. Everyone who was anyone was out to be seen, and of course, to see if you were of any import to them.

Another rider passed, and then, suddenly, there she was. Her red hair glowed like a living flame in the late afternoon sun, and her deep green walking dress hugged her every curve. His heart thudded heavily in his chest as desire bubbled up—unwanted and wildly awkward as he stood on a public promenade.

"Good afternoon, Wolf." She tilted her head, causing her bonnet to shift precariously. She then reached up and caught the hat before it could fly off. "Oh, I knew I should have worn my usual bonnet. This one is too tall to be functional."

He smothered a laugh as she settled the head covering back into place. "It's quite fetching, height notwithstanding."

She preened a moment, which made him inordinately pleased.

"How are you this fine afternoon, Jules?"

"Well enough, I suppose. Though I am afraid I do need to speak with you. I appreciate your coming on such short notice."

Short notice? If he had been required to wait for even a minute more, he would have been a candidate for Bedlam. "Think nothing of it." He took one of her hands and tucked it in the crook of his arm. "Shall we walk and talk?"

She wrinkled her nose. "I suppose we should. After all, I did draw you out on that exact pretense."

"Yes, you did, and since I've been hunched over my desk all day, my legs could use the stretching."

They started off amongst the throng of people. As they walked in companionable silence, Wolf fought off the urge to hurry her along with whatever she wished to discuss. Instead, he focused on politely nodding at various acquaintances as they passed, while not looking overly pleased with himself. He was enjoying having her on his arm, even as he began to notice the reaction of people around them. As he paid closer attention, he realized that most of the women were glaring at them, or rather at Jules. And most of the men either offered a lascivious perusal, or eyed her with curiosity. He resisted the urge to sigh. It would seem her ploy to stir up scandal had been *more* than effective. Add him to the picture, because of course he had caught at least one less than circumspect comment on the breeze about how they made a fitting pair.

And why not? He was widely rumored to be a bastard—though his father had claimed him as his son and heir. Of course, most of the gossipmongers didn't know that the rumors were absolutely, unequivocally true. But he did. Her dead husband had made certain of that.

So, the bastard and the... He tried to imagine how Society might frame them.

The bastard and the light-skirt?

Then Julia broke into his scurrilous thoughts. "The reason I asked you to walk with me today is to discuss your previous offer."

Curious, he continued to walk, though he refrained from commenting until she explained herself further.

With her cheeks pinkening, and obviously not from sun exposure, she presented a fetching picture. "I'm afraid I spoke out of turn and declared our betrothal to Lord Wallthorpe and my parents this morning."

Wolf felt the jolt of excitement straight down to his toes, though he merely inclined his head. "I see."

She looked at him as though waiting for more of a reaction from him, as they continued to stroll. When he said nothing else, she pursed her lips a moment, and then pressed on. "Is that all you have to say, after I stubbornly refused your offer twice?"

"I can see it does put you in something of a predicament, as I have not recently—say in the last day—made such an offer again. Am I to assume you are here seeking some assistance in this matter? Or are you simply alerting me to the fact, should I be unexpectedly questioned?"

He kept their pace up as the crowd thinned around them and they meandered off the main thoroughfare.

Jules shot him an annoyed glance. "Wolf, do not be obtuse. Yes, I am here seeking your assistance. An engagement in name only will not suffice, as my mother and father have now taken up Lord Wallthorpe's cause."

A surge of pleasure bubbled up inside him as he considered how to leverage this turn of events in his favor. He would, of course, help Jules, regardless of what he wanted, because it was *her* asking. However, he very much wanted an opportunity to get to know her again, to learn about the woman she had become. "I suppose I could make myself available to you for a few social calls, and the like. Simply to establish the fact of our courtship, of course."

Her face lit up then, and his heart stuttered in his chest. It was an achingly familiar expression to him, and yet wondrous in the newness of it, from the woman who so intrigued him. "You are a real brick," she said.

He stopped them near a small copse of trees that offered them some privacy. "Oh, ho. Do not sing my praises just yet, Jules. I'm afraid I want something in exchange for my assistance."

Her green gaze sharpened as she eyed him warily. "And what is it you want?"

"Do not look at me as though I were Spring-heeled Jack." He stepped closer to her, taking her hands in his. "I simply wish to have you in my bed again. The one night at The Market was not enough to satisfy my desires."

She didn't move, but her hands trembled in his. "And if I say no?"

Wolf sighed. "You are well aware that I would help you, no matter how you reply. I'm not such a cad as to desert you." He tugged her hand, drawing her into his arms. "But I want to learn who you are *now*, so I can appreciate the changes your life has wrought, as well as those things that remain the same. I need to taste and touch you, to see your hair spread across my pillows as I drive into your heat, and to hear you call my name as I pleasure you. I want you to let me make love to you."

And then, before she could answer him, he snared her lips in a kiss. Licking into her mouth, he tasted, explored, and discovered. The sweetness of her breath mingled with his own as he grew drunk on her. His cock hardened, pressing against her. Then a loud whinny shattered the moment, causing them to pull apart, even as they gasped for breath.

Wolf tipped her face up so he could look into her sparkling emerald gaze. "Your answer, Jules?"

Worry flitted over her face as she bit her lower lip, the one swollen from his kiss. "Yes. But you must remember that the engagement is a ruse. We will reach a point where one of us will need to break with the other. I am happy to allow you to be the one to do that, since marriage is not a concern for me. I'd not rob you of your future family."

He ignored everything she'd said after replying yes. He had little chance of a future family, but he refused to point out the truth of the matter, since it changed nothing. "Where would you prefer to meet for our trysts? I am happy to come to you."

Her eyes widened. "Oh, no! Ros would certainly notice your visits."

"Yes, I suppose she would. And you can't very well be seen coming to and from my residence. I suppose we could continue to make use of The Market. Though I would suggest you come masked and with a cloak, since there is little point in continuing to invite scandal."

A warmth he could not explain enveloped him.

"Very well. I am sure my mother will desire to have us over for dinner, so I shall be in touch soon. Now, it seems we should stroll back and make something of a show of our being enamored with each other." She winked saucily at him. "Though I suppose your rather obvious erection may illustrate the point just as well."

Wolf felt his own cheeks heat at her comment. "Give me a few moments, and I shall bring my wayward cock to heel."

He turned away and tried to think of anything that might aid his predicament. Unfortunately, the soft scent of jasmine wafted from Julia, teasing and tormenting him. Willing his erection to settle down was not working with her so near. With a growl of frustration, he took a step further away from her scent, and deeper into the copse, where he could not be seen from the nearby path.

Standing with his eyes closed and his hands fisted, he drew a deep, cleansing breath. With the next one, however, the jasmine returned. He opened his eyes to find Jules had followed him, and was even now studying him. And when his gaze clashed with hers, desire flared hot and bright between them.

She stepped up to him, removed her glove, reached out, and cupped his straining erection. "Let me help you."

Wrapping his fingers around the delicate bones of her wrist, he warred with himself. A gentleman would refuse her offer, but he reminded himself that he was no gentleman.

He was a bastard, after all. "How?" he asked in a raspy voice, while fighting for control.

She opened the placket of his trousers and freed his hard shaft. Despite the cooling shade of the copse of trees, a light sheen of perspiration broke out on his brow as he stood in a public park with his cock exposed.

She shot him a coy look from beneath lowered lashes. "I could stroke it for you."

As she put action to words, his knees wobbled. The warmth of her hand contrasted with the air around them, only high-lighting how good her touch felt. "Yes," he groaned.

His hips jerked forward, pushing his length into her firm grip. Lids lowered to half-mast, he watched as her tongue snaked out to trace her lower lip. He wished it was *his* tongue tracing that plump line, but at the moment, it was taking all his focus just to remain standing.

Then she looked up at him. "Or..."

She suddenly sank to her knees, careful of her skirts, and his heart skipped multiple beats.

"I could kiss and lick it for you."

And again, she followed through on her suggestion.

As her lips touched his cock, his blood thundered through his veins. For a moment, it felt as though his skin was no longer capable of containing his blood, his pleasure, and everything that he was. The stroke of her tongue had his knees giving out, yet he somehow remained standing. Jolt after jolt of bliss shot through him when she wrapped her lips around him and swallowed his cock. She took him deep into her throat in a single motion that had him gliding into heaven. When she pulled back and then sucked him in again, his body shook as his balls drew up tight.

"Jules, I'm going to come."

He pushed the warning past clenched teeth as he tried to hang on long enough to give her a chance to release him.

Instead, she reached up with her ungloved hand and cupped his sac as she gently rolled it over her fingers. Lost to the pounding need to blow, he gave up his fight and came hard. She continued to work him with her lips and tongue as he pumped his seed into her mouth. Without missing a beat, she caught every drop, and even delicately swiped at him as she pulled away.

He stood there dazed by his intense orgasm, while she tucked his now softened cock back into his trousers and stood up.

With a naughty smile and a wink, she shook out her skirts. "We'd best return to the main path, so we can be sure to be seen together. I'd hate for anyone to think we weren't truly enamored of each other."

Wolf followed her from the protective copse of trees, at a loss for how anyone could think he wasn't utterly taken with the enchanting, sensual creature before him.

Chapter Eight

Julia stood with Wolf on the front step of her parents' home while butterflies danced in her belly. In truth, she was more worried they would say something offensive to him, and not that he would somehow slip up and reveal that their engagement was fake. So, when the front door opened and their longtime butler stood there, it was with some trepidation that she greeted him.

"Good evening, Thompson."

He helped her with her cloak, and then took Wolf's coat from him.

"I assume Mother and Father are in the parlor?"

"Indeed, my lady."

The white-haired old man bowed, and then shuffled off to put their outerwear away.

"Are you ready to beard the lion in its den?" Julia asked Wolf, winking at him and feigning a confidence she did not feel.

One of his golden brows lifted. "It can't possibly be so dangerous as that."

"My mother may look sweet, but she has claws. Never forget it," she drawled, as she placed her hand in the crook of his elbow.

His forearm was heavily muscled, something she could tell even through his jacket. She loved the tensile strength he exuded, despite his finery. Taking comfort in his calm demeanor, she led him into the parlor. As they strode in, her parents and Ros all stood.

"Mother, Father, you remember Lord Wolfington?" Julia kissed each of them on the cheek.

"Of course." Her father shook hands with him. "Welcome, my lord."

"A pleasure to see you again, Mr. Fairchild." Wolf nodded, then turned to take her mother's hand. "Mrs. Fairchild. You look lovely this evening."

"Thank you, my lord." Her mother curtsied and offered a polite smile. "Dinner will be served shortly. May we offer you something to drink?"

"A glass of sherry wouldn't come amiss," Wolf replied, and then greeted Ros.

They all took a seat as her father poured the drinks. He presented both her and Wolf a glass before taking a seat as well. Silence reigned as they sipped from their glasses.

The moment was on the verge of growing awkward when Ros spoke up. "Wolf, have you heard that Father has been able to secure rights to import Darjeeling tea?"

Wolf sipped his sherry. "I had not heard. Congratulations, sir."

Mr. Fairchild smiled. "I am quite pleased with the arrangement. It is only in the last few years that tea gardens have been established in that region. While it's not an exclusive right to import, I am one of a very few importers who have made the proper connections. My investors were rather excited when I delivered the news earlier this week."

Thompson entered the salon then and pronounced, "Dinner is served."

With something akin to relief, Julia stood and walked with Wolf into the dining room. At least now they would have the excuse of eating to explain the lack of conversation.

The meal stretched interminably. At least, that's how it felt to her. If it hadn't been for Ros, she and Wolf would have been practically having a private conversation. By the time dessert was served, her father had engaged a bit more in the discussion, though his contributions still felt slightly stilted and awkward. Her mother, silent unless directly asked a question, was a better hostess than that, but Julia knew she was deeply unhappy about the engagement. Determined to have a private word with her later, Julia set her napkin aside.

Then her father rose from the table and started toward his study. "Wolf, why don't you join me for a cigar and an after-dinner drink?"

Dutifully, and because it was obvious that it was a command and not a request, Wolf followed her father out.

Pleased for the semi-private moment with her mother, Julia waited for the study door to close in the distance. As soon as the sound assured her the men were secluded, she launched her attack. "Mother, I cannot believe you are behaving in such a poor fashion. I have *never* seen someone treated so shabbily in this home."

Mrs. Fairchild let her eyes widen as she pressed a hand to her breast. "I do not understand what you are suggesting, Julia."

"I am not suggesting anything. I am saying straight out that you are behaving as a very poor hostess. Were it not for Wolf's better manners and Ros providing most of the conversation, dinner would have been all but silent. You are, in short, being extremely rude."

Her mother's gaze wandered about the room, looking anywhere but at her daughter. "Oh, for heaven's sake. What a ridiculous thing to say. It is hardly my fault if he has poor conversation skills. One can only offer so many sallies."

Ros tutted. "Mother, do not be so perverse. You know you've behaved abominably all night."

Julia tried to keep her temper under control. "He is a good man, Mother. I loved him once, but I did my family duty at the time and married as you demanded. Do I not deserve to marry as I wish now?"

"Demanded!" Her mother rose, her face turning beet red. "I did what was *best* for you. I ensured you were married to a titled man, someone with means and the social cachet to bring London to your feet. And how did you thank me for that excellent guidance? When your aging husband died, you remained abroad, where that social currency was completely useless!"

Julia's temper slowly cooled. She had always known her mother had social-climbing desires, but she had not realized to what lengths she was willing to go until now. A coldness permeated Julia's body as part of her heart broke at hearing her mother speak the truth so plainly. "Only for you. My title served me well where I was, but I would have happily forgone such service in order to marry the man I loved. Do not expect any future family dinners of this nature. I would not wish to burden you with my fiancé's lack of social cachet."

Shaken by her mother's selfishness, Julia quietly retreated to the parlor.

A moment later, Ros was there, her arms circling Julia's shoulders. "I am so sorry. She's terribly self-serving."

"It's not as though we didn't know that, but she has taken great pains to hide it from us in the past." Julia sighed and leaned her head against her sister's shoulder. "Perhaps I should go and rescue Wolf from Father's clutches, so we can depart?"

Ros let go and straightened up "He seemed to be holding his own at dinner, and he's a very fine man now. I imagine he can manage on his own for a short while more."

Their mother walked in a moment later, followed by Wolf and their father. To her dismay, it seemed the men had bonded over a cigar and a drink, while her own relationship with her mother had irreparably fractured.

Wolf sniffed the contents of his bell-shaped glass, then paused as he glanced about the room. "This is a fine cognac, Mr. Fairchild. I've not had its equal."

To Julia, it was obvious that something had shifted in the atmosphere among the women of the room. She and her sister stood huddled together by the fireplace, while her mother sat in a wingchair near the window.

"If I may," Wolf began, speaking into yet another awkward silence. "While I know Julia is no longer under your auspices, it was important to me to have your blessing."

To Julia's surprise, her father nodded in encouragement.

Then Wolf turned and set his glass aside. He strode over to where she stood, lowered himself to one knee, and produced a rather stunning opal and emerald ring. The opal was a cabochon with small emerald solitaires encircling the edge.

"Julia, it seems our lives are destined to be intertwined. And while our time together may be limited...to this life, I cannot imagine another woman I would wish to spend it with. Will you be my viscountess?"

Though his words possessed layers and layers of meaning, most of it couched in terms of the short nature of their engagement, she couldn't help but be moved by the words and the gesture. They had not discussed him presenting her a ring, and so she truly was surprised. Holding out her left hand, she smiled. "Of course. Yes."

Then Wolf slipped the ring on her finger and stood to take her in his arms. Pleased that he kept their audience in mind, he pressed a chaste kiss to her forehead and simply embraced her.

Peering over his shoulder, she saw the look of annoyance that her mother did not bother to hide, but her father looked rather pleased with the outcome. It was a surprising turn, since he rarely went against his wife's wishes, and in this case, he had all but ignored a direct order.

As they parted, Ros, and then her father, descended on them to wish them well. With a flurry of hugs and smiles, it took her a moment to realize her mother had slipped away.

Chapter Nine

Wolf fussed with the silverware for what had to be the hundredth time in the past ten minutes. The candles were lit, the table set, the linens crisp, but his mind was a stuttering, nervous mess. He would have thought that seduction was the easy part, but as he stood in the glow of the romantic setting he'd arranged, he suddenly realized how important all this was to him. *How* important *she* was to him.

It was possible he had tried to cease loving her over the years, but the feelings had never truly gone dormant while they'd been apart. And there was no denying the fact that he still harbored deep-seated feelings for Jules. He was well aware of them, however he refused to examine them too closely at the moment.

Taking a deep breath, he attempted to calm the whirlwind of his emotions and let his mind settle. There would be time enough to show her how he felt once she arrived.

A knock sounded just before one of The Market's footmen opened the door, allowing Jules to enter. Still masked and covered by a heavy, hooded cloak, he wouldn't have been sure it was her if a single, flame-colored tendril hadn't peeked out from the green velvet swath she wore.

The servant quickly departed, leaving them alone.

"Good evening." Wolf helped her with her cloak, and then tugged at the strings of her mask. "No need for this while we are alone in here."

Setting her cloak and mask aside, he took in her beauty. With her startlingly red hair and vivid blue gown with white trim, which cut low across the tops of her breasts, she was a stunning study in contrasts. In lieu of the pale white skin common to most redheads, she had somehow managed to still retain a sun-kissed glow that invited his touch.

"Good evening to you." She glanced around. "What a lovely room. I imagine on a sunny afternoon, it must be overwhelmingly cheerful."

Wolf smiled. "I can't say I have ever been here in the afternoon to know."

"Well, it is a comfort to know you are not so dissolute as to engage in debauchery at all hours of the day or night."

Her playful wink removed any sting her words might have contained.

He chuckled. "I am merely your basic debaucher of women. I stick to the night shadows for my business."

They both laughed for a second.

Then he pulled a chair out for her. "May I pour you a drink? Dinner should be served any moment."

She took the offered seat with a shy smile. "Thank you."

Once her drink was poured and dinner served, he settled into the comfortable quiet. From the first moment he'd seen her parading around downstairs, he'd been plagued by the urge to revisit the past, if only to heal old hurts—mostly those he knew he'd caused.

"Jules, I owe you an apology."

She stopped eating, clearly a little surprised by his statement. "For what, exactly?"

He swallowed his pride, or at least what he could manage of it. "For leaving you alone on a London street corner in the middle of the night when we were to elope. I wasn't the man you required me to be at the time, and it still discredits me to this day."

He could not look at her as he said the last part, unwilling to let her see the full scope of his shame. The rumor of his being a bastard she would likely learn soon enough, as she moved among their peers, but one only he or his father could corroborate it. And neither had done so as yet, though each for their own reasons.

The warmth of her touch as she laid a hand over his drew him from his own bleak musings.

"I must admit I was shocked by the surge of anger upon seeing you again the night you won me. Everyone I loved and trusted failed me where Wallthorpe was concerned. You, my parents, and even myself. And while I could wish that things had been different, I won't deny that I have led a life that many would envy as a result of the path I was thrown onto. I do not regret the life I've lived."

Wolf was snared by the sincerity in her gaze, and what he could only call an echo of old love. Was there some chance that they might resurrect what had once existed, and fan the flames anew?

"Such sanguine thoughts on our tumultuous history. But then, you were ever the one to find the positive in any situation."

She smiled ruefully, while letting her hand slip away from his as her gaze dropped. "Perhaps not *every* situation."

Cold swiftly chilled his skin, where she had just touched him with such care. To distract himself from the loss, he reached for his glass of wine and took a sip.

"I can remember a late summer day when we visited the river not far from your house. It was so hot we decided to cool off in the water. I was about twelve, you were nine, and Ros was seven." The memories flooded back to him and made him happy, as they often did when he let them come. "You were so very careful of your new dress, taking it off and setting it to hang on a branch, so it wouldn't be dirtied. Ros refused to come in with us, but she happily stood on the banks as we played in the water. When we crawled out of the river and realized how dirty our underthings had become, there was no question that we were going to be in trouble. But you, Jules—you assured me your mother would be pleased that you had been careful with your new dress. You even made Ros carry it home, so as not to damage it in the slightest with your muddy, wet underclothes."

She chuckled, her smile lighting up the room far more than the candles he'd lit. "You know I missed dinner and breakfast for that stunt? I swore she was never going to let me run off to play with you again after that. Strangely, my father intervened, pointing out to her the fact that I had been so careful with my dress. Though I did have to promise never to go swimming again."

Wolf grinned. "Which you promptly did the next day, as I recall."

"Of course! I was simply much smarter about it. I secreted the required accessories to ensure I could repair myself well enough not to get caught." She matched his grin with one of her own. "We did have wonderful times together. Who would have thought we would be such good friends?"

Leveling his gaze on her, Wolf allowed some of what he was feeling to be seen on his face. "We were well matched then, as we are now."

She drew a deep breath, one that caused her breasts to rise and nearly spill from the low neckline of her dress. He was captivated both by her sensuous display, and by the blatant desire he could see lurking in her green eyes.

"I cannot disagree, though I like to think I am conceivably more of a leader and less of a follower now." She let her gaze dip down before looking up at him again. "I've been my own master for nearly a decade, and I can tell you, I'll never give that up again. Not for any man."

Wolf tried to tamp down the urge to challenge her then and there. He wanted to prove to her how good it could be. With *him*.

He'd never been the most dominant of his friends—Stone carried that title without a doubt—but something about Jules roused the protector in him. Drove him to try to shield her, to swaddle her in the softest cotton, and ensure that nothing and no one could ever hurt her again. It was entirely possible that made him the biggest hypocrite in history, since he knew he had hurt her so terribly ten years before.

He held her gaze steadily as the silence drew out between them. "With the right man, you wouldn't have to."

"Be that as it may, I still have Wallthorpe to deal with. And deal with him I shall. In the meantime, I do appreciate the breathing room you've given me with our false engagement." Relief shone in her eyes.

"It doesn't have to be false, Jules. If you'd marry me, you would be fully protected. Safe."

Anger unexpectedly welled up from deep within him. She shouldn't *need* protection. She shouldn't have to be fending off the attentions of a man who wouldn't take no for an answer. But then a wrenching dose of shame and sadness punched him in the gut. She shouldn't have had to marry a doddering old man ten years before, either, but she had. And he had only himself to blame for not saving her then, no matter what she said now.

She rose from the table and spun away from him, presenting her back. Her shoulders hunched over as she trembled. He stood as well, taking a step toward her, intent on offering comfort, but she straightened up and faced him.

"No. I've already told you: I shall not marry again for any reason but love."

It was on the tip of his tongue to say he did *love* her, but he would not do so until he was absolutely certain. For one, she would never believe a declaration like that in the moment, not after making her stance so clear. *Again.*

And second, he wasn't sure if he truly loved her, or if he simply needed to make reparations for his past sins. He refused to play her false ever again, and he needed time to figure out if his jumbled emotions were love or regret. She deserved that much, at least.

A woman like her, one so strong and confident, ought to be loved for herself alone, and not have it tainted by the past. If and when he was certain he could give her that, then and only then would he offer for her hand once more.

"As you wish. I shall not press the issue, though I still believe it would solve your pesky problem."

She sighed and offered a sad smile. "It would no doubt end Wallthorpe's incessant attempts to garner my hand in marriage, yes. But if I have learned nothing else in the last ten years, it's that I wouldn't be happy in a marriage of convenience—even to someone as handsome as you."

Latching on to her compliment, he deliberately shifted the direction of their conversation. "Ah-ha! At least I know now that you aren't refusing me because you think I'm an ogre."

She laughed. "Don't be ridiculous, Wolf." She hesitated, but then stepped closer to him. "You know I have always found you attractive. I remember the first time I spotted you across a ballroom, after you returned home from school."

"The Blakelys' ball."

His memory easily called up an all-too-familiar image of a red-haired goddess aglow in the candlelight. He'd been stunned to realize that the beauty who had instantly stolen his heart was his former playmate and best friend.

A small gasp escaped her—if he'd been further away from her, he might have missed it altogether, it was so soft. "You remember that?"

"Of course I do, Jules. You took my breath away back then. Allow me to return the favor."

Not remember the Blakelys' ball? It wasn't possible. He repressed a snort. Ready to end the conversation, he swept her into his arms and captured her parted lips.

The faint sweetness of the red wine they'd had with dinner teased his senses as he plundered and explored her mouth. Never one to surrender control, she met him stroke for stroke, their tongues sliding sensuously together. She melted into him, her corseted breasts pressed against him, teasing him with their proximity.

Determined to suck on the tight buds of her nipples, he began working her dress open at the back. All the while, he continued to sip of her lips and savor the taste that was all her own. Once he finally had her gown loosened and gaping in front, he reached down and lifted one breast free of its confinement. There were too many more layers of clothing to get through to wait for the pleasure of sucking the tip of her breast. So as he continued loosening her clothing, he took her pebbled nipple into his mouth and drew on her succulent flesh.

She laced her fingers through his hair and moaned as he tugged on the sensitive point. When he finally had her corset loosened as well, she pulled his mouth from her breast and turned around.

"Finish undressing me. I want to feel your chest hair chafing my nipples as you kiss me, your skin hot against mine."

She cast a sly smile over her shoulder as she waited for him to do as requested.

His already-hard cock seemed to grow even harder at her expression, as lust blew past all his restraints. With an efficiency he could only credit to his driving need to bury himself inside her, he quickly divested her of her clothes and all her underthings. Naked and unabashed by her natural state, she turned around, grabbed his jacket, and pulled it down his arms. As soon as he had one hand free of the garment, he was tugging at his necktie, while she finished removing his jacket. Then she was pushing his shirt up over his chest, until his skin was bared to her.

Her green eyes flared with heat as they shoved his shirt over his head together. By the time he had freed his hands once again, she had pressed her torso against his, and proceeded to rub against him like a cat. Any moment he expected her to start purring.

"Mmmm... I do love a man with chest hair."

She even nuzzled his pecs with her nose.

After a few moments of simply holding her as she chafed her breasts against him, he groaned when she reached down and opened his trousers. He toed off his shoes, while his remaining clothes fell away from his body under her busy hands. Trembling with need, he stepped free from his pants and was about to scoop her up for another kiss when she immediately dropped to her knees and caressed his groin.

"Did you know Arab men remove their pubic hair?" she asked, as she tangled her fingers in the coarse hairs nestled at the base of his shaft.

His reply was strangled in his throat for a moment as she caressed his sac. "I did not."

She took his length in a firm grip and stroked from base to tip. "They do. The practice has its merits, and its weaknesses."

She flashed a smile at him and then took the tip in her mouth.

As the warm, wet heat of her mouth engulfed him, shivers chased over his body. Wolf was no stranger to all forms of pleasure, but when Jules sank down his shaft until he lodged in her throat and then swallowed, he nearly came. Taking control over the interlude, he shoved his fingers into her hair, causing pins to fall out as her coiffeur was dismantled from his rough handling. And then he withdrew until just the tip of his erection sat between her lips.

"Jules, look at me."

Her bright green gaze shot straight to his face.

"Good girl. Tap my leg three times if you need me to stop. Do you understand?"

His voice came out harsh, as the need to plunder her mouth rode him hard.

She nodded, and then he pushed back into her mouth, sinking all the way to the root. She choked a bit on the first stroke, but once he pulled back and slid in again, she accommodated him with ease. Pleasure skimmed across his flesh as he lost himself in the warmth of her mouth, the tight clasp of her throat, and the sweet song of her moans.

Lost in the moment, she took him by surprise when she slipped her hand between his legs to fondle his sac. Then she shifted further back. With her finger coated by saliva, he supposed, she wiggled between the cheeks of his arse until she found his tight pucker.

Wolf groaned as she penetrated his hole, sinking deep inside him. Then she touched something within him that almost caused him to explode. Despite the fact that he was working his cock in and out of her mouth, fucking her thoroughly, she had once again stolen control.

Again, she rubbed that spot deep inside him, and his body seized. With his balls drawn tight against him, he cursed and then sank deep into the tight grip of her throat. With each pulse of his orgasm, she stroked that sensitive spot in his arse and swallowed around his cock. By the time she had finished drawing out his climax and removed her finger from his backside, his legs shook with the effort to stand. Withdrawing from her mouth, he stumbled to the bed and sank down before he collapsed.

As he calmed his racing heart and regained his composure, he glanced over to find Jules kneeling where he'd left her. With her hair disheveled and a pleased smile gracing her swollen lips, she was the most beautiful woman he'd ever seen.

"Come to me."

Chapter Ten

Julia shifted forward onto her hands and knees. Power and desire pulsed thickly through her veins as Wolf's heavy-lidded gaze rested on her with a gravity that made her feel strong, yet feminine. Determined to retain the control she had wrested from him, she crawled across the rug to where he sat on the bed. Thinking of how she'd once seen a tiger stalk its prey, she stayed low and long, working to affect a sensual quality to each slow move forward. Her breasts swayed, drawing his focus for a moment before his eyes retrained on her face.

Need slithered along her spine to coil low in her belly and between her thighs. She licked her lips, savoring the remnants of his musky taste, as well as the slight tenderness from his rough fucking of her mouth. Nearing his legs, she couldn't help but draw a comparison between this man and Tariq, the desert sheik she had taken as a lover. One light, the other dark. Both commanding lovers, but one's command stemmed from his force of personality, the other his birthright as the leader of his people. Both were fit men, but she could not deny that Wolf's broader frame and thickly roped muscles appealed to her in a way that Tariq's more sleekly muscled body never did.

Stopping before the man she'd known forever, she waited as her body yearned for his touch. It was a bit disconcerting to realize just how strong a pull he still had over her.

His clear blue gaze had grown darker, almost a stormy gray. "Stand."

Doing as he directed, she tucked her toes and rolled back to her feet to rise. He spread his legs and reached out, laying one hand on her hip to draw her closer. After adding his other hand to the opposite hip, he smoothed them up over the curve of her waist, stopping to span the distance. Then he leaned into her stomach and pressed his face to her softly rounded belly. For a moment, he seemed to be lost in the moment, absorbed in the crackling intensity that arced between them every time they touched. Then he pressed his lips to her skin and slowly peppered kisses over her stomach until he moved up over her ribs. With his hands trailing up her sides, his kisses gave way to nips and licks that had her body flashing hot and then cold, as lust swelled up from the tips of her toes.

Her breathing grew labored as he caught the underside of her breast with his teeth, only to switch to the other one and drag his tongue over the sensitized flesh. Her knees weakened with each touch, yet he refrained from lavishing her nipples with the same attention. As he teased and tantalized her, desire overrode her patience. She fisted her hands in his hair and tugged his head back so she could see his face.

"Suck on my nipples. I need to feel your mouth on them."

A sensual but determined gleam came into his eyes as he stared up at her. "No."

She inhaled sharply, desire warring with her self-control.

He jerked forward, ignoring the hard pull of his hair as her fist remained tight, and nipped the side of her breast one last time. Then he stood, forcing her to release her grip, and shifted around her until his chest was pressed to her back.

What was he going to do?

Uncertainty caused her excitement to soar as she waited. And waited.

"Bend over."

His brusque command came out low and raspy.

Determined to retain some control, she leaned forward, pressing her hands to the mattress and wiggled her backside against his groin.

"All the way, sweetheart. I'm the only one in control here." Then he pressed his hand against her back between her shoulder blades and forced her down until she had to turn her cheek. "Don't move unless I give you direction."

In that moment, with her soaked pussy rubbing against his hardening cock and her face pressed to the bed, she had never been so turned on. Because if Julia was honest with herself, as much as she liked her independence, it was exhausting always having to fight for her power, and her freedom.

"Jules, you need to understand something about me. I am a dominant man, and in the bedroom, *I* am the one in control. My only desire is to please you, but I shall go about that in my own way."

He stroked her backside, first one cheek, and then the other.

"I've had demanding lovers before, and have a full understanding of the rules."

She tried to lick her lips, but her mouth had gone dry with wanting. Wanting him pressed against her. Wanting him inside her. Wanting… She pushed aside the yet unformed desire, because she knew in her heart of hearts it was not something she could afford to acknowledge.

He grunted at her answer. "Perhaps, but the first rule you'll need to learn is that if you attempt to wrest control from me, there *will* be consequences. This time, it will be ten swats to your arse to remind you who holds the reins in here."

And then he smacked her right cheek. Heat bloomed over her flesh, but it was a relatively light blow. If he'd asked her, she could have told him she'd had worse, much worse punishment in her life. Though certainly not with the promise of explosive pleasure at the end, and there was no mistaking his intent.

Then he landed a smack on her left cheek.

This was no brutal punishment of the sort that Wallthorpe had doled out early in their marriage. Or even of the caliber Tariq had handed down to her when he felt she had exceeded the bounds his masculinity could accept within his culture. While he had been an enlightened man, a Cambridge man even, some of her transgressions could not be overlooked in order to save face with his people. Having a white infidel as a lover was already asking too much.

Two more slaps landed, one on each side. And then two more.

Heat spread through her, and with it came the desire, the need that always flooded her when she was treated to that erotic bite of pain. She bit her lip to keep her moan in check. She didn't trust him enough yet to fully disclose her less-than-proper preferences. But if he kept up this pace, he would soon figure it out, whether she wanted to reveal the truth or not. Her quim was soaking wet, and her legs trembled with desire.

He rubbed his palm over her warm backside and moaned a little behind her. "Your bottom has turned a delectable rose color, but we're not done yet. Four more to go."

Was he reminding her or himself?

Not that it mattered, because she was so ready to feel him inside her.

Two more spanks landed. Then he dragged his shaft between the globes of her backside and pumped between them like he was fucking her for a moment. When the last two blows landed, it was all she could do to keep from coming as she rubbed her mound against the edge of the bed. Just a little more pressure would do it.

Then one hard and very unexpected spank landed across both cheeks. "Cease trying to bring yourself off. You'll come when I take you there."

His gruff demand sent shivers up her spine, and cranked her want a little higher. She whimpered with the pulsating need to release, like a steam kettle about to blow. "Please, I ache."

Wolf nudged her feet wider apart, spreading her open to him as she lay bent over the bed. "What was our lesson this evening?"

Her head spun until she could barely form a coherent thought. Every word he spoke felt like someone had plucked a violin string, except the string was buried deep inside her and drawn taut between her nipples and her clit.

He'd asked a question...

"What was the lesson, Jules? I need an answer before we move on."

He put his hands on her bottom and squeezed, sending sparks of pain mixed with desire shooting through her body. Desperate for the answer, she knew she knew it. She raked her scattered thoughts together, until a single word clicked.

"Control." She licked her lips, wetting them once more. "You're in control in the bedroom."

Oh, God, please let that be the answer he wanted.

"Mmm...very good. Now, a reward for a lesson well learned."

He shifted around behind her, possibly even lowered himself to his knees, she thought.

The first swipe of his tongue over her drenched slit caused her legs to shift from trembling to full-on quaking. Her hands fisted in the sheets as he stroked over her clit and drew his tongue back to her entrance. Then he plunged inside her and twirled it around. The next swipe over her sensitive nub had her exploding. "Wolf!" she cried out as pleasure burst through her.

Relentlessly, he dragged his tongue over her plumping folds, lapping at her desire as the promise of release danced just out of reach. Then he ran his tongue from her clit back to the entrance of her sex. She waited eagerly for the sensation of his tongue sliding within, swirling around once more...but he slicked right past her entrance and moved a bit higher. As he gripped the still-tender globes of her bottom and spread them wide, she gasped with the pleasure-pain as her need crept another notch higher.

Then he swirled his tongue over her tight whorl. Her whole body shook with need as she relaxed and then clenched around nothing. A keening cry of emptiness careened out of her. "Please!"

"You may not come yet, Jules. Hold back for me."

His gruff command settled the wildness that had grown in her until she wasn't sure she could contain it any longer.

He continued to lap at her tight entrance, even as he slid two fingers inside her pussy. The pressure returned to building, and she knew she couldn't last forever. But then he pulled his fingers out of her quim and pushed them past the tingling, tight ring of muscle.

He plunged inside her and then retreated. Over and over. And then from underneath her, she heard the words she'd hung on for, the signal of her freedom.

"Come for me. Come now."

His demand, followed immediately by the sucking force of his mouth on her clit, tossed her over the edge, and she exploded.

He licked and lapped as he continued to drive his fingers inside her, until her knees gave out and she sagged onto his face. She whimpered at the added pressure to her sensitive tissues while sparks of ecstasy shot through her. As long moments stretched out she reeled from his sensual assault. Finally, with his support, she found her legs as she reveled in the deep pleasure of the climax he'd wrung from her.

He stood up and eased her onto the bed. All the while he stroked and petted her, until she had fully returned to the moment.

He nibbled on her ear as he spooned her, and then whispered, "I need you. I need to fuck you hard. And I don't think I can be gentle."

She tilted her head back toward him, catching his expression from the corner of her eye. "I do not recall asking you to be."

With a growl, he rolled her back onto her stomach and urged her onto her hands and knees. Moving with an economy of motion she could not credit, he donned a French Letter. Then he lined his cock up with her cunny and drove into her in a hard and fast move that had stars dancing before her eyes. Her swollen sex felt stretched, and so full of him. Then he drew out, dragging his shaft along all that sensitive flesh, and shivers broke out over her body.

"Do it again."

And he did. He slammed into her hard, and then drew back in the most sensuous slide, that sent her desire spiking once more. He started fucking her, pounding into her from behind, with a pace that made her head spin and her heart beat like a moth's wings. His balls slapped against her thighs as he shuttled in and out. His need was escalating quickly with each pump of his hips, as was hers. She could feel the frantic quality of his thrusting, and yet he'd not exploded.

"Reach between your thighs and rub your clit. Make yourself come for me."

His command answered the question that had popped into her head only a moment before. And so, she did as he instructed. She reached down and stroked over the extended nub. As he continued to fill her over and over, she worked her clit until her orgasm slammed into her like a runaway train. She screamed his name as she pushed backward into his thrusts. Two strokes later, while she swiftly dropped from her high, he stiffened up behind her.

"Yes! Jules, yes!"

The warm heat from his seed seeped into her through the barrier of the French Letter as he continued sliding in and out with much less aggression. With each plunge, his hips slowed until he sank inside her and draped himself over her back.

She reveled in the heat of him, his weight, and the feel of all those muscles wrapped around her. A sense of contentment she had not felt in many years settled over her. She refused to examine it too closely, because she knew she could not afford to feel anything for Wolf.

They had no future, because she refused to be tethered to any man again. Not to mention trusting anyone was nearly impossible. She was the only person she could rely on.

Chapter Eleven

Julia and her sister had decided to take some air. It was early spring, and a particularly warm day, which was why half of London had decided to do the very same thing. Strolling along Rotten Row was a necessary evil—the only upside of which was that one was not expected to stop and chat. Much. People spent the majority of their time smiling and nodding, and both she and Ros excelled at this mundane interaction.

"Are we almost to the turn off?" Ros asked through her teeth, as they strolled arm in arm.

Julia continued to smile and nod. "It's just ahead."

They walked for a few more moments, and then came to a fork in the path where they could depart the more crowded route. As they left the notable set behind, they relaxed their sore cheeks and stretched their tight necks.

"Oh, at last!" Ros let go of her sister and reached up to rub her neck. "I couldn't take much more of Society. Truly, I do not know how you stand it."

Julia rolled her shoulders and offered her sister a genuine smile. "I'll tell you, it has been much easier this time around. As a woman steeped in scandal—not to mention being a widow—I have far more leeway than during my come-out. There is no question you made the right choice when you ran off with Archie and got married."

She darted a quick glance at Ros, instantly regretting her absentminded reference to her sister's dead husband. Ros' emerald green eyes—exactly like her own—dimmed a bit as the ever-present sadness that haunted her returned.

Julia grabbed her arm. "Oh, please forgive me! I know how much you miss him, still."

"It has been five years, but yes, I do miss Archie. Though I have begun to suspect I miss being married more."

At that, Ros blushed—fetchingly.

Julia was not above admitting that her sister's less violent coloring allowed her to do things like blush and weep without turning a virulent shade of magenta. She, on the other hand, avoided both blushing and weeping with a vengeance. With her bright red hair, she had long ago learned that it did not make for an attractive appearance when emotional. Fortunately, in the last ten years, she'd had little to cry about. Blushing, however, still sometimes proved problematic.

"Oh, ho! And what part of being married is it you miss most?"

Julia could not think of a single aspect of marriage she had enjoyed. But then, that had likely had more to do with the man she had been wed to, and less about the state itself.

Ros narrowed her gaze. "Well, of course I miss the intimate activities." She rolled her eyes. "But truly, I miss having someone to share the day with. To share my life. Archie would come home at the end of the day, sweaty and tired, and I loved taking care of him, hearing about his day, seeing the stress slide from his face as we talked and touched." Ros fell silent, as though reflecting.

Julia sighed softly. If her marriage had been more like that, she might not abhor the notion of it so greatly. Her experience had been *far* different. She shuddered with the errant memory.

"You make it sound so lovely."

The greenery of the park stretched out around them as they continued their sedate walk.

"Oh, it was, but that was because I loved Archie. Had we not been so crazy about each other, I imagine the life of an army man's wife would have become wearing. It was a hard life, with all the washing and cooking, and the daily cleaning of the house. We simply did not have the funds to afford help." Ros stared off in the distance as they walked. "I thought he might divorce me at least once a week during that first year. I couldn't do anything right," she said, laughing.

Julia laughed as well. "I remember your tearstained letters. But you've always been full of ingenuity. I knew you would figure it all out eventually."

"And I did, thank goodness!" Ros tilted her head and looked at her sister. "If marriage was so terrible for you, why have you agreed to marry Wolf? Honestly, I thought you'd remain a widow for the rest of your days."

Julia let her gaze drop to her toes as they strolled, and tried to form as true an answer as she could muster. She hated lying to her sister, but Ros had no ability to prevaricate. It simply wasn't in her to employ guile in any manner. "I hadn't any intention of remarrying, as you know, but Wolf caught me in a weak moment, and I said yes."

Ros frowned. "You do not love him?"

Julia's brows drew together. "I suppose I care for him. He has always been a great friend, but I do not love him."

I can't.

The sound of hooves slapping the ground had them stopping to look back at who had caused such a clamor.

"Well, hello, ladies."

Wallthorpe rode up to them, as though he had spied them from a distance and chased them down. His poor mount's sides heaved as though he'd been run hard, which seemed neither practical in Hyde Park, nor very kind.

They both curtsied and murmured, "My lord."

He swung down from the horse and turned, as though he expected to walk with them. Julia gritted her teeth as Ros stiffened beside her. The younger version of the old brute she'd married scared the devil out of her sister, and Julia hated that she was responsible for bringing such a vile creature near her gentle sibling.

"What can we do for you, my lord?"

"I simply spied two lovely ladies out for a stroll and thought to accompany them. Must I require something more than your fine company?"

He offered a pleasant enough smile, but Julia watched his eyes, as she always did. As she had learned to do with his father. His smiles never reached his flat brown gaze.

She pressed her lips together in annoyance. "No, if that is all you seek."

"Well, a private word would not come amiss, Lady Wallthorpe."

Then he looked pointedly at Ros.

"Oh, I can certainly fall back a few steps if you'd like, Julia."

Ros looked to her to say yes or no. Julia had a choice, but each option held consequences. If she did not give him the moment he sought, he would turn cruel, and say something untoward about her—or worse—her sister.

With a sigh, she nodded. "Perhaps you could give us a moment?"

Ros quickly fell back, offering them some semblance of privacy.

Julia decided to take the bull by the horns. "Say your piece, my lord. I do not wish to leave my sister lingering long behind us."

His lip curled up at this, but he quickly smoothed it out. "I wished to revisit our previous conversation. There is still time for you to change your mind about this farce of an engagement to Lord Wolfington. *I* am the man you should be marrying."

"I am afraid I disagree, my lord. I am quite happy with my choice of future husband."

Julia worked hard to keep her tone neutral, despite the fact he made her skin crawl. He always had, even when she was a debutante.

Wallthorpe stopped and turned her to face him. "Lady Wallthorpe, you are a marchioness! You do not have to lower yourself to marrying a mere viscount."

She stepped back from the obtuse man, jerking her shoulders free of his hands. Then she resumed walking. "My lord, whatever title my fiancé bears is inconsequential to me in the course of determining his suitability as a husband."

"I see." He tucked his hands behind his back as they continued on. "Well, then. I suppose I shall have to cast my eye in another direction."

He then looked back over his shoulder, in the direction of Ros.

Julia stopped short. His threat was clear, and her throat closed, as if he had physically wrapped his fingers around her neck and squeezed. Somehow, she managed to heave in a breath. "My lord, I believe I am feeling unwell. I should return home. You will, of course, excuse me."

"Of course." He executed a half bow. "I do hope you are feeling better soon."

She nodded and strode toward where Ros stood, a short distance away. Once she reached her, they retreated back toward Rotten Row—and escape. Julia fought back the nausea that threatened to blossom as she frog-marched her sister home. All the while, Ros remained silent while she struggled to maintain the bruising pace Julia had set.

Once they were both safely ensconced in their parlor, Ros looked at her sister. "Tell me what that odious man said to upset you so."

Julia refused to repeat the implied threat. "No. There is no need for anyone else to be disturbed."

Her sister's brows drew together. "What could he possibly have said?"

"Nothing worth repeating." Julia paced over to the secretary, opened the drop desk, then promptly closed it and paced back toward the fireplace.

She moved over to the window and looked out at the hustle and bustle as people passed their home. How could she protect Ros from Wallthorpe? Certainly, she was a grown woman capable of saying no, but she was such a gentle soul. It would fundamentally change her to have to thwart Wallthorpe's advances, and Julia refused to allow that to occur. Pressing her fingertips to her temples, she knew she needed help with this situation. There was only one person she could call upon to offer assistance.

With a determined stride, she returned to the secretary, opened the drop desk, and pulled out a paper and stylus. Wolf would know what to do. Julia was certain he could find a way to protect her sister, and it would not include one of them breaking their fake engagement.

It simply couldn't.

Chapter Twelve

W olf stood on Julia's front steps with her summons in hand. The correspondence held a frantic note that concerned him, which was why he was knocking earlier than what might otherwise be considered acceptable.

The door opened to reveal a butler—not especially tall, and not especially remarkable. His brown hair was graying at the temples, however, and offered up a distinguished air when paired with his simple livery.

Behind him, Julia hovered as though she might just push the man aside and take over his duties.

"Good morning," the butler said.

"Good morning. Please tell Lady Wallthorpe that Lord Wolfington—" Wolf was cut off by an impatient Julia.

She huffed and stepped around her staid servant. "Oh, for heaven's sake, I am right here, and I can plainly see who is at the door, Johnson. Go back to whatever you were doing."

She shooed him off.

"My lady, it is simply not done for someone of your stature to answer her own door."

Johnson seemed far more affronted by her actions than either Julia or Wolf. In fact, he couldn't hide his grin as she tugged him inside by his coat sleeve.

"Pish, Johnson. No one but *you* is standing on such propriety. I haven't lived in England for a decade, and Wolf is an old friend."

She towed him into the front parlor.

With a disgruntled rumble, the butler closed the front door and retreated to the rear of the house.

Wolf was still swallowing her offhand description of him as a friend. He knew her far more intimately than any *friend,* in his experience. He'd tasted her sweet-tart honey, and watched her come apart in his arms. They were decidedly *beyond* friends.

Undoubtedly lovers, but could he convince her to be his wife?

If he were honest with himself, he knew now that he'd never be able to let her go again. His head spun with the unexpected realization.

"Thank you for coming." Julia released his sleeve and spun around to face him. "I was up all night working out a plan."

Wolf took his agitated fiancée by the shoulders and forced her to hold still. "Take a deep breath, and tell me what is going on."

She tried to dislodge his hands with a shrug. "Oh, do stop. I'm fine, just concerned."

"Jules, look at me."

He used what he thought of as his commanding voice, the one that normally made women pay attention and do as he desired.

Her green gaze locked with his.

He drew his hands over her shoulders and up to cup her delicate jawline. "Whatever it is, we will tackle it together. But I need you to settle down and explain what has happened."

She drew a shuddering breath, and then nodded. "Of course. My apologies."

She quickly explained about Wallthorpe's unexpected appearance in the park, and his veiled threat toward Ros.

Wolf's brows drew together. "And you're certain he intends to pursue her?"

Julia pinched the bridge of her nose and sighed. "Am I certain? No. Am I worried? Very."

"Can she not simply refuse him?"

He could tell Jules was deeply upset by the notion of Wallthorpe switching his focus to her sister.

She let one brow rise in annoyance. "Certainly. Ros can refuse his advances exactly as I did, but with the same likely result."

Feeling a bit abashed, since he was currently embroiled in Jules' own plot to extricate herself from the persistent

Wallthorpe, he nodded. "I suppose you are correct. He has not abided by Society's standards of conduct so far."

"Precisely. And I am afraid if he went to my parents and addressed his suit, they would put even more pressure on her to remarry." Jules drew a steadying breath. "But I have a plan. If I can find her a suitor—someone who will protect her in the short term, and then allow her to end the connection once it's safe, as we have agreed to do—she, too, can fend Wallthorpe off."

Wolf's brows both rose. "So, you are saying you expect a man to court your sister publicly and then allow her to call off the engagement, at the end risking possible damage to his reputation?"

She turned to face him, her brows drawn together in the most adorable display of confusion. "You're doing exactly that for me, aren't you?"

He wanted to snarl and tell her that he had no intention of letting her go once this fake engagement was over. But he knew if he did such, she would end everything at once, putting herself at great risk again.

No, he could not show her the truth of what he wanted. Not yet.

He plastered his card face on and did his best to look unflappable, even as he seethed beneath the surface. "Of course, but I've known you for years and years. Does Rosalind know any men who might be willing to perform this same service?"

The crease between her brows remained as her lips curved down in disappointment. "Not that I am aware of. There is that very nice officer from her husband's unit who has visited her once or twice, however."

Wolf huffed. "Have you even discussed this with her?"

Jules looked wary—though that crease had finally disappeared. "No. She will just refuse my help."

"Bloody hell! Jules, even if we could find a man willing to aid your sister, he cannot very well do so without her consent."

Not to mention, Wolf had his doubts that some poor, unsuspecting officer would have the wherewithal to manage this particular situation. Not many untitled men would choose to work in direct opposition to a peer of the realm.

Jules glared at him. "Help me find a man first, and then we can argue about what to tell Ros."

"And what is it you are plotting to hide from me now?"

The woman in question walked into the room, her strawberry blond hair caught up in an artful twist that accentuated her long neck. With her soft green day dress, she looked very elegant, though slightly cross at the moment.

Jules shot daggers at Wolf with her eyes, even as she turned to smile at her sister. "Nothing, dear."

Ros looked from him to Jules, and then back to him. He knew what was coming, because between him and Jules, he'd always been the easy mark.

"Wolf, don't let her bully you into keeping secrets from me."

Ros looked at him with her big green eyes—so much like Jules'—and he simply caved.

The Fairchild sisters both seemed to have him in the palm of their hands—though one usually held a much more fun part of him.

"Wallthorpe has alluded that if he can't have Jules, he will come after you next. So she's scheming to have a man—one yet to be determined—take up with you as a suitor, until Wallthorpe can be dealt with properly."

He could hear Jules cursing under her breath before she tried to land a preemptive strike and appease her sister. "Ros, I just wish to protect you. You shouldn't have to contend with an unwanted suitor simply because I rejected him."

Her sister pinched the bridge of her nose. "But really, Jules, you were not going to tell me?"

Her cheeks turning a delightful shade of magenta, Jules said, "I was, once I worked out a suitable man to protect you. Which I had hoped Wolf could help me with. I was just working my way around to asking if one of his friends might assist us in this." She let one brow rise.

Wolf mentally sighed. Jules was quite the managing baggage when she chose to be. He'd forgotten that about her—rather inconveniently, he realized. "Well, I..." He swallowed.

Who among his set might he trust to protect Ros?

She was much too sweet for any of his friends.

"Come now, there must be one amongst your friends who might aid us?" Jules pushed.

He stalled, trying to imagine which of his friends might be the most believable as her suitor.

Undeterred, Jules upped the ante on him with an evil grin. "I suppose I could see if that nice Mr. Lucifer might be able to offer us some help."

Wolf wanted to curse. Loudly. And with great vigor. Instead, he did what he always did when it came to these two women and gave in, despite his better judgement. "I shall see if one of my friends might be willing. It is possible Linc would take on the task."

Ros harrumphed. "Well, you needn't make it sound so onerous. I am not an ogre, last I checked the mirror."

"I meant no such insult. I am just trying to picture you with one of them, and Linc seems the most likely fellow. He's quite the charmer." Wolf nodded then, as much to himself as to them. Yes, he would be the best choice. Certainly the most believable. "I suggest we all go for an outing, so Ros and her intended may meet."

He couldn't keep his lips from twitching.

"We could all attend the Weatherly ball later this week," Jules suggested.

"Maybe something less formal. Mayhap a picnic would be better? We can include all the Lustful Lords to ease any awkwardness."

Wolf didn't suspect his friends would be overly eager to attend a ball, and with the crushing crowds, it would be harder to keep Wallthorpe away from Jules and Ros.

"No, we need something more public, where a connection between Ros and your friend will be noticed."

Jules' voice carried a confidence that Wolf did not share on the matter. A ball seemed like a terrible idea.

"Absolutely not," he retorted in his commanding voice. "A ball will be too crowded. And even if I could convince the other Lustful Lords to attend, it will be far too difficult to protect you both in such an environment."

To his dismay, Jules utterly ignored him.

"Excellent. We already planned to attend, so why don't you *and* your friends meet us here Thursday evening, and we can go together? We'll see you at half past nine."

He tried again. "Julia, I said *no*."

"Wolf, be reasonable. If we do not make a very public display, the effort will be useless. Trust me when I tell you, Wallthorpe and my parents will simply ignore anything else."

Then she pressed against his arm and unleashed her emerald weapons. He looked into her eyes and called the loss.

"Fine. We will see you then." He ground his teeth and gave up the fight. When she dug her heels in, he knew there was no budging her.

Thursday night came and Wolf arrived at Jules' house first. He was shown into the parlor to wait. Flint was coming with Linc, since they had planned to have dinner beforehand, and just to add a bit of polish to the effort, Stone and his wife, as well as Cooper and his new bride, were also joining the party. Arthur had fallen ill with a cold and had elected to stay home—balls not being his cup of tea.

Of course, none of the Lustful Lords were avid attendees of such soirees. They typically only went when forced by family, duty, or their wives.

Wolf suddenly heard the rustling of skirts, and then Jules appeared in the doorway. She looked stunning in a vibrant purple gown that could never have been mistaken for mourning garb. The off-the-shoulder dress bared far more of her shoulders and bosom than he would have preferred, though he could not deny she looked stunning. Her dress nipped in at her waist before belling out into full skirts. It was simple, with few adornments, but it fit her perfectly.

"You look ravishing this evening."

She smiled brightly. "Do save the sweet words for when everyone is here. They are wasted without an audience."

"The truth is never wasted, and I couldn't care less if any-one is here or not."

He stalked toward her, drawn to her by the need that con-stantly thrummed in his veins. She took a step backwards toward the door, but he caught her around the waist before she could escape.

Jules pressed her hands against his chest. "Wolf, what are you doing?"

"Kissing you. I should think it were obvious."

"But my dress—"

He cut off her objections by sealing his lips over hers. Des-perate to taste her unique blend of sweet and spicy, he drove his tongue past her lips and teeth to explore her mouth. A soft little moan escaped her as she pressed closer to him, as though seeking his warmth. His cock lengthened and grew hard while they continued to feast on each other. Finally, on the verge of doing something unthinkable, he tried to pull back.

But she clung to him and whispered, "I need you. I need your hands on me."

With a groan, he sank deeper into the kiss, and reached down to hitch her skirts up. Pawing at her petticoats and crinolines, he finally found her pantalets. With her skirts crushed between them, he delved through the opening and found her wet center. She moaned as he stroked along her slit, rubbed over her clit, and then pushed a finger inside her.

With a soft gasp, she clenched around him as he slipped his finger in and out. Lost in the throes of pleasure, she broke off the kiss as he circled her clit. And then she cried out as she came, dousing his fingers.

He captured her lips once more to smother her cries of pleasure. Trembling in his arms, she slowly regained aware-ness. Her eyes were wide as she regained control over her body and straightened up. With her cheeks flushed—either from her climax, or from embarrassment, he couldn't be sure—she ducked away from him. Giving him her back, she proceeded to shake out her skirts.

He took a moment to gather together the threads of his control. He needed to tamp down his own lust. The woman pushed him to the edge of sanity, it seemed, but he couldn't remember feeling that way about her a decade ago. Without a doubt, he'd loved her then, but it had been—even for him—a young, naïve emotion. An experience fraught with stolen kisses, gentle touches, and restrained desire. Maybe curiosity more than anything.

It wasn't that he had been inexperienced then, but conceivably he'd seen Jules in a different light?

He'd been raised to see a gentlewoman and act accordingly. *But now?*

After the auction at The Market, sharing her with Linc, and their night together alone, his perspective had changed. Jules was no less a lady now than she'd been before, but his understanding of women and their innate desires had greatly expanded. His awareness of her needs had also changed. She was a woman who embraced her own natural instincts and needs.

How could he not feel differently? Not embrace her willingness to indulge in sexual pleasure? After all, he was merely a man. Whether his heart was engaged or not, his libido certainly was.

A sharp knock at the door drew his attention back to the moment. He turned, and his gaze locked with hers.

Dear God, the woman absolutely simmered with passion.

"We will discuss this interlude later, Jules."

Chapter Thirteen

Julia's heart still raced, and she was positive her cheeks were flushed. They still felt warm after that unexpected moment in Wolf's arms. As his friends walked in, she tried to smooth the creases in her skirts that his amorous attentions had caused. Not that she regretted either.

"Lady Wallthorpe, may I introduce Lord and Lady Stonemere?"

Wolf's rumble sent shivers along her overstimulated frame.

The imposing man and his vivacious wife—she fairly sparkled with life—seemed an unlikely match. But then the man smiled indulgently as she tossed all formality out the window and hugged Julia. Shocked by the intimate gesture, Julia hugged her back.

"I'd apologize, but since we are going to be great friends, I figured we should dispense with all the pomp and circumstance up front. And please, call me Theo." Then the slightly shorter woman stepped back. "Stone, say hello, and stop looming."

He rolled his eyes at his wife and took Julia's hand, bowing over it. "Lady Wallthorpe, a pleasure to meet you."

She smiled at the couple. "Please, call me Julia. Both of you."

Then Wolf motioned another couple forward. "And this is Lord and Lady Brougham."

The handsome blond man would have made Greek statues weep for his beauty, and with his equally lovely wife by his side, they made a stunning pair. He, too, bowed over Julia's hand. "A pleasure, my lady."

"Julia, please. Such formality seems a bit overdone, as you are all friends of Wolf's."

She drew her hand back, only to have Lord Brougham's wife pull her into an embrace, as well.

The women were quite the hugging group, weren't they? Julia smothered the laugh that threatened to escape.

"Please, call me Emily. It's a good thing you've given in to the informality already. Theo is a bit of a runaway loco-motive when she has determined she will be friends with someone."

The pretty brunette winked at her, and then cast a fond smile at Theo.

The other woman merely grinned. "She's not wrong."

And then she shrugged as everyone chuckled.

Another knock heralded the arrival of the last of their party, though a lone man walked in. He was around the same height as Wolf, but his hair was as dark as night. In contrast, his eyes were bright blue—though something dark lurked behind them, making the fine hairs on the back of Julia's neck rise up. While the man appeared pleasant enough, there was a menacing quality to him.

"Flint, you're late," Wolf said, by way of greeting.

He tugged at his coat sleeves. "Apologies, I ran into a few issues."

Wolf's brow rose, but he quickly shifted topics. "And where is Linc?"

"Afraid he won't make it. Came down with whatever Dun-mere has."

Wolf groaned. "Well, doesn't that beat all?" He frowned and looked at her. "Sorry, Jules. Seems Ros' suitor is not going to make an appearance this evening."

Disappointment and worry seized her lungs. "Oh, no."

"Who isn't making an appearance?" Ros asked, as she float-ed into the room, glowing and smiling at the group.

Sometimes it unnerved Julia how quiet her sister could be, even when wearing layers of crinolines and fabric. "The man who'd agreed to act as your suitor has taken ill, I'm afraid."

Ros' smile faded. "Oh, why, that's terrible news. I do hope he will be all right."

The dark-haired man stepped forward then, his gaze locked on Ros. "It's just a cold. He should be fine in a few days."

Her sister looked up at him, and seemed to hesitate before she spoke. "Th-that's good."

Did her sister just stutter?

Julia had never heard a misfired syllable from Ros in all her life. How odd. "Well, I suppose we shall have to close ranks around Ros then during the ball. I had hoped having an obvious suitor would stave off Wallthorpe."

"I'll act as her suitor."

The dark man—Flint—boldly made the offer as he stepped closer to Ros.

She immediately turned a fetching shade of pink.

Wolf looked as worried as Julia felt. "Are you sure, Flint? It can't be just for tonight. This issue may drag on for a bit."

Flint stole another look at Ros, and then nodded. "I'll not let anything happen to such a lovely lady."

Julia's internal alarm sounded as she watched the byplay between the two. "Wolf, perhaps you should introduce your friend, before we make any changes to the plan?"

"Apologies, Lady Wallthorpe, Mrs. Smith. May I present Lord Flintshire?"

He bowed over each of their hands, though he lingered much longer—obviously so—over Ros's.

"My lord." Her sister's breathless reply continued to cause concern for Julia.

"As I said, I'd be happy to offer my protection, if Mrs. Smith requires it." Flint repeated the offer once more, his words not revealing any strong emotion, one way or the other. Yet his intense gaze continued to drift to where Ros stood.

Wolf and Julia spoke at the same time, tripping over each other.

"Excellent!" he said.

"No need, my lord," she replied, and narrowed her gaze at Wolf.

Everyone looked at her in surprise.

"Well, we can simply close ranks, as I suggested before. Then, when Lord Lincolnshire is feeling better, he can take up the role, as previously planned."

Flint tensed at this, his hands fisting.

"Julia, I would feel better accepting Lord Flintshire's offer." Ros' softly spoken assertion caused the obvious tension in the man to relax.

It shocked Julia to see such a physical reaction from him. Warily, she glanced back and forth between the pair, and then her gaze finally settled on her sister. "If you're sure. I want you to be comfortable with this."

Ros looked up at Flint and smiled softly. "Yes, I'm quite sure."

"Well, now that that has been decided, perhaps we should go?" Wolf motioned the group toward the front door.

The ballroom was packed to the gills, as expected. Julia stood shoulder to shoulder with Wolf, and tried not to focus on her whirlwind of thoughts. Her mind kept circling back to her sister, who stood beside Flint, and then to the shared moments with Wolf, before everyone else had arrived. Her body kept swinging between hot and cold, even as she scanned the crowd for signs of Wallthorpe.

"Perchance you should attempt to appear to be enjoying my company?" Amusement tinged Wolf's voice.

She huffed in response. "I am too busy worrying over Wallthorpe, and now my sister and your friend." She angled closer to him. "Did you see how Ros behaved with him? I haven't seen her act in such a fashion since her late husband was alive."

"Do not make more of what is likely to be only a passing curiosity for them." He stroked her shoulder with his gloved hand, sending goosebumps rippling over her skin.

"Possibly."

She wanted to agree with him, but some part of her refused to let go of her concern. Then a movement out of the corner of her eye drew her attention. She cast her gaze to her right, and found Wallthorpe moving toward their group. "Here he comes."

Wolf made some movement with his hand, and Flint swept Ros away, along with Cooper and Emily.

Julia and Wolf faced her pesky suitor together.

"Good evening, Wolfington, Lady Wallthorpe," he said, as he bowed to each in turn.

"Wallthorpe," Wolf replied, almost growling at the man.

Wallthorpe glanced at Stonemere and Theo, who stood behind them. "And where is that lovely sister of yours?"

Julia took a breath, and hoped their gamble would pay off. "I believe she is off spending time with her suitor."

Wallthorpe's gaze narrowed. "Suitor? I had not realized Mrs. Smith had garnered such attention."

"Yes, well, it seems she has. I believe you are acquainted with Lord Flintshire?" Julia worked to keep her features in a neutral place. It wouldn't do to sneer at the man.

Wallthorpe paled.

She found it a strange response, but if the mere mention of Lord Flintshire caused such a reaction, maybe his supposed interest in Ros would be more than enough to keep her safe.

Her stepson visibly swallowed. "I'm surprised you would allow such a brute near your tenderhearted sister."

"Yes, well, the heart does as the heart wants. I'm afraid they took an instant liking to each other upon a casual meeting." She pressed a hand to her chest. "You can imagine everyone's surprise at the discovery."

"Indeed," Wallthorpe drawled. "Well, it was lovely visiting with you both."

And then he moved along, through the crowd. Julia watched him closely as he crossed the room, and then made his way toward the foyer of the Weatherly's home.

Wolf captured her hand between his big palms. "Jules, are you well?"

She drew a deep breath. "I believe I am. He seemed rather disconcerted by Flint's pursuit of Ros."

Wolf grunted in reply.

Her curiosity piqued, she turned to face him. As always, his chiseled features elicited her admiration and had her heart skipping necessary beats. "Is there ought I should know of his character? I must say, Wallthorpe's reaction makes me curious to know more about him, particularly as he called him a brute."

Wolf shoved a finger into his collar, and seemed to be seeking a bit more room. "Well, he *does* have a bit of a reputation as a boxer."

Julia stared at Wolf. "A boxer? That seems a bit mundane for such a reaction. Many gentlemen box. What aren't you telling me?"

He looked down at his feet. "He is also something of a bare-knuckle brawler."

Julia could not hide the horror she felt. "Wolf! You cannot mean to say you have sent my sister off in the clutches of such a man?"

"Do not be so overdramatic. Not only is Flint a perfect gentleman, but he would never dream of hurting your sister. And if Wallthorpe were to become overly aggressive, Flint would be the man to call on to end such behavior."

"I suppose that may be true. But I do not like their pairing, even if it is a hoax."

She turned to find her sister among the crowd. When she spied Ros across the ballroom, her sister's cheeks were pink as she held on to Flint's arm.

Neither Julia nor her sister were in great demand for dances, so they were free to dance or not as they wished. She watched the couple for a while, and noticed that as the man loomed over her sister, most of the men who had claimed a dance with her approached, but never made it close enough to claim their partner.

She couldn't be sure if Flint caused them to scamper on purpose. It could merely be a byproduct of his brutish presence or, she supposed, his reputation alone repelled the less intrepid men. Nevertheless, Ros did not seem at all perturbed to be standing next to him. In fact, she glowed.

A waltz was then announced, and Julia decided it was time to cease worrying about her sister. She was clearly safe for the moment. "Wolf, come dance with me."

"Only if you are finished brooding about your sister." He let one brow arch, which caused her own cheeks to heat.

Friends could be such a hassle.

"I'm done. While I'm not sure about Flint as a stand-in suitor, I *am* confident she is secure under his care for the moment."

Wolf nodded and took her hand to escort her onto the dance floor. As the waltz began, he gathered her into his arms and the first sweeping twirl of the dance. "Flint may have been the better choice of my friends, actually. I'm abashed to say I simply did not realize the strategic value of having him escort Ros."

Curiosity wouldn't allow her to let the topic go. "I assume you are referring to his violent reputation?"

"In part. Because of his reputation, he rarely—no, he *never*—attends Society's entertainments. Which, of course, means seeing him here tonight, *and* in the company of your sister, all but marks them as engaged."

The crowd around the edges of the ballroom streaked by as Wolf continued to lead her through the waltz.

"Well, that is…concerning."

His blue gaze trapped her as surely as the strong band of his arms did. "I thought that was what you sought? To have her claimed in such a public fashion that Wallthorpe could not pursue her in lieu of you."

She swallowed past the lump in her throat. "I did, but I thought…" She broke off. "It doesn't matter what I thought. You're correct in that his presence has been more than effective. Wallthorpe turned tail and ran, and Ros appears well and truly claimed."

"As do you, if you would only smile at me a little," Wolf chided.

Then he pulled her closer to his chest—indecently close, if she were still considered an innocent. At the far end of the dance floor, the terrace doors stood open, allowing the evening air to cool down the overheated attendees.

With a finesse she had not expected from him, he maneuvered them to the outer edges of the dancers and out the doors as they passed. Once the shadows swallowed them, he brought their dance to a halt, but did not release her from his hold. Her heart raced from the dance as much as the anticipation of his kiss.

"I've needed to taste your sweet kiss again since earlier this evening."

Then he leaned in and captured her lips before she could say a word.

And truly it did not matter, because she would have happily said yes, anyway. As her breasts pressed tight against him, her body melted. His tongue sought hers out, and twined together in a sensual dance that had her crying out for his intimate touch once more.

Time slipped past as he tasted, touched, and nibbled at her mouth. He was showing—rather than telling her—how much he wanted her, and she was helpless to do anything but reply in kind. Because despite her better judgment, she wanted this man more than her next breath.

As they slowly parted, the cool air finally penetrated her lusty haze and caused her to shiver.

He curled his arm around her shoulders. "You're cold. We should go back inside."

"May we go? It seems as if we've achieved our goal this evening."

Julia wanted to steal away to The Market and spend the rest of the night in Wolf's arms.

He looked down at her, and she was confident he could see the desire in her eyes. Even in the shadows, it would be hard to miss.

"Let us go find the others, and see if they are ready to depart." He hesitated. "You'll come to me at The Market later?"

She reached down and stroked his hard shaft. "Oh, yes. I have need of you again, after the orgasm you gave me earlier. It was too short, and too fast."

He smiled as he took her in from his hooded eyes. "Agreed."

Chapter Fourteen

April, 1862

The late morning sun shone down, making the day feel unusually warm, even for spring. But it suited his purposes as Wolf knocked on Julia's front door. Then Johnson opened the entry and allowed him to pass. A few moments later, Julia sailed into the front parlor, looking splendid in a golden-brown driving dress. The coppery color of the garment set off her hair, and made her green eyes sparkle.

"Hello," she said. "My, you do look handsome today."

He let the compliment settle in his chest. After the Weatherly ball, a week earlier, he'd made love to her all night long. He still feared that she might begin to pull away from him if she detected the truth still crowding his thoughts. He couldn't let her know how he felt yet, and if he didn't play his cards correctly, he could lose everything.

And he had come to realize that she was, in fact, *everything*.

"As do you. That is a smashing dress."

He smiled as she playfully preened a bit.

Placing her small, jaunty bowler hat on her head and pinning it in place, she looked up from under her lashes. "So, where are we off to?"

"That is a surprise." His smile stretched wider at her moue of disappointment. "Trust me, you'll enjoy it."

Giving in with good grace, she smiled back. "Very well. Take me away. I am yours for the afternoon."

In short order, they were seated in his blue-and-yellow spider phaeton and moving through London's streets. Ever observant, she immediately spied the blankets piled on the rear bench seat behind them.

"Blankets, Wolf?"

Her tone belied her amusement, even as she tried to appear stern.

"Sit still and stop trying to ruin the surprise," he ordered.

She laughed outright. "But trying to discover the secret is half the fun!"

He sighed. "You are a troublesome baggage. Always were."

"Which is why you love me."

The words flew out into the companionable moment, utterly crushing their comradery. She looked as surprised as a debutante caught kissing her beau.

Needing to dispel the awkwardness, he winked. "It may or may not be one of the reasons I tolerate you."

His heart ceased beating as he waited for her to react to his taunt.

"Tolerate me? You always were a brute."

She let her mock outrage carry her past the moment.

Then his heart returned to its regular state of beating, and their conversation carried on as they discussed their childhoods. But what he *really* wanted to know was more about the woman she'd become.

By the time they reached the outer edges of London, where the city gave way to countryside, and the Thames carved through green grass instead of cobblestone streets, they had fallen into a comfortable silence once again. When he reached the spot where the river curved and a thatch of trees created a hideaway nestled between the banks of the river, Wolf was more than ready to eat...possibly more than just the picnic lunch he'd brought.

They spread out the blanket along the bank of the river. The sun-soaked day was warm enough that he stripped off his coat and left it in the phaeton. With the basket settled between them, Jules immediately set about unpacking their feast. She pulled out cured meats and bread, a bottle of wine, and even an assortment of delectable fruits, all the while chatting about some of the foods she'd tasted while living abroad. By the time they'd eaten their fill, he had shared some of his own—far more limited—food experiences.

Satiated, he leaned back on his elbows and let the warmth soak in to his clothes. "It sounds as though you enjoyed the last ten years outside of England."

She stretched out on her back, letting her hair fall loose around her shoulders, to spread out over the blanket. "I did. As much as I detested Wallthorpe, I equally relished the freedom and independence that came after he died. I loved seeing India, and then Arabia. It was fascinating to see how women were treated in other cultures. In some ways, I had far more freedom in those lands, and in others, far less."

"And now? Are you happy to be home?"

A sick feeling burbled in his stomach as he waited for her response. If she wasn't happy in England, then she would leave again, eventually.

She turned her face toward him and smiled. "Strangely—despite young Wallthorpe and my parents—I find I *am* quite happy." She hesitated then, glancing at him with a vulnerability that only reinforced his desire for her. "I wasn't sure, at first. I thought perhaps I had made a mistake in returning, but as old friendships have been renewed and new ones discovered, I am finding myself quite satisfied to be here."

Contentment like he'd never known filtered in through all the self-doubt and self-recrimination he'd heaped on himself over the years. Between his father's anger and animosity, and his own, he hadn't been truly happy—let alone content—in over a decade.

Not since he had left for school. That was the year everything had changed for him.

"I wonder if I had intervened with Wallthorpe, if things would have turned out differently for us. Maybe we'd be happily married now, and raising two children."

She raised up on one elbow and angled herself so she could see him better. "Do not think such things. Had we tried to run, Wallthorpe would have made his son's pursuit of me look like child's play. If I learned nothing else in the short time I was married, it was that my husband was a relentless and mean monster. I can tell you now that there is nothing he wouldn't have done to secure me, like some prized broodmare. I was simply a trophy to mount on his wall, along with all the others he'd collected over the years."

Wolf grunted in response. He had his doubts, but then, he had not been the man he was today back then. If he had, he would have just whisked Jules away and married her. It was a regret he had learned to shoulder, though the burden seemed to have grown heavier since their renewed intimacy. "Was your time with him so awful?"

She sighed. "It was far from pleasant. I was a shell of myself with him."

He closed his eyes tight and asked the question he'd needed to know the answer to for a long time. He had his suspicions, based on things she'd said, but he needed confirmation. "Did he hurt you physically?"

Jules shifted, sitting up and angling herself slightly away from him. "Does it matter? I have moved past my unwanted marriage. Can you not?"

He sat up and scooted to sit just behind her. "*Yes*, it matters. If you suffered, *it* matters...because *you* matter."

He pressed a kiss to the skin exposed where her neck and shoulder joined. She shivered despite the warm spring day, but he didn't know if it was a reaction to his touch, or to the subject at hand.

Her voice dropped then, her tone low and haunted. "I was a smart woman, possibly *too* smart. He only beat me twice in the year we were married." She stopped, drew a breath, and seemed to pull herself together. "The first time was on our wedding night, for some perceived infraction. He determined I was behaving lewdly when I groaned, because he had hurt me as he took my virginity. I sometimes wonder if I had explained that he hurt me, instead of letting him believe I was enjoying his attentions, whether he might not have hit me. But then I remind myself if it hadn't been then, it would have come soon after. It was merely an excuse to do as he wished. He beat me so badly, I remained in bed with poultices on my back for days."

Wolf growled, his hands clenched into useless fists.

"After that, I studied him. I learned his moods, and what his triggers were. Mostly I avoided confrontations with him. When I couldn't, I simply gave in and apologized to keep the peace. He slapped me a few times, and pinched me often enough, if he thought I was being too chatty or not responsive enough, but mostly I managed to keep his temper at bay. And it worked for almost a year." She drew a shuddering breath that rattled both her and him. "But then he grew restless, antsy even. I wasn't sure what the issue was, but I could tell he was agitated and spoiling for a fight. I knew there would be no avoiding the argument, and no placating him. That was the day he died."

She licked her lips as though she were parched, but pressed on before he could offer her a sip of wine. "He decided the house we were living in was unkempt, and that I had failed in my duties as the mistress of his domain. I apologized, and promised him I would try harder. Do better. But none of it mattered. He came at me, slapped me across the face, and shoved me onto the couch in the study." She trembled, her gaze glassy, and her focus somewhere else. "He hovered over me, raising his riding crop high above him. Then, instead of lashing at my back with the weapon, he simply seized up and keeled over."

Shaken to his very core by what she'd told him, Wolf wrapped his arms around her and pressed her into his chest. "I'm sorry I couldn't protect you."

A mirthless laugh escaped her, sharp and a little bitter. "I wasn't yours *to* protect. That was the job of my parents, but they failed in that one task. They failed *me*. And what makes me so angry now is that they refuse to acknowledge that fact." She turned into his arms and faced him, tucking her head against his chest as she practically sat in his lap. "When I first told them what had happened on our wedding night, they refused to accept the truth. So I peeled my dress down in their dining room and showed them the healing marks from the beating. And do you know what they said to me?"

"No." It was all he could manage in that moment, since he was so overwhelmed with helpless anger and despair at how badly he'd screwed up.

"My father looked appalled, but my mother—heartless in a way I had never imagined—suggested I must have done something to deserve the beating, because no normal man would do that to his wife, were she not deserving of it. My father refused to gainsay her, and merely shut down after that. Not unsurprisingly, he preferred to avoid an argument with her rather than protect me."

A full body quake shook her then, and he heard the first sniffle. As he wrapped her tighter in his arms, her tears dampened his shirt and shredded his soul. If the brute was not already dead, Wolf would have gladly killed him.

For a while they sat there as she cried, until he couldn't take anymore. "Jules, I'm so sorry. So very sorry I didn't do more."

She wiped her tears and sat back a little. "There was nothing you could do. But you can imagine why a younger version of that man is not of any interest to me. I couldn't survive a lifetime of marriage to someone who would be so callous. So harsh. There is no way I shall ever marry his son, and there is no way I shall allow him to trap Ros. I simply cannot."

"I won't fail you this time, Jules. Ros is safe for the moment, as are you. We will find a way to achieve a more permanent arrangement, I promise."

He couldn't control the gruffness of his voice as his words rumbled out, unfiltered by his surplus of emotion. And while he'd driven so far out to spend a lazy afternoon with her—possibly even coaxing her into making love outside—at the moment, all he wanted to do was hold her and keep her safe.

Forever.

Chapter Fifteen

J ulia stared at Wolf as he prowled around the blue room in The Market. She'd arrived early and had decided to get comfortable with the aid of one of the housemaids. Swathed in nothing but a silk robe, she currently found herself wishing she had stayed dressed.

"You want to do what?" she asked him again, because the first time she'd posed the question, it had come out as a breathy whisper.

Wolf's smile barely met the criteria despite any resemblance to the gesture. The man was downright predatory. Tariq had once come to her in such a state. He had confronted an enemy and challenged the man to combat, only to have the coward throw himself on his own sword. Deprived of his target, and with no substitute to vent his spleen on, he had come to her seeking succor. Tariq had used her hard that night, availing himself of her body to release his tension.

It seemed plausible that Wolf was suffering similarly.

He made a tsking sound. "Do not pretend you did not hear me. I said that I wish to tie you up and fuck you."

Part of her rejected the notion—the very idea—of making herself so vulnerable to a man again after her experience with Wallthorpe. She'd told Wolf of the beating, but not all of the humiliating details. She'd not revealed how her husband had tied her to the bed and whipped her. How the beating had gone on for hours, the old man only pausing to allow his arm to rest, so he could resume where he'd left off.

With a shake of her head, she pushed the old memories aside. It had been years since she'd dealt with the aftermath of her marriage. Years since she'd accepted her fate and moved on, and Wallthorpe held no further power over her.

She refused to allow him control, even in death. So, with a brutal will to live, she pushed the fear back down, where she locked it away, and focused on the part of her that relished the idea of giving control to Wolf. He'd proven to be everything she could have desired in a lover: commanding, confident, evenhanded, and determined to ensure her pleasure along the way.

She had nothing to fear from him—except possibly losing her heart a second time. Could she trust him? Did she? She had once before, and the man had abandoned her. But things were different now. Weren't they?

She swallowed, licked her lips, and grabbed on to her courage. "Yes."

She didn't know if she was answering her own question or his, but the result was the same. Merely saying the word unlocked a familiar warmth within her, which chased away all the darkness and fear thoughts of her dead husband had summoned. She wrapped herself in the certain knowledge that despite everything, she wanted to trust Wolf. It was a truth that ran deep within her core, and it calmed her inner monologue.

He paused a moment and absorbed her words. His eyes closed, and then a true smile stretched his sensuous lips. "Thank you."

His simple acknowledgement caused her heart to squeeze, and smothered the last of any thoughts about her dead husband. Now there was only Wolf and her.

He crossed to her and pressed against her back, his heat easily penetrating the thin silk of her robe. She relished the warmth and the feeling of safety that always accompanied having him near. With a gentle touch, he stroked down her shoulder, and then wrapped his arm around her stomach. With his right hand, he tipped her head to the right and dragged his lips the length of her neck. Along the way, he stopped to kiss and nibble her sensitive flesh.

Need shifted beneath her skin, a slight ripple of sensual awareness. He caught the lobe of her ear between his teeth and tugged, causing her body to slowly come awake. Then he whispered, "I need you, Jules. I need you to take this ache away, to let me make you feel so good that you'll scream my name as you come."

A full-body shiver sliced through her as he reached up and cupped her breast in his hand. Then he brushed her pebbled nipple through the silk, heightening the sensation. He continued to caress her tip until the hard buds poked out through the fabric. With a firm—but not cruel—pressure, he squeezed one tip between his thumb and forefinger, and then rolled the point. A low moan escaped her as her head fell back against his shoulder. She reached behind and gripped his thighs, desperate for purchase as her legs turned rubbery with desire.

"I'm yours. Use me however you need. *Make me scream.*"

The rumble of his chuckle vibrated against her, adding to the maelstrom of lust that he had whipped up with a few strategic caresses.

"On the bed, and drop your robe on the way."

Determined to tease him as much as possible, she slowly untied her robe as she walked to the bed. About halfway there, she let one side slip from her shoulder. She took a few more steps, and allowed the other side to drop, exposing her bare back to him. Finally, as she approached the bed, she let the silk waft from her fingertips and down to the floor. Bared to him, she crawled onto the mattress, into the center, where she reclined on one hip, with her legs crooked to the side.

"Mmmm... Very nice."

He stripped off his coat and walked toward her. His trousers already bulged, revealing his aroused state, yet he made no motion to remove the rest of his clothing.

As she watched him, she knew she was in deep trouble. Her heart pounded in her chest as he stalked toward the bed, and finally the first inkling of real fear set in. Not fear of Wolf, but of *herself*. Of the knowledge that she could lose herself in this man, and she wouldn't care. She knew with him, she wouldn't bother trying to fight back and retain her independence.

And then he was hovering over her on the bed, wrapping one hand around the back of her neck underneath her long red hair. He leaned in and captured her mouth. He licked and nibbled, kissed and tasted her, all the while levering her back until she lay flat on the bed. Then, with one hand, he stroked up her side and then under one arm, urging her to lift it above her head. As she stretched up, still caught in his lips, he moved his hand from her neck and broke their kiss. Dazed, she stared into his deep blue eyes—lost to the satisfaction and desire that swirled in their depths.

Then a coolness wrapped around her wrist as the leather cradled her skin. She tugged gently, an uncontrollable reflex, and her eyes shot wide open as a flash of a memory shot through her—the burn of silk tied too tightly against her tender skin.

But instead of flat, lifeless brown eyes, she fell into the heated azure depths of Wolf's gaze. She drew a steadying breath and moved her wrist in the leather band. Something soft, like lamb's wool, brushed across her flesh. There was no mistaking where she was, and with whom.

"Are you well, Jules?" Wolf's brows had drawn together, creating a crease between them.

She pushed the last remnants of her past aside. "I'm with you. How could I not be?"

He reached up and cupped her face. He stared at her for a moment, and then shook his head. "I saw the fear in your eyes. We should abandon this."

"No." She reached up with her still-free hand and stopped his movement toward her bound wrist. "I want this. I want *you*. Nothing else. Don't abandon this. Don't abandon *me*."

Wolf stared at her for what felt like an eternity as he seemed to war with himself. Finally, he nodded. "If you need to end this, or need me to release you, simply say *carriage*, and I shall release you without hesitation."

Suddenly her heart lodged itself in her throat, which made speaking a supreme effort. "Thank you."

Then he was kissing her again as he stretched her free hand up on the other side. When he pulled away and secured the leather strap that was connected to the bed, she was well and truly trapped, spread out for his pleasure.

He drew back once more, kneeling between her legs as he looked down at her exposed flesh. "Bloody hell, you are a beautiful woman."

He cupped her face for a moment as something flashed in his eyes. She wondered what he'd been thinking, but his hands shifted down her neck and over her breasts, quickly pushing all thoughts from her head. Her nipples beaded beneath his touch, sending sparks of pleasure along her limbs. Then he plucked at the tight peaks, pinching lightly and heightening her pleasure.

On a moan, she arched into him, needing more. But he was determined to control their interaction, and he moved on, dragging his hands down her torso. He molded her curves, sliding over her hips until he stopped to place a kiss on the flat of her stomach. Of course, the soft flesh of her belly quivered at the feel of his lips, and she couldn't help but feel grateful she was lying down. But then he moved lower, and dropped a kiss on the top of her mound, before he backed off the bed and stood.

She lay there, a quivering mess as her body seemed to reach for him with every fiber of her being. Need lashed her as she remained strapped in place, and entirely at his mercy.

"Tell me what you want, Jules." His raspy voice revealed how close to the edge of control he rode.

Her breathing grew choppy, despite the fact he no longer touched her. "You, inside me."

One brow rose. "And?"

Stringing a coherent thought together was proving more difficult with each passing moment. Her body quivered in anticipation of what he planned. "Fuck me. Hard. As you promised."

His clothes flew off his body then. It was the only way she could describe it. He was dressed one minute, and then he wasn't.

"I had intended to take my time, but I find seeing you spread out so delectably has sapped my meager supply of self-possession."

And then, with a French letter in place, he plunged into her in one hard push. She reached over the cuffs at her wrists and gripped the ropes that somehow attached to the bed, and met him thrust for thrust. With each stroke, he filled her again and again.

Her pleasure crested on a sudden rise as his hips slapped against her. "Oh God, I'm close. Don't stop."

He maintained his steady pace, his blue eyes dark with need. "Scream my name, Jules."

His demand cascaded over her, a jolt of added stimulation to what was already bordering on too much. And then she shattered into a million pieces as she came. "Wooolllf!" she cried out on a long, drawn-out scream of pleasure.

All the while, he shuttled in and out of her, his arms straining with the effort of balancing himself over her, and then his whole body seemed to tense, even as his hips moved faster. With a shout, he stilled and shook as pleasure carried him away.

Julia once more relished the weight of him as he pressed her into the mattress. As much as she enjoyed being bound to the bed for his pleasure, she wished to touch him. To feel his muscles ripple beneath his skin as he recovered from their shared pleasure. Instead, she placed a kiss against his shoulder, where it met his neck. A shiver coursed through him as he moaned softly and eased up to look at her with bliss-clouded eyes.

She glanced up to her wrists. "Release me."

He shook his head, as if clearing his thoughts. "Of course."

She watched as he withdrew from her, stretched up, and freed her from the restraints. As each limb was freed, he stopped and pulled her wrist to his lips, where he placed a gentle kiss before rubbing her arms. Her heart squeezed and did a slow roll in her chest in response to the tenderness of the gesture. Long moments stretched out as he took care of her, fussed over her, and displayed a caring side she neither wanted nor expected.

The problem was, she wasn't immune to it. Not in the least.

Chapter Sixteen

Wolf stood beside Jules and tugged at the collar of his formal wear as dancers moved past in a stately formation. He'd once more found himself acting as a guard for Julia and Ros—not that Flint would have let anything happen to the latter woman. As stunning as it was for all of the Lustful Lords to comprehend, Flint had taken a shine to Mrs. Rosalind Smith. Jules was also under their care, of course, though she would have argued otherwise had he phrased it as such. It was wiser to merely be on guard, rather than have a pointless quarrel.

He knew now that he would protect her with his life, which came as a bit of a shock.

Unwilling to consider how far gone he was over his fiery redheaded wanton, he focused on watching the crowd instead. Wallthorpe had yet to make an appearance.

Then Jules turned to her sister and smiled. "I believe your next partner is approaching."

Ros grimaced. "Oh, do shut up. You know I detest galloping about a ballroom." Then she smirked. "Besides, I see your next partner approaching, as well."

Wolf watched as two gangly young men, barely out of university and still wet behind the ears, approached the lovely sisters, who were currently working hard to paste on the appearance of enthusiasm. Neither he nor Flint cared for seeing the women off on the arms of *any* man when they were trying to keep them safe. But propriety demanded the women dance with any men who asked, and Ros had long since chastised Flint about glowering at the younger men who dared to approach. And so, they were off to engage in a youthfully exuberant galop—a much less sensual cousin to the waltz.

Flint and Wolf stood closer together as they watched the women disappear on the other side of the dancing crowd.

"When must you dance next?" Wolf asked, a sense of glee causing him to smile at Flint's obvious discomfort.

His friend grunted. "I lost my dance card."

Wolf shifted his gaze from tracking Julia to stare at his companion. "But you'll break some poor debutante's heart by not appearing for your dance!"

"I also forgot to request any dances, except for the waltzes on Mrs. Smith's card. Besides, I can't very well keep her safe if I'm traipsing about the ballroom with some ridiculous chit who is more scared of me than anything."

He glared briefly at Wolf, and then returned to watching the dancers. Or one in particular.

Wolf sighed. Flint had even less use for Society than he did, but he *did* have a driving sense of justice and honor. Once he'd stepped up to protect Ros, Wolf knew his friend wouldn't relent until she was completely safe. If that meant suffering through a series of balls and other lesser gatherings, he would do it.

Wolf then turned his thoughts and gaze toward Jules. The woman moved with a natural grace that most had to practice relentlessly to achieve. A slow, simmering ember of lust stirred within him, because he'd seen that ability of hers used to best effect in the bedroom—not just on a ballroom floor. Perchance it was a bit possessive of him, but he relished that no other man in England could say the same.

He chose to ignore the qualifier. He'd certainly not been a monk all those years apart. Besides, whether she would admit it or not, she belonged to him now.

A soft curse beside him drew his focus back to the dancers. "What is it, Flint?"

"She's disappeared." Flint rose up on his toes, as if he could levitate up over the crowd in order to spot his quarry.

"Ros?" Wolf quickly scanned the crowd, and spotted Jules still swirling around the dance floor.

His friend grunted. "Who the bloody hell else would I be talking about? They were coming around the bend, ducked behind a couple, and then they were gone."

"Go look for her. I'll collect Jules, and we shall be just behind you. She can't have gone far."

Flint nodded, and then they parted. Wolf edged around the floor until he found an opportunity to step up and cut in. After an awkward moment with the disappointed young man, he and Jules were moving through the crowd to catch up to Flint. His friend had just come out of a curtained alcove and was shaking his head.

"I haven't checked all the rooms down here." He pointed to a long hall off the main foyer. Wolf and Jules took one side, Flint the other. They'd only checked two rooms when a loud crash sounded in the next room on Flint's side. They all barreled in, Flint leading the charge.

As they spilled into the library, two things were immediately obvious: Wallthorpe and Mrs. Smith had been struggling, and she was clearly winning the battle. Regardless of the success she might have been having, Flint dashed in and belted Wallthorpe, laying the man out with one extremely hard blow to the face.

The villain landed flat on his back, but he was not unconscious. He lay on the floor, holding his face and moaning as Jules scooped her sister protectively into her arms. Wolf had to hold Flint back from landing another powerful blow.

"You, sir, are as good as Seven-Dials scum hitting a man unawares."

With Wallthorpe's hands covering his nose, which bled profusely, the complaint was both muffled and yet shrilly petulant.

Flint shrugged out of Wolf's grip and straightened his jacket. "You're lucky a bloody nose is all you'll walk away with, you pompous lout."

Then Flint opened and closed his hand, flexing his fingers, which drew Ros' attention.

Immediately she extracted herself from Jules' arms and rushed to Flint's side. "Were you hurt?"

Flint looked up at her, surprised by her open display of concern. "It's nothing, really. Barely felt it."

"Come, let me at least get you a cool rag to ease the swelling."

Ros was leading him toward the open door as Flint's cheeks began to turn a little pink.

Wolf smirked, even as he turned to deal with Wallthorpe. But the unprincipled cad had vanished. He sighed.

"He slipped out." Jules watched her sister walk with Flint into the hallway. "I imagine he'll think twice before trying such a thing again, though I am curious as to what happened. How did she go from dancing with that young man to being alone with Wallthorpe?"

"An excellent question. I suppose we should go find the young gentleman in question."

Wolf held out his arm and waited to feel the warmth and weight of her hand as she tucked it into the offered crook.

Jules nodded and set her hand on his sleeve. "A capital idea."

They left Ros to fuss over Flint, who looked even more uncomfortable as a maid joined them and assisted Ros in showering him with female attention of a distinctly non-carnal nature, something he was not at all accustomed to.

After making a circuit of the ballroom, Wolf and Julia found the young man who'd originally partnered with Ros. As they approached, he turned white. Since Wolf knew he had himself refrained from scowling, he glanced at Jules. Even in profile, he could see that she had murder in her glittering green eyes.

"Easy now, love. He's just a young man, prone to foolish mistakes."

She snorted, but she did make some attempt to smooth out her features. Once they stopped before the gentleman, Wolf made the requisite introductions. Facing the young Mr. Jessop, he posed his question in a calm—even casual—manner. "I do hope you can help us clear up how it came to pass that Mrs. Smith was dancing with you and then, before the set had ended, she was not."

Mr. Jessop jammed a finger down the collar of his shirt and made a futile attempt to separate the fabric from his neck. Unfortunately for him, it appeared that someone in his household had appeared to be overly liberal with the starch in his winged-tip collar. "Well, you see... my lord," he said and continued to fidget.

The young man's father, Sir Jessop, appeared at that very moment. "Lord Wolfington, is all well?"

Wolf turned to the older man, who he'd had occasion to chat with. "I'm afraid your son was just about to explain how he was dancing with Mrs. Smith one minute, but then somehow wasn't the next, which led to her being manhandled by a rather unsavory sort."

The young man's father sighed. "Edwin, tell Lord Wolfington what occurred. Stop dawdling."

Wolf stood silently and waited, even as Jules crossed her arms in obvious impatience. Also, if she wasn't careful, her breasts just might escape her rather plunging neckline. His cock twitched in the most inconvenient way as his focus was now split between the nervous Mr. Jessop and Jules' bosom, which seemed in eminent danger of spilling free.

"Well, my lord. I was dancing with Mrs. Smith, and then Lord Wallthorpe cut in." The young man shrugged. "I'm afraid he did not give me an opportunity to reject his request, and despite the lady's protests, he swept her away."

Pinching the bridge of his nose, Wolf reached for calm. "And yet you did not come seek out myself or Lord Flintshire to apprise us of the situation?"

"I- I-" The young man's cheeks turned bright pink. "I was ashamed I failed to stand up to him. She very obviously did not wish to dance with him."

"My lord, please take my humble apologies for my son's inaction. I shall certainly have a conversation with him regarding appropriate etiquette in such a situation, should he encounter a similar one in the future."

Then Sir Jessop snapped his heels together and bowed, clearly a retired military man.

"Don't be too hard on him. Other than failing to alert Mrs. Smith's chaperone, there was little he could have done under the circumstances."

With a nod, Wolf turned and drew Jules along with him.

"Well, you certainly let that young man off easily," she huffed as they stepped away.

He grunted and sidestepped a lady whose unruly skirts were swaying as she strode forcefully past them. "If you believe young Mr. Jessop is going to get off lightly, you are mistaken. His father is a decorated soldier with a strong sense of discipline. I imagine his son shall not make such a mistake again."

She looked back over her shoulder, and then returned her gaze to him. "He won't harm the boy, will he?"

"Not at all, but I do imagine the young Mr. Jessop will have a challenging day tomorrow. My father would make me join the stable boys in shoveling out the stalls as punishment if I failed"—he hesitated, surprised he had spoken of the man—"to meet his standards."

Julia stumbled a bit, maybe equally surprised by his mention of his father. However, unwilling to further discuss his unbending parent, he steered them toward the shadowed terrace.

"Now that we have solved the mystery as to how Ros ended up in the clutches of the dastardly Lord Wallthorpe, I have another matter I wish to address."

"Oh?"

He looked at her, but with the shadows sliding around them, her expressive face was shielded. Then he backed her against the wall at the far end of the stone patio and pressed against her. "I have come to realize that your gown is bordering on indecent."

She gasped. "You are no judge of women's fashion."

"True, I am not. However, I am an excellent judge of the potential for a lady's assets to be unintentionally displayed." He reached out and traced the edge of her neckline with a fingertip, caressing the soft, creamy flesh of her breasts. "And yours, my dear, have spent a fair portion of the evening in grave danger—most recently by crossing your arms when you grew annoyed with Young Jessop. In fact, I am not certain if he was embarrassed by his own actions, or the precarious situation you presented him with." He didn't bother to hide his smirk, whether she could see it or not.

She smacked his digits away. "My breasts are quite safe, my lord, and are in no danger—other than from your wandering hands."

"I don't disagree with regard to the source of the most immediate danger; however, I suggest you follow the rules of etiquette and refrain from such an...aggressive posture in the future. While I understand your previous desire to effectively stir up a scandal, I believed you had moved past that strategy. And having your lovely breasts spill from your neckline in the midst of a ball would, without a doubt, cause quite a scandal."

She placed her hands on his chest and urged him backward a step. "Do not be a bore, Wolf. I shall dress as I see fit."

"Can you blame me for merely wanting to shield what is mine from the view of others?"

He taunted her with their engagement, though, if he were honest with himself, there was far too much truth hidden in his words.

Her emerald gaze narrowed as she glared at him. "*Yours?* Have you turned Bedlamite?" She stepped into him and jammed her finger into his chest as she hissed her displeasure. "Do I need to remind you that this engagement is a farce, and will be over just as soon as Wallthorpe is no longer a threat?"

Wolf grinned as he grabbed her finger and then wrapped her in his arms. "Do I need to remind you how you melt against me when I kiss you?"

She pressed her hands against his chest, whether in self-preservation or to relish their closeness mattered not as the heat radiated into him despite the chill her words caused.

"Do not grasp at things that can never be."

"Ah, I see I *do* need to remind you."

And then he leaned in and captured her lips with his own. As he sought entrance to her sweet mouth, she remained rigid. But then as the smell of orange blossoms and spice wafted around him, her lips softened, granting him access. The sweetness of her taste burst across his palate as he delved deeper, letting their tongues twine together in a sensual dance. Her body melded into his, there in the shadows of the Hamptons' terrace.

Lost in the headiness of their shared attraction, Wolf couldn't imagine ever letting *his* Jules escape him now. Not a second time.

Chapter Seventeen

May, 1862

Julia sat in her front parlor, reading the sensational novel *Lady Audley's Secret* by M.E. Braddon. She was so engrossed in the riveting tale of bigamy and murder she did not realize she had a visitor until Johnson interrupted her.

"My lady, Sheik Tariq Azzam Hassan requests a word with you." He stood waiting for her reply without even raising a brow.

Surprised to hear that her former lover was in England for a visit, she set her book aside. "Please, show him in. And please have Mrs. Paulson prepare some tea."

"Very well, my lady." Her butler bowed and went to fetch her guest.

Nervous, both about seeing Tariq and about what he might wish to discuss, she stood and edged closer to the door. She had learned a great deal in her time with him, and though receiving him while sitting might have given her the upper hand, it would also be insulting, considering their former connection. Besides, she still considered him a friend.

Johnson appeared once more. "Sheik Tariq Azzam Hassan, my lady."

Then he bowed and left the handsome man from her past standing in her parlor, looking every inch the desert sheik. From his flowing robes and gold gilded headdress to his beringed fingers, he radiated his power and status, though of course, he would know none of it mattered to her.

"Julia, you are still the most delicate English rose I have ever laid eyes on." He stepped closer and bowed over her hand.

"Tariq, married life appears to suit you."

She refused to lavish him with compliments. The man had always had far too healthy an ego for his own good. Extricating her hand from his grasp, she motioned to the seating arrangement behind her. "Please, come in and sit."

He took a seat on the settee, and she returned to the nearby chair she had occupied. Disappointment flashed across his swarthy-yet-handsome features. "Come, sit here with me. We were once such close friends."

No fool, she shook her head. "I think not. I imagine Fatima, your first *wife*—let alone the second wife you have since taken—would not welcome the knowledge of this visit. Should they hear of it, I have no intention of courting more of their ire than is strictly necessary."

He chuckled. "Fatima *is* a jealous woman, though in fairness to her, she knows you have always held a special piece of my heart."

Julia hated that he still harbored feelings for her. "I find that sad for her. No woman should have to know that she does not hold all her husband's interest."

"Yet you know this is the way of my people. We take more than one wife so that we may bear many children. It is also to protect the women. I, in particular, must do so to strengthen political alliances with other families. I am on wife number two now, but I love them both equally."

His gaze stroked over her curves, and down the long length of her covered legs.

The man knew what she looked like naked, stretched out before him like a pleasurable feast. And she knew too well the look of desire that sparkled in his eyes. "I find it difficult to believe you do not have a favorite." Disquieted by his lusty scrutiny, she shifted in her chair. "Be that as it may, I am certain you did not come here to discuss the state of your personal affairs."

To her relief, Johnson chose that moment to roll the tea cart into the room, and placed it firmly between them. With a simple nod of his head, he exited as quickly as he'd come.

Once the ceremony of pouring tea was completed, Julia settled back and tried to imagine what Tariq sought from her. The desirous way he continued to look at her was growing more uncomfortable by the moment. "Tell me, to what do I owe the honor of this visit?"

He sighed. "You were never one to hold your tongue, were you?"

She snorted.

He nodded sagely. "You would have made a magnificent wife, but also a troublesome one."

Refusing to rise to his bait, she sipped her tea and let him work his way around to what he wanted to say.

"Despite this knowledge, I have been unable to rid my body of its desire for you. In your absence, I have fucked both my wives until I am spent and exhausted—no easy feat, as you may remember—and yet, merely a stray thought of you, and I find my cock grows hard with need once more."

Julia swallowed the tea she'd drunk and blinked as it seared its way down her throat. She coughed and sputtered, grateful for the momentary reprieve to gather her wits. What did a woman say to a declaration of that nature?

"While I am certainly flattered, Tariq, I told you before I left that I could not marry you."

"And yet, here I am, in hopes you have missed me as much as I have missed you. That your sexual needs have grown so strong that only I can fulfill them."

She set her teacup down with a rattle. "I am afraid that is not the case, Tariq. I have moved on from our time together, though I cherish it greatly. I am afraid I still have no desire to be married."

He frowned, his caramel-colored gaze growing dark. "Then why is it that I have heard you are engaged to be *married* to some pasty Englishman who could not possibly be a fraction of the lover I am?"

Dread settled in her stomach then, making the tea she'd drunk slosh about. "Yes, well. That is an unusual circumstance. You see, my connection to an old friend is of a temporary nature."

Bloody hell! One of the reasons she had refused Tariq's proposal, besides the fact she did not love him, was that his ego made him incredibly difficult to deal with at times. This, she suspected, would prove to be one of those times.

Tariq's brows drew closer together, deepening his frown, as well as the crease between his nearly black eyes. "This man does not intend to follow through on his vow to marry you?"

"Well, no." She hesitated, worried about trusting Tariq with the truth. He could easily spoil her plans if he felt the need to inflate his own sense of self-worth. "It is more that *I* do not intend to marry him. He is merely aiding me in rebuffing another man's unwanted advances." She silently cursed all men in that moment. "It really is rather complicated, but please, trust me when I say that I have no desire to marry *anyone*."

Tariq, perpetually handsome, with his broad shoulders, stunning caramel colored eyes, and sunbaked skin tone, did not look pleased with her answer. "You have always been an elusive one, Julia. It is reasonable to believe that is why I find myself still enamored with you."

"Please do not say such things. Think of Fatima and your other wife. I would never have married you, Tariq. I'm just not sure I could ever marry anyone again. Please let me go from your head, and from your heart."

His features smoothed out a bit, but stubborn as he was, he still did not agree. "I do not see a way to do so. Is it my wives that hold you back? I would renounce them for you."

She gasped. "Tariq! That is an awful thing to say! And clearly, they were not the issue when you first asked me, as you were not married then. My answer was still the same. *Is* still the same."

She tried to be gentle with him, since she knew him to be a passionate man, who at times surrendered his better judgement to that passion.

He rose now, anger bubbling beneath his calm exterior. "This is not over. Whatever it will take to woo you, I shall do. I must have you as my wife, Julia."

Nervous, and increasingly uncomfortable with the situation, she rose as well. "I believe you should go. There is no good that will come of us continuing this discussion, now or in the future. Go home, Tariq. Take your wives and *go home*. Make many babies. Grow your tribe to be strong and resilient, as you are."

"This is not over." He turned on his heel and strode from her home.

He was merely confused, not so much angry. Or perhaps a bit embarrassed at yet another rejection from her. But she would never have married him, and would never have converted to Islam in order to do so.

Of course, her visit with Tariq had reminded her that the question of Wolf lingered, as well. The man was impossible. He was bossy, demanding, too alluring for his own good, and he was overly attentive to her. She was already half in love with him again, despite her resolve not to fall. If she didn't find a way to make Wallthorpe cease his pursuit, she would be in far greater trouble than she could have ever planned for, because the only thing worse than being forced to marry a second time would be to fall in love with the man who only married her out of a sense of obligation.

Determined to put both men out of her mind, Julia headed upstairs to dress for a dinner party at Lady Maccomb's home. A widow, she often entertained small groups with food and games. It was a light affair usually, and one that she and Ros often attended in lieu of some of the more grandiose soirees.

The evening was proving to be cooler than expected, but once she was in Lady Maccomb's foyer, it made little difference. Having greeted their hostess, Julia followed Ros into the parlor, where many of the evening's guests waited. To her surprise, Wolf and Flint were both in attendance. Before she could say a word to Ros, her sister was making her way across the room to where the men stood. Ros had already greeted them, so she said her hellos as well.

"I had not realized you were acquainted with Lady Maccomb."

Wolf shrugged. "I knew her husband more than the lady herself, but I believe she extended Flint and myself the invitations more because of our associations to yourself and Ros."

Surprised by that notion, she glanced at her sister to find her making cow eyes at Lord Flintshire. "I suppose I should have expected such a thing, what with us making our engagement so public."

"Indeed. It's conceivable we should start coordinating our social calendars." The statement held a hint of laughter, but also a determined note of seriousness.

Wary of any such further entanglement, she smiled. "Oh, there is something to be said for the surprise of finding ourselves at the same function."

"Is there?" Wolf let one brow rise in question.

Clearly, he did not agree. Well, such was life. Disappointment was something he should have become accustomed to when it came to her. It was inevitable. "Oh, indeed. It's quite entertaining, though my parents *have* begun asking when we will set a date." She leaned closer to him so her sister would not hear. "We should come up with some excuse why we have not, shouldn't we? Perhaps we could fake a death in your family? Do you have any aunts lurking about we could kill off?"

She repressed the feeling of being an addlepated fool, but she knew she needed to slow things down with Wolf. After all, they would be parting ways eventually.

He was about to reply, but Lady Maccomb interrupted everyone's conversations.

"Ladies and gentlemen, I am very excited to introduce a dear friend of mine and my husband's, who has joined us this evening. And all the way from the Far East..."

Julia's stomach knotted and flipped.

There couldn't be more than one sheik in London right now, could there?

She closed her eyes and prayed she was wrong, that some other berobed Arabic man was about to walk through Lady Maccomb's entryway.

"Sheik Tariq Azzam Hassan, and his wives, Shaykhahs Fatima Hassan and Aaleyah Hassan."

Julia opened her eyes and blinked. That was most certainly her former lover standing there grinning at her, while Fatima glared. Not to be outdone, just behind her, Wolf growled.

She should have known a quiet evening out was beyond the realm of possibility. After all, she'd been courting scandal for so long now that it seemed to just find her through no particular effort on her part. As Lady Maccomb began making personal introductions, the conversation of the other guests returned to its normal, dull roar.

Taking the opportunity, Julia turned to Wolf. But before she could say a word, he cut in.

"That is the man you spent the last decade with?"

She bit her lip and huffed. "Not the *entire* decade, for heaven's sake. He was my lover for six or seven years. But it has been nearly two years since I left him." She drew a deep breath and rushed through the part that mattered most. "He appeared on my doorstep this morning. We visited, and he indicated that he wished to continue our intimate relationship. I made my lack of interest in rekindling a connection more than clear."

Wolf's beautiful blue eyes were more like a cold blue-white than their normal mesmerizing sapphire. A muscle also ticked in his jaw, pulsing in time to the rapid pounding of her heart.

"I would posit that he did not receive your message, since the man has barely taken his gaze from you since he arrived. And you may be interested to note that one of his wives is visually driving daggers into your back as we speak." He sighed. "You are a siren, Julia, tempting normally sane men to throw themselves upon the rocks, in hopes of capturing you. All despite the promise of certain death."

Anger surged through her. As if the insanity of men could be laid at her door! "Need I remind you who the *survivor* is here? *I* survived an abusive, disastrous marriage." She did not say that it was Wolf's fault, but the thought still lingered for her...and certainly for him, if the paleness of his face was any indication. "*I* survived being a widow in a foreign land full of men who desired nothing more than to own me. *I* survived being an infidel in a tribe that welcomed me merely because their leader wished it. And *I* have so far survived the unwanted courting of a man who has not taken no for an answer. I am but one woman, who is in no way in control of the stupidity of men as a whole. If you will excuse me now, I think I am in need of some fresh air." Her nose wrinkled up in a haughty sneer. "Something rotten is perfuming the air in here."

In full dudgeon, she turned on her heel and stalked through the party and out the back door. Ros was just behind her as she hit the terrace, which was surrounded by ivy and other flowering plants that Julia wouldn't have recognized, even if she'd had a guidebook handy. Furious over Wolf's comparing her to a mythological destroyer of men, she paced the length of the flagstone space.

Ros stood there wringing her hands. "Julia, perchance you were a bit excessive in your response to his comment."

Greatly wishing to bash something—or more aptly, *some-one*—over the head, Julia ignored her sister and continued to stride back and forth in an effort to work off her anger. The nerve of him to suggest she purposely lured men to their doom! She had not asked to be born with red hair and the proportions that seemed to draw men's eyes. The only man she had ever wanted to want her had walked away when she'd needed him most. And now, after giving him a second chance, in a moment when she needed his support, he'd turned on her, and blamed *her* for the situation!

"Julia, it is lovely to see you again so soon." The rich tones of Tariq's voice only added fuel to the fire of her fury. But in an effort not to cause a further scene, she banked the flames and stepped as far from him as she could.

"Sheikh Hassan, it is a pleasure to see you again."

He winced. "So formal?"

"Merely proper. We are no longer so intimately acquaint-ed, and I do not believe either of your wives would appreci-ate a more intimate greeting. May I introduce my sister, Mrs. Rosalind Smith?"

Ros curtsied as Tariq stepped over to her, took her hand, and placed a kiss on it. "Another lovely English rose, from the same bush."

A low growl from the shadows of the house suggested that Ros was being watched, and that her protector did not appreciate such attention from another quarter. It was a response Julia could well understand and value, as opposed to an accusation of responsibility.

Ros blushed as she stepped back. "Thank you, Sheikh Hassan."

Then Wolf strode out of the shadows, followed by Flint. The men took up positions by her and Ros' sides, respectively. Tariq eyed the men with interest, particularly when Wolf placed a hand against Julia's lower back.

He flashed a predatory smile. "There you are, dearest. Leave it to you to have already met Lady Maccomb's esteemed guest. I am Lord Wolfington, and this is Lord Flintshire."

Tariq nodded at each man. "A pleasure to make your acquaintance. And how is it you are acquainted with Lady Wallthorpe?"

"May the good Lord save me from posturing men," Julia snapped, glaring at each man in turn. "Lord Wolfington and I are engaged to be married. Now, all three of you, cease this childish behavior at once. Sheikh Hassan, I am sure your *wives* are wondering where you have wandered off to. Wolf, another word, if you please."

And then she strode off onto the garden path, leaving the others to disperse as directed.

"Good evening." Tariq cast a dark glance her way before he made his departure from the terrace.

A moment later, her fiancé joined her where she stood waiting, furious with his behavior. She heard Flint and Ros walk back into the house before she turned to confront Wolf once more.

"That man has far more serious intentions toward you than a rekindling of your connection."

The roughness of his voice indicated how agitated he was, but it did little to soothe her ire.

"I am well aware of his desires; however, I have already dealt with the situation." Feeling waspish about the whole scenario, she did not hold back. "As for you..." She pursed her lips and glared at him. "You were well aware of the terms of our agreement. I shall not be treated like a possession to be paraded about or fought over. You would do well to remember I am no simpering miss."

Wolf inhaled sharply, his nostrils flaring in the dim glow of the lights from the terrace. "God, you are stunning when you are angry."

"You will not distract me with such flattery. Your behavior is unacceptable, and I shall not be a pawn in yet another man's machinations. If you cannot control yourself, my lord, our arrangement must come to an end."

She let her fury fill each word with a seriousness that he could hardly miss.

"Magnificent," he mumbled, as he swooped in and captured her mouth with his own.

Unable—or more accurately, unwilling—to push him away, she melted into his kiss. The bruising power of his desire melded with the searing heat of her lust until the two of them nearly set fire to Lady Maccomb's lovely garden. With their tongues entwined, Wolf walked her deeper into the shadows. Somehow, even as they continued to taste and explore each other, they maneuvered onto a bench and sank down.

After a tug on the front of her gown, her nipples peeked over the edge, drawing first his touch and then his lips. He suckled one rosy tip and then the other, until her breath grew as sharp as the need pulsing between her thighs. With a deft hand, he opened his trousers and freed his impressively hard cock.

Hungry for the taste of him, she reached over and stroked his shaft, making sure to draw the moisture from his tip onto her finger. Then she lifted it to her lips and licked the salty-sweet essence that was all Wolf.

"Fucking hell, woman, you destroy my common sense."

Then he shifted them so she sat on the bench, her thighs wrapped around him.

A husky chuckle escaped her, her anger forgotten in the heat of passion. Then her amusement was abandoned when he drove his cock inside her with a single hard thrust. Grateful for the ease of access of her pantalets, she absorbed each hard thrust of his shaft as he claimed her in the most elemental fashion. She reached backward to grip the edge of the bench as he pumped into her over and over again, a man lost in the throes of animal need. Her breasts bounced each time he bottomed out inside her as she held on.

And then he pulled out until just the tip of his erection remained inside her. "Who do you belong to?"

His demand caught her by surprise as she reeled from the need to have him fill her once more. Unable to follow his words, she shook her head. "What?"

"Say it. Say that you're mine. That you belong to me."

His growled demand made her pussy grow impossibly wetter, even while her heart pounded in her chest. Her eyes widened as she stared up at him.

Her heart and body warred with her head.

He slammed into her once more, only to retreat and hold still again. "Say it, Jules."

She moaned. "Please, Wolf."

Her hips bucked, seeking more of him.

He shook his head.

Despite the protests of her mind, she finally whispered the words. "I'm yours."

"Mine," he groaned in triumph, and then resumed pistoning in and out of her channel.

He fucked her hard, and with a demand she could not deny. Her body welcomed his claiming until she strained and shook, while bliss overtook her fears and doubts. She burst apart at the seams as he continued to slide in and out of her, fighting the tight grip of her pussy with each thrust. In and out, he worked her body until he stiffened and thrust twice more before he withdrew to spill his seed on the ground.

Reclined and watching him right his clothing, Julia wondered how this would change things. Because there was no doubt in her mind everything had just shifted between them, whether he knew it or not. A tear slipped down her cheek, because she knew there was no more denying how she felt. No more protecting herself from this man.

Fool that she was, she had fallen in love with him. *Again.*

Chapter Eighteen

W olf stood with Flint in the front parlor of Mr. and Mrs. Fairchild's home. They each had a brandy in hand, which Flint appeared to need far more than he. His friend scowled fiercely as he listened to Mrs. Fairchild prattle on about how wonderful it was that Ros and Flint had experienced such a whirlwind romance.

"These people know nothing about me, yet based on the fact I have a title, they would hand their daughter over without a single qualm," Flint said in an aside to Wolf, as he swallowed down half his glass of liquor.

Wolf snorted. "Not just because you have a title. Consider that I *also* have a perfectly respectable title, and I was *never* an acceptable suitor for Jules."

"All the more terrifying that that poor girl might be foisted off to some cretin once we end this charade," Flint muttered softly.

Wolf's brows rose in surprise. "Well, if you are that concerned, I suppose you could just go through with it and marry Ros. But I'd point out that she is no girl; she is a widow. And not just a widow, a *battlefield* widow. She followed her husband to war, endured harsh conditions, cared for the wounded soldiers in the aftermath, and then, when her own husband was taken, she sought out her sister and lived abroad with her."

Flint gulped the remainder of his drink. "And yet, she's still too innocent by half."

"My lords, I was just saying that the girls should consider a double wedding," Mrs. Fairchild said loudly, cutting into their private conversation.

Jules tried to bring her mother's meddling to a halt. "Mother, it is far too soon for such thoughts. We have yet to even set a date."

But the steely-eyed Mrs. Fairchild was not to be deterred. "All the more reason to plan a double ceremony. You can all come to an agreeable date. It is a second marriage for both of you, so it's not as though you will have so much pomp and circumstance as your first weddings."

Wolf looked to Jules to see how she wished to field such a slight. But before she could say anything in response, Flint spoke up.

"Mrs. Fairchild, if I may, it will be *my* first marriage. I cannot imagine forgoing the usual traditions, but I shall bow to the wishes of my betrothed in this matter."

All eyes turned to Ros, who turned a pretty shade of pink. "I, too, think it is a bit early to be discussing this matter, but I promise we will consider all of it very soon, Mother."

While Mrs. Fairchild did not look pleased about being put off, she seemed far less likely to argue with Ros than with Jules. But that was no surprise to Wolf, since Ros had always been a bit of a peacemaker in the family—especially between her mother and sister.

Two hours later, they were nearing the end of the meal. Wolf had not expected such a lavish dinner. Then he caught Jules staring at him once more. Throughout the dinner, she had cast long, lingering gazes at him, which was not at all her usual style.

He couldn't help but wonder if it was possible that she, too, had felt the shift in things between them after he'd claimed her in Lady Maccomb's garden? Incensed by the air of possession the sheikh had exuded when it came to Jules, Wolf had felt the need to clearly mark his territory. Not that he believed for one moment Jules would have tolerated such a notion. In fact, she had picked up on his most basic need and squarely bashed him for giving in to the urge.

Of course, once they'd been alone in the coolness of the garden, he'd still laid his claim. And somehow, it had been more than mere words or actions. It had been as if he'd finally pierced a protective shell that had been erected around his Jules' heart. He'd felt the connection between them grow stronger, and warmer. It was hard to explain, and not something he'd expected, but he could not say it was unwelcome.

He'd known the moment he'd deserted her that he'd made a mistake, but some mistakes took time to correct. Even years.

"Lord Wallthorpe came by this afternoon, you know."

Mrs. Fairchild was a calculating woman, but she'd yet to understand that Jules could be very much like her when pushed to her limit.

The feisty redhead who owned his heart simply smiled. "Did he, now? I can't imagine what he could have wanted."

Her mother frowned at the subtle hint, but she persevered. "He was simply visiting. I've told you, we are quite close friends with him. Such a handsome young man, and a marquess to boot. Such a shame that he hasn't yet found a woman receptive to his interest."

Jules sighed. "Yes, well, I am sure he would find a lovely bride among the season's debutantes if he were but to *look*."

"Oh, he has, but he says it is exceedingly difficult to find a bride in these modern times. Many of the girls come filled with these notions of being treated as equals. I, for one, blame that Wolstoncrab woman."

"*Wollstonecraft*, Mother. Mary Wollstonecraft is the author you are thinking of. And she has many a capital notion. You would do well to read her treatise."

Jules gave her mother a pointed look. One that was clearly lost on the woman.

Mrs. Fairchild huffed. "I should say not. Men have their roles in this world, and we women have ours. Caring for our home and families is not demeaning work."

"Now, Patrice, you know the younger generation has more modern sensibilities. They aren't like we were, when we married." Mr. Fairchild attempted, however gently, to turn his wife's thinking more toward understanding.

Mrs. Fairchild darted an angry glare at her husband. "A good man will always see to the care of those dependent on him. It's how it has always been."

"And what of a husband who does not hold to that standard, Mother? What should a woman do then?"

Green fire snapped from Jules' eyes, but Mrs. Fairchild completely missed the warning signs.

Wolf did not.

"May I suggest we adjourn to the parlor for a digestif?" Ros suggested, as she set her serviette aside.

Jules and her mother stared at each other for a moment longer, and then her mother nodded.

"An excellent idea, Rosalind. Gentlemen, will you join us?"

"In a moment, my dear," Mr. Fairchild replied, delaying their departure.

As the women filed out of the dining room, silence settled over the men while the servants bustled around the table, clearing the bulk of the dishes. Finally alone, Mr. Fairchild sat back and rubbed his protruding stomach. "My lords, my wife means well, but I'm afraid she is not always one to see the situation as clearly as I do."

Wolf and Flint glanced at each other. Worry niggled at Wolf as he braced for whatever might come next.

"I did not think it strange when Julia resumed her friendship with you, Lord Wolfington. You two have been peas in a pod for ages. But when Lord Flintshire—no slight intended, my lord—suddenly took an interest in Rosalind, I could not help but wonder."

"Wonder what?" Flint asked, a dangerous edge to his voice that had Wolf on alert.

Jules' father sat forward, a crease in his brow. "I know that Lord Wallthorpe merely courts my wife's attention to serve his own purpose. I was unsure what that purpose might be until Jules related his aggressive courting. I still had my doubts, unsure if she merely misunderstood his enthusiasm for something more. But now that she is engaged to you, Lord Wolfington, I like to believe she is protected from any unwanted advances." He paused and turned his focus to Flint.

"What I am *not* sure I understand is your interest in Rosalind, Lord Flintshire. While I love my daughter, I fail to understand her sudden willingness to marry, when she has rejected every suggestion to that effect since her husband was killed. What, my lord, are your intentions toward my daughter?"

Flint shifted in his seat, causing the delicate cherrywood to creak ominously. His hands clenched into fists for a few moments, and then he appeared to consciously relax them. "Mr. Fairchild, I seek only to protect your daughter."

With his brown hair and green eyes, Jules' father looked at Flint with a hard stare. "Do you not care for her? Perchance even like her? I could not condone a connection based on so little as a simple desire to protect her. I once made the mistake of entrusting a daughter to a man based solely on his title, and his claims to wish to protect and care for her. I shall not be so foolish again, my lord."

"She is all that is fresh and innocent, Mr. Fairchild, and yes, I wish to protect that. But I also want to bask in the kindness she exudes, for as long as I am permitted."

The words felt forced from Flint, but were delivered with a grinding honesty that shocked even Wolf.

"Very well, then. I think we should join the women, before my eldest daughter and wife come to blows."

Mr. Fairchild then rose and strode from the room, fully expecting them to follow.

Chapter Nineteen

J ohnson closed the door behind Julia as she stepped onto the sidewalk. A young man, Jeremy, held the reins of her sleek little phaeton, and the handsome, matched pair she'd purchased after her return to England. Her vehicle was stylish and on the smaller side, nothing too flashy or over the top. At the time, she'd thought she would be moving home and fading into the hustle and bustle of London. Instead, she'd found herself caught up in one tangle after another.

First was Wallthorpe, a knot she'd yet to fully unravel. The man was dogged in his pursuit of her, and she simply couldn't fathom the why of it. She was starting to worry that if she didn't get to the bottom of that question, she'd never manage to convince him to leave her alone.

Then, in an attempt to solve her first problem, she'd managed to ensnare herself in a second, far more pleasurable—yet equally confounding—knot. Wolf was a man who was proving to be very different from the one she remembered. The gregarious young man she'd spent summers traipsing around with had been replaced by a thoughtful, calculating man who showed a tendency to brood. He also seemed to be very comfortable with their arrangement, yet there was something about it all that didn't quite fit.

Another puzzle to solve, though certainly far less sinister than the first.

And then Tariq had appeared on the scene, muddling an already complicated problem. The enigmatic man was un-accustomed to hearing the word *no*, which was obviously proving to be an issue. Though it had been nearly two years, he obviously had not accepted her refusal to become his wife—or her decision to return to England.

Who followed a woman halfway around the world and dragged his two wives along with him? And how on earth had she managed to attract three such different men?

Or conceivably, at their core, all three were more alike than appearances suggested?

Without question, Wolf and Tariq were closer in nature. Both were men of privilege, with their birthrights teaching them that anything could be acquired if they desired it. And Wallthorpe could certainly be lumped in that group, but somehow, he struck her as different. There was a core of principle in both Wolf and Tariq that she did not sense in Wallthorpe, which would make sense, considering who his father had been.

She settled behind the reins and set the vehicle in motion once Jeremy hopped on the rear bench. She had an appointment with Madame LaFleur, who she'd been waiting a month to see in order to sort out a few wardrobe changes. She'd kept up with the latest fashions, but since she'd been spending more time in Society than planned, she needed to add a few more gowns to her arsenal.

Having arrived a few minutes early so she could browse for any fabrics that caught her eye, she was considering a lovely clover green silk when she was rudely interrupted. A hand latched onto her arm and spun her about, until she faced an all-too-familiar woman.

Fatima stood there, small of stature, but fierce and angry. Julia had learned very quickly not to let the woman's diminutive height fool her into seeing her as harmless. She was a tigress, willing to fight as dirty and viciously as required to hold her place in the world.

"You pasty whore infidel! I knew he sought you once more."

Julia sought a calm she simply did not possess at the moment, but she did not wish for more of a scene than the outraged woman had already caused. The two other women in the shop were furiously staring at whatever fabric they held, as opposed to staring at her and the stranger in foreign robes.

"He came to see me, but I told him the same as I did before I left. No."

"You lie! He sent you away because he was angry. His ire has been forgotten, and now he has come to bring you back."

The other woman's dark eyes snapped with her fury—and fear, if Julia was not mistaken.

Taking a deep breath, Julia pushed a loose strand of hair off her forehead. "I do not lie. I left when he asked me to marry him, and I told him I would never be accepted by his people. I could not be a good wife to him, as you would be."

Fatima's grip on her arm loosened, though it did not fall completely away. "Why do you not want him? No other man can compare."

Julia resisted the urge to snort. It was not hard to fathom how Tariq's ego had become disproportionately large, between his natural handsomeness and his birthright. With the women who surrounded him and fawned over him, it was unlikely he would remain unaffected by such excessive adoration.

"Maybe for you. But for me, there has always been another who held that special place in my heart."

The other woman's kohl-lined eyes widened in surprise. "You never loved him?"

She shook her head. There was really no need to elaborate further.

Fatima sighed. "I do not understand you, but it seems I understand Tariq even less."

With the fear drained from her, she released Julia's arm entirely as her shoulders sagged.

"Whether he knows it or not, he has always cared for you a great deal."

Jules could remember sitting with him at meals as he watched the beautiful, doe-eyed woman dance.

"I am, how do you say? Common to him?"

"Ah, you mean too familiar." Julia nodded. "Possibly even too eager to please him. I believe that was one of the things that made me so alluring. I was elusive for him."

"Elusive?"

The foreign word did not roll nicely off Fatima's tongue.

"Yes, unavailable. He had to chase me. I was a challenge." She tapped her lower lip as an idea sprang to life. "Fatima, perhaps we can help each other?"

Suspicion glinted in her dark gaze. "And why would you wish to help me?"

Julia smiled. "Because by helping you, I help myself. If Tariq finds you more of a challenge, then he will divert his attention back to you, where it belongs. And I can also rid myself of one of my current problems."

By making her assistance sound self-serving, Fatima would be more accepting of the help. In her world, nothing was done for purely unselfish reasons.

The wary woman nodded. "How will this work?"

"We are going to turn you into a properly dressed English woman. I assume you have access to any funds you may require?"

"Of course. My husband is a generous man."

Julia remembered how Tariq had tended to lavish gifts on a woman in lieu of discussing his feelings.

With their arms interlinked—she couldn't risk Fatima changing her mind—Julia turned an eye toward finding just the right fabric to complement the other woman's olive skin tone. Something bright and eye-catching was the order of the day. The culturally restricted woman would likely never wear it outside of her residence, anyway, so there was no such thing as too bold a color choice.

Madame Le Fleur appeared from the rear of the shop and nodded to the two women who were still shopping before she approached Julia. The shop owner's fake French accent cut through the remaining tension between the women. "Lady Wallthorpe, are you ready for your appointment?"

"Indeed, I am, but we may need a bit more time than originally planned. May I introduce Shaykhah Fatima Hassan? She is the head wife of Sheikh Tariq Hassan."

Madame Le Fleur looked briefly speculative, and then very pleased by this development. "*Oui*, welcome to my shop."

Fatima nodded, but said nothing. Obviously still wary, she slowly followed the two other women into the back room.

Madame glanced from one woman to the other as they settled on the settee in her showroom. "Now, how may I help you, ladies?"

Julia settled her skirts and smiled. "I need to add a few gowns to my wardrobe. I have been unexpectedly attending more social functions, and am finding my selections too sparse. And then we need to outfit Shaykhah Hassan with one or two gowns of the latest fashion. I'm thinking a day dress and a ball gown. Something modern, yet sensitive of her culture's expectations for a woman."

"No," Fatima interrupted. "I want what any infi—" She stopped and cleared her throat. "I want what any London woman would wear. He must see me as he sees you."

She spoke firmly, and decisively.

"Well, then, you heard the Shaykhah. Nothing less than the most modern fashions for us both."

Julia smiled and wished she would have the chance to see Tariq's face when his first wife transformed herself into a London lady.

They spent the next few hours discussing dress design, fabric, and men. Along the way, Julia made sure to offer carefully couched advice on how to draw Tariq's attention. Of course, Fatima knew what to do once she had it. While demure and modest in appearance, Julia had lived around the women of Tariq's tribe long enough to know they had the amorous arts well in hand.

As she and Fatima left the shop much later in the day, the other woman turned to her. "I do not understand you." The woman hesitated, not unsure but maybe more uncomfortable. "Why you would wish to help me with Tariq, but I am grateful for your assistance."

"I hope that we can be friends. My time with Tariq was a period of healing and growth for me. It was something I needed, and I am thankful every day for what he did for me. For what *your people* did for me. I could never repay that kindness in full, but maybe this is one small way I can try." Julia grinned. "I also really wish I could be there the first time he sees you in that ball gown. The deep red is a stunning shade on you. He will be transfixed, I assure you."

Fatima smiled. "It is possible you will get your wish."

Then they embraced and parted ways. Julia hoped that she had given Tariq both a bit of happiness, and something of a challenge. Because Lord knew, the man did not usually like the easy path. With a pleased sigh, she headed home.

After all, she was to attend a masked ball tonight, and she suspected her escort had nefarious plans.

Wonderfully *naughty* nefarious plans.

Chapter Twenty

The Crystal Palace glittered like a diamond on black velvet. The evening's outing required two carriages to carry everyone, but all of Wolf's friends and their wives had been excited for the event. A masquerade ball at The Crystal Place was not one to be missed, particularly when it was rumored to be hosted by a secret guild of courtesans.

Jules looked stunning in her violet gown and matching mask. The purple made her red hair and golden skin glow in the gaslight.

He grinned and contemplated the adventures that would soon find them. "Come, my fair maiden. A magical evening awaits you."

Julia laughed as she swept from the carriage. "And are you my knight in shining armor?"

With his blood thrumming through his veins, desire bubbled just under his skin, making him feel as though caterpillars crept all over his body. "It may be a bit tarnished, but I would don armor for you nonetheless." He leaned in close and lowered his voice. "Of course the magic really happens when we discard the armor altogether."

"Indeed, my lord, I suspect far more is accomplished when men set aside their armor. After all, I've never made a very good damsel in distress." She reached down and caressed the paltry fabric that covered his now partially erect shaft. "I've always been more of a welcoming widow, happy to assuage a man's more lusty needs."

"Your practical nature has always been one of my favorite things about you. Now keep your hands to yourself lest we scandalize even the most bawdy of London's populace." He grabbed her hand and dragged it from his aching cock so he could both place a kiss on her palm and help his need settle down. It would likely be hours until he could have his fill of this woman who drove him mad with desire.

Ros, Theo, and Emily swept Jules into their little group to wend their way through the garden paths leading up to the building. Stone, Cooper, and Arthur walked behind, discussing something quietly while keeping an eagle eye on the ladies. Wolf strolled with Flint and Linc.

"Are you boys enjoying the tightening noose of possible matrimony?" Linc asked with a cheeky grin.

Flint shot him a dark look, his shoulders set in a rigid line. "You know very well that Ros will release me as planned, once Wallthorpe is dealt with."

"Do I?" Linc let one brow rise in question. "I see the way she looks at you. The woman is completely taken with you."

A burst of laughter from the women had all of the men looking to the head of the group, until Theo shushed them after casting a wary glance backward.

Wolf had also begun to worry that Ros was a bit more caught up in the fake engagement with Flint than was wise. His violent tendencies would be a worrisome prospect for any well-bred woman. But marrying a rougher sort of female wasn't an option, not even for Flint.

"If she won't do it willingly, I'll give her a reason to hate me before the charade ends. You know I shall never marry." Flint sounded almost as though he was angry about the whole situation.

"Hopefully we can resolve the question of why Wallthorpe is so determined to have Jules before then. I haven't heard anything from the private man of inquiry I hired. But he is the man Stone and Cooper have both utilized, so I expect something soon enough."

Julia had little to hide beyond some lurid details about her life between her marriage and her reappearance in London. Slowly she'd been sharing it with him. The hardest to hear had been the truth of her marriage. It still made Wolf want to kill the man. Too bad he was already dead.

Arthur dropped back to join them. "Those two married types are deadly boring. All they can talk about is how the markets are doing, their investments, and their *babies*." Emily's brother shuddered.

Linc laughed and slapped Arthur on the back. "Those two have always been sticks-in-the-mud. The real fun lies back here, with us."

"I hope there will be dancing partners aplenty at this shindig," Arthur replied with a grin and a waggle of his brows.

Linc's eyes glittered with mischief in the light of the torch-lit path. "The doves will be ours for the plucking, my friend."

Wolf and Flint looked at each other and groaned. Those two were still high on the bachelor life. When their time came, they would learn that one good woman far outweighed having many passable women in their lives. In the meantime, Wolf supposed there was nothing wrong with them living it up. As long as Arthur continued on the straight and narrow, Cooper and Emily would remain content. And well, Theo and Stone appeared to be living in a dream where he was the master of his castle...and likely his woman, though none of the Lustful Lords would deign to speculate on their private life.

A squeal of excitement burbled through the ladies as they neared the glass monstrosity that contained their evening entertainment. For once, this would be a ball worth attending. Without all the stiff formality of the *ton's* usual entertainments, tonight should prove to be a rollicking good time for everyone. As the path opened up to a large graveled area before the entrance to the building, Wolf nodded at his friends. "Excuse me, gentlemen."

"Dear God, another one among us has fallen prey to the desires of a woman."

Linc had a flair for the dramatic, one that Wolf mostly appreciated, but not so much in the moment.

With a snort, he moved forward to claim the arm of Jules, because there was no possibility he could stand by and allow another man to mistakenly believe she was unescorted. Cooper, Stone, and Flint also claimed their ladies, leaving Linc and Arthur to trail behind.

Inside the illuminated bubble, the musicians were warming up as the crowd milled about. Jules grinned at him from behind her half mask, but refrained from speaking, considering the volume of the din around them.

Finally, they found a corner for the group to claim, and they settled in for an evening of revelry and bacchanalian delights.

A few hours later, as the crowd found themselves generally deeper in their cups, Wolf wished he could steal Jules away. Unwilling to strand part of their group by leaving, he decided to lure his feisty redhead into the gardens for a quick tryst. As she returned to his side once more, her dance partner bowing gallantly, Wolf tucked her hand in the crook of his arm.

"Come along with me, mistress. I can show you even more delights beyond the glare of The Crystal Palace."

She grinned and then batted her lashes ever so innocently. "Whatever can you mean, kind sir?"

"Ah!" He knew she'd be a game one. "There are magical things beyond the glow of the lights. Come with me, my pretty, and let me show you paradise."

She worried her lip and truly hesitated for a moment. "Wolf?" Her voice grew serious. "I've heard it can be dangerous in the gardens. Are you sure this is wise?"

He released her hand and turned to face her. Cupping her cheek and mask in one hand, and resting his other on her waist, he looked deep into her eyes. "I would protect you with my dying breath before I let anything bad happen to you again. Haven't you realized that by now?"

Something dangerous—something that looked suspiciously like love—sparkled in her green gaze. "Yes. That's what scares me."

The noise of the ball, the music, the dancers, and the conversation that ebbed and flowed around them all faded into silence as his heart ceased to beat. Their gazes locked as the unspoken words hung there between them, like ripe fruit waiting to be plucked.

And then someone bumped into him, and the moment was lost as the chaos around them swept back in, like the tide crashing against the shore.

Worried he'd scare her with a declaration then and there, he opted to send them rushing headlong back down the path to pleasure. He tucked her hand in place and urged her forward. "Then come with me to experience the delights that await us in the garden."

And with a wicked smile, he drew her away from the crowd, where he could relish her touch, her beauty, and the pleasures of her flesh in relative privacy.

With the tension dissipated, she fell back into his game, her lusty side coming out to play. They strolled along a busy path until they found a branch that led them off into one of the darker corners of the grounds. Then Wolf discovered a stone balustrade that carved a kind of overlook. With a torch nearby to offer some small bit of light, he pressed her against the stone rail.

In the dull glow of the light, her creamy flesh beckoned him to caress her softness. With a single finger, he traced the delicate curve of her collarbones from one side to the other, and she shivered under his touch. Need that had simmered all night began to boil over. His cock hardened and his desire flared. He leaned over her and pressed his lips to the swell of her breasts just above her neckline, savoring the sweetness of her skin. Hungry for more, he tugged down on her bodice until her breasts rode up, freeing a nipple. Eagerly he sucked the puckered tip, relishing her moan as she dug her fingers into his hair.

As he worried the point with his lips and teeth, he eased his hands down to slowly gather her skirts. Then her hands were working with his, as together they wrangled her unwieldy gown until he found smooth skin above the knee. He stroked her leg higher, and shockingly found nothing but more bared skin.

Releasing her nipple, he sought her gaze. "My lady, I believe you have misplaced your knickers."

"No, I don't believe I have misplaced them in the slightest. They are right where they belong. At home. In my drawer."

She offered him a wicked smile, and then reached up with one hand to pull him down into a kiss. She explored his tongue and mouth as though staking a claim, one his cock eagerly accepted.

Concern for her missing clothing vanished as he gave in to the lust that flooded his veins and reached between her thighs to find her core soaked with her own need. Slipping two fingers deep inside her, he absorbed the heat that surrounded him. She was on fire, a living flame in his arms, and he was ready to be consumed.

He pumped his fingers in and out of her, adding a third, and resumed his steady pace. She moaned and ground against his hand. A tremor raced through her body, one that he felt all the way to his bones. Watching her delicate features in the dim light as pleasure chased across her face had his shaft growing longer and harder. He ached to feel her wrapped around him, but his release would wait. She deserved every ounce of bliss he could offer up in this moment.

In any moment.

"Yes, Wolf. Don't stop." Her hips bucked, grinding her clit against the heel of his hand as he braced her with his body.

Her climax was close. He could tell by the jerky, uncoordinated motions of her body and the stiffness in her limbs as she struggled to let go. Determined to help her along, he leaned in to her and demanded, "Come for me, Jules. Come now."

And then he slipped a finger out of her clenching heat and stroked over her swollen clit. She lit up for him, her orgasm arriving in one great rush. Shoving her face into his chest to muffle her cries of passion, he worked her slick flesh until her body gripped his fingers in a vise that pulsed in time with the throb of his erection. As the pulsing slowed, she returned to the present under his gentle caress, even as he worked to keep her desire alive. He needed to feel her wrapped around his cock soon, or he might explode himself. Withdrawing his fingers from her core, he reached for the opening of his trousers, when he suddenly found himself flat on his arse, with a ringing in his ears he could only attribute to the sudden pounding in his head.

Shaking his head in an attempt to clear his thoughts, he regretted that decision instantly. But then Jules' voice sliced through the muddle and spurred him to action.

"Wolf!" she cried out, fear and panic in her voice.

He looked up and saw a man garbed all in black, trying to drag her away. As she dug in her heels and battered his head with her free hand, the villain grunted and then faced her.

"Hush your blathering, missy."

The man then took a menacing step toward her, but rather than be cowed, his fiery redhead socked the bastard right in the nose.

Just like Wolf had taught her years ago when they were children.

Sparked to action when the man released her in favor of protecting his face, Wolf jumped to his feet and pummeled his assailant. Fury surged through him as his fists crashed into the hard bones of the man's face over and over again. But then the darkly clothed man reared up unexpectedly and slammed a fist into Wolf's gut, causing all the air in his lungs to escape. Yet adrenaline and pure determination pushed Wolf until he cocked his arm back and swung. The blow landed square against the villain's temple, knocking him out.

By the time he'd subdued the cretin, a small crowd had gathered. Spotting a young boy in rags hovering nearby, he waved him over. With a shilling in his pocket and the promise of a second, the boy was off to retrieve their friends. He refused to either leave Jules or the bastard who attacked her, even for a moment. Hovering over the now-cowering man, Wolf glanced over at Jules, who stood trembling at his side. Reaching out to wrap an arm about her shoulders, he was pleased to see she had found an opportunity to right her clothing before too many people had gathered.

It seemed like hours before Stone, Cooper, and the rest of their group appeared, and even longer for the Metropolitan Police to arrive. By the time the whole mess was sorted out and the uncooperative villain was taken away, there was no doubt in Wolf's mind that Jules had accumulated another scandal to her credit. There was little doubt that her strolling in the dark gardens of The Crystal Palace—even with her fiancé—would make the rounds. Unfortunately, he doubted greatly that such a scandal would have any impact on Wallthorpe's determination to marry her, and clearly, he was *very* determined.

Wolf glanced at Jules, and she looked about as wilted as he felt. It was past time to take her home, so he gathered her in his arms and tipped her face up to his. "You look exhausted. Let me take you home."

Her green eyes widened. "Home? I don't think I want to go home right now. I have no desire to be alone."

Wolf cursed softly, and then turned to the others. "If you all wouldn't mind finding another way home, I'm going to take Jules with me." He hesitated, hating to say it, but needing to. "Ros, you'd best come with us as well. I don't think it's safe for you to stay alone at your home tonight."

Flint's arm curled protectively around Ros. "You'll take me then as well. I'll not leave her unprotected while you are tending to Julia."

There was little chance anyone could have missed the look of relief that crossed Ros' face as Flint offered his presence. With a nod, the four of them headed off through the gardens to where Wolf's carriage would be waiting. Many of the spectacle goers had long since left the ball, though some revelers remained. Wolf's spine tingled and his every sense seemed very much on alert the entire walk to his vehicle. He imagined Flint felt much the same. Once they were settled in his carriage, the tenseness melted from his shoulders, even as his mind began to whirl with questions.

Who was behind the attack?

Because there was little doubt the brute who'd tried to snatch Jules could not have been working on his own recognizance. Of course, only one answer came to mind: it had to be Wallthorpe. Though Wolf also refused to discount Jules' former lover. Sheik Hassan seemed mighty determined to have her back in his bed as well, and the man had traveled thousands of miles to find her.

He looked down at Julia, who was huddled against his side. He wanted to marry her. Not only was it the best way to protect her, but he was ridiculously in love with her. Despite his efforts to make her fall for him, she had yet to change her mind.

Was tonight's attack enough to sway her thinking on marriage?

Chapter Twenty-One

J ulia stood in the foyer of Wolf's town house as the indomitable Mrs. Gordon put everyone and everything to rights. She wasn't cheery, she didn't laugh, she didn't smile, but she was welcoming in an efficient sort of way. Julia had known her for all of three minutes, and she wouldn't dare think of crossing the woman.

"Lord Flintshire, you may take your usual room. My ladies, I shall have rooms prepared for you in a trice."

She turned to hustle off, but stopped as Wolf cleared his throat.

"Mrs. Gordon, Lady Julia will sleep in my quarters."

Julia looked up, surprised yet overwhelmed with relief at his blunt announcement.

"My lord!" The housekeeper pressed her hand to her chest. "Why, that's scandalous!"

That his cheeks were dusted pink amused Julia, even as he appeared simultaneously embarrassed and put-upon.

Wolf sighed. "Be that as it may, I shall not sleep separate from her after this evening's events."

Flint looked even more uncomfortable than Wolf, but spoke up, as well. "And I'll need a room adjoining Mrs. Smith's. We can't be too careful after tonight's incident."

Mrs. Gordon's brown gaze narrowed, and if she could have thrown daggers at the men, Julia was certain she would have.

"I, for one, shall sleep better knowing Lord Flintshire is close at hand." Ros spoke so softly that Julia wasn't certain anyone else heard her. But then Mrs. Gordon's disapproving brown eyes softened a bit.

Julia bit her lip and admitted her own relief as well. "I wouldn't sleep a wink without Wolf after nearly being abducted." She glanced up at him and let her desire show in her eyes. "I may not sleep at all, even with him at my side."

And just like that, Mrs. Gordon tutted and scooted away to see to their rooms.

Wolf cleared his throat in the awkward silence. "Yes, well. A nip of something bracing seems in order while we wait for our rooms to be prepared. Wouldn't you agree?"

Half an hour later, Julia found herself in Wolf's chambers, soaking in a steaming bath before a small fire. It was warm for May, when the sun was shining, but the nights still held a chill. Not to mention the cold fear that still lingered well after the incident. She'd only stopped shaking once they'd settled in Wolf's carriage and she'd been able to press herself against his side. There was no doubt in her mind, she wouldn't have been able to sleep in her own bed that night. Though when she'd asked him to stay with her, she'd assumed he would take her to The Market—not his home. But Wolf was always defying expectation—or at least hers.

She hoped Ros was soaking in an equally delightful bath, though with slightly less of an audience than she had at the moment.

Wolf hovered near the tub, looking masculine yet comfortable standing in his shirtsleeves, trousers, and bare feet. "May I get you anything else?"

Julia sighed a little. The worst of her shock and fear proved to be dissipating, along with the tendrils of steam. "I'm quite well at the moment, but thank you."

He kneeled behind her at the edge of the tub. "Would you allow me to scrub your back?"

She thought about it for a minute, drawing the moment out almost teasingly. But then she raised the scrubbing cloth out of the water. "Mmmm...I think I shall."

His presence behind her was both reassuring and exciting. Then he leaned close to her ear. "Sit forward, my lady."

As he reached down into the water and searched out the soap, his wandering hand stroked and caressed all of the flesh he could find. Eventually, he found the small bar and set about his task. The light roughness of the cloth and the slippery feel of the soap combined in a pleasurable way with the pressure he applied to further relax her tense muscles. She wouldn't have asked for a bath at such a late hour—and, in fact, hadn't—but she truly appreciated that Mrs. Gordon had arranged for one so quickly.

Curious, now that her emotions had settled down, she considered who her assailant might have been. There was truly only one logical answer in her mind. "Wolf, do you think the man was sent by Wallthorpe?"

Her bath attendant sighed behind her. "I do suspect that to be true, though I am unwilling to entirely discard the notion that your sheik might also have played a hand in tonight's events."

She gasped and half turned in the tub so she could see his face. "You cannot mean that. Tariq is many things, but he is no abductor of women."

Wolf's brows rose up to his hairline. "Did he or did he not travel thousands of miles to woo you back into his bed?"

Her cheeks heated, and it had less to do with her bath or the fire, and more to do with discussing her former lover. "He did come to do that, yes, but he had other business interests to attend to as well. I was merely one of a number of concerns on his agenda. Not to mention, I suspect he will be far more occupied with one of his wives in the future, leaving him little time to court me. But I still believe that Tariq would not have done such a thing. Tonight's dastardly deeds have Wallthorpe's hands all over it."

Wolf huffed a little. "I mostly agree, but, out of an abundance of caution, I plan to have both men examined closer. I'd already started checking Wallthorpe's circumstances, but tomorrow I shall add your sheik to the list as a precaution."

Anger prickled her skin as she turned back around. "I'm telling you that isn't necessary. Tariq is no threat."

Wolf grumbled. "And I am telling you, as a man who once lost you, it is very necessary to eliminate all possibilities."

"Oh, stupid men," she mumbled, as she leaned back against the curve of the tub.

He leaned in close to her ear again. "I'm right here, you know, and I can clearly hear you."

"Well, bully for you."

She wanted to be angrier, but she understood his desire to be certain about Tariq.

Wolf then dragged the cloth from her upper back to her shoulder, and then moved it across the front of her collarbone. "Pouting does not become you, Jules."

He was right, but she would not agree so easily. "I am *not* pouting. I am merely having a difference of opinion with you. But as long as you continue to touch me like that, I am less likely to be so adamant about my opinion."

He chuckled, but then he hung the cloth over the edge of the tub and stepped away, only to return with a drying sheet. "Come out of that cooling water, before you become chilled and undo all the good the heat did."

She stood, feeling like Aphrodite rising, and waited for all the water to sluice from her body before she stepped out of the tub. Then he was there, wrapping her in warmth once again. Her heart fluttered in her chest, but she refused to give in to the sensation. Love would only lead to heartache when they parted ways once more.

He finished drying her off and then smacked her bare bottom. "Into the bed with you."

Laughing, she did as directed, crawling in after bypassing the prim nightgown that lay on a nearby bench. Sleeping in the nude was far more advantageous when lying next to a man like Wolf. And despite the evening's drama, she found her body pulsing with a need to touch and be touched. Perhaps it was the result of the night's events, or maybe it was merely being close to a man she desired, but she still wanted him. No, she *needed* him in a way she had never needed another man. Deep down inside, there was a part of her that still felt cold, and she was certain that only Wolf could thaw it with his desire.

Propped against the pillows on the bed—*his* bed—she allowed the haze of lust to drop over her as she watched him remove his clothes. He stood where she could watch as he divested himself of his shirt, then his trousers, his undershirt, and finally, his drawers. He paused there a moment, letting her look her fill of his body. She took in the thick muscles that roped along his arms, his wide shoulders that tapered to a trim waist, and the long, well-defined legs that carried him. His cock lay long and thick in a semihard state, but it was growing with each moment she observed him.

"Come here, Wolf. I need you. I need to feel you touching me. Again."

She shivered then, both her need and the cold within her growing again.

He crossed to the bed and climbed in, but he hesitated. "I think it would be best if you simply rested tonight. You have had quite a scare."

His words warred with the aroused and very erect state of his shaft.

She was absolutely certain about what she needed, and it was not rest. At least not yet. "I did have quite a scare, you are right. For a moment, I feared losing you once more. I feared being taken away, never to see or touch you again. Now, let me be reminded that you are in fact here with me." She reached out and wrapped her hand around his length. "That I can touch you as I please, and please you as I wish."

She stroked along his length and watched as all vestiges of chivalry and gentlemanliness disappeared, to be replaced with stark desire.

A soft growl escaped him. "I don't know if I can be gentle tonight. I fear I'm still rather wound tight, having nearly lost you."

She pressed a kiss to his jaw, right where a small muscle ticked. "I don't recall asking you to be gentle. I merely asked you to let me touch you."

She continued to stroke his cock, gathering the bead of moisture that gathered at the tip and using it to slicken her movement. Done with talking, she focused on doing as she wanted, so she pressed a series of kisses to his chest, and then eased her way down his body as she continued to work his length. Then she reached her objective and quickly engulfed the head of his cock in her mouth. Replacing her hand with her lips, she sank down on him, swallowing him until her lips neared the base of his shaft.

"Bloody hell." His mumbled words came as he sank his hands into her hair.

She reveled in the power of being able to draw such a response from him so quickly. But never one to sit on her laurels, she dropped one hand down to cup his balls as she continued to suck his cock. And when she stroked the expanse of skin between his sac and his rear opening, his hips bucked, forcing him deeper into her mouth, until he breached her throat.

As big and broad as his body was, he shook with his need to come, and she wanted him to, but as his movements grew more agitated, his hips flexing, driving deep into her throat, she reached back and pushed the tip of her finger into his backside.

He nearly leapt up off the bed. "Fuck, yes!"

As he came down, her finger went a little deeper inside him. Then his balls tensed up in her hand, and suddenly he pulled out of her mouth, rolled her on her back—dislodging her finger from his backside—and came all over her breasts.

Surprised by their sudden shift in positions, she lay there breathing hard as she watched his face tighten in pleasure. Eyes closed, he pumped his cock over and over, spurting his cum until nothing more came out. As he kneeled over her, cock still in his hand, he opened his eyes and looked down at her.

A dark smile played over his lips, an unexpectedly sexy look of desire and possession. "You're mine, Julia."

Her eyes widened at the use of her full name versus his pet name for her.

Then he dragged his fingers through his seed and rubbed it into her skin. "You're mine, and I shall never give you up again. Do you understand?"

Shocked by such a primitive action, she found it hard to choke a simple "yes" past the desire that had clogged her throat. As he continued to rub his semen into her skin, she felt beautiful. Desired. Claimed in a way that unexpectedly appealed to her, and only drove her need for this man higher.

He straddled her stomach and shifted to using both hands to massage her breasts, then shifted to plucking her nipples as the last of his essence disappeared and dried up. "Say it, Julia. Say you understand."

He pinched her nipples, hard, and she arched up off the bed, loving the bite of pain with the pleasure. "Yes. I understand."

And she did. She understood that he had claimed her. That somehow, married or not, this was the last man who would ever touch her. And while her mind still struggled with the notion, her body opened and welcomed his claiming. Her heart nearly burst with the joy of it.

Then Wolf eased down her body, and to her utter shock, he licked over her nipple and sucked it into his mouth. Then he followed suit on the other side. As he continued kissing down her body, he paused to look up at her. "You taste of me, because you belong to me. *Mine*." His declaration was followed by a low growl, and then returned to moving down her body. When he spread her legs, he smiled again. "I dare say I've never seen your pussy so wet. I think you may have appreciated me making my claim as much as I enjoyed making it."

Aroused and needy, she hurtled right past dirty talk into begging. "Please, Wolf. Lick my pussy. Make me come all over your tongue. I need to feel you inside me, any part of you."

"Any part?" He slid his pinky inside her pussy.

She moaned, barely feeling the penetration, yet all too aware of it. "More. Please, give me more."

He placed one hand on her thigh and changed fingers. She couldn't see what he was doing now, but she could feel something thicker inside her.

He worked the digit in and out a few times. "Better?"

"Don't tease me. I need you." She practically cried out the words, her voice cracking at the end.

Guilt quickly replaced his smile, as he laid down between her legs and spread her wide open. His tongue swirled around her hole and then up over her clit, before swooping back down and driving inside her. Her hips bucked off the bed as she sank her hands into his hair. He continued to hold her thighs open, effectively pinning her hips as he stabbed his tongue deep into her, only to drag it up over her nub, again and again. She moaned as the pressure grew to unbearable levels, and then suddenly he sucked her clit into his mouth and shoved two fingers inside her and she exploded.

Her orgasm rushed in like a tidal wave, slamming into her with such force that the breath was knocked from her lungs, making it impossible to cry out. But the bliss continued as he sucked and stroked her pussy. Finally drawing breath again, she was woozy from such intense pleasure when she suddenly realized he was inside her.

Wolf sank into her welcoming heat and tight grip, shuddering as he bottomed out. His cock ached with the need to fill her, even after having already come once. He could not have explained his earlier actions. It certainly had not been planned, but somehow, in that moment, with her lips wrapped around his cock, he had needed to stake his claim.

To mark her in the most primeval fashion.

And now, even as he sank into her pussy, it still didn't feel like enough. He needed to *own* her. To own her pleasure, and her heart. And—as uncomfortable as it was to admit—to own her soul. He wouldn't take less. Couldn't. So he pounded into her as a reminder to them both.

The primitive impulse remained strong enough that he pulled out and flipped her over onto her hands and knees. He eyed the tight pinch of her rear entrance, remembering how exquisite it had been to fuck her there while Linc had filled her pussy. He'd have her there again, but right now, he needed to fuck her hard. So he sank into her wet heat and relished her cry of pleasure.

He pulled out until just the tip remained, and then sank deep once more. Again, and again, he shoved inside her until his thighs slapped against hers and his balls smacked her clit with each surge. Then she was pushing back into his thrusts, meeting him stroke for stroke as they both raced headlong into another wave of bliss. Determined to get her there again, he reached down and stroked her swollen flesh, finding her nub and pinching it.

Her body squeezed down on his cock as they kept moving, but she cried out. "Yes! Oh God, Wolf. Yes!" Her voice was hoarse, raspy with the pleasure he was delivering.

Her passion-spent cries sent him over the edge, and he slammed into her once. Twice, three times, and then came, pumping everything he had deep inside her. His desire, his need, and his love.

Slumping over her, his body slick with sweat, he struggled to catch his breath. She sank down, carrying both of them to the mattress. As they landed, he rolled off her, not wishing to crush her after such an intense fucking. She was amazing, and he had to find a way to show her how much he appreciated that.

Chapter Twenty-Two

J ulia and her sister were safely ensconced back in their home, with each of the Lustful Lords taking a turn acting as their guard, although Flint was almost always there. Wolf would be joining him shortly, but first he had a meeting to keep with his investigator. The man had sent a note around that he had information to share at Wolf's earliest convenience. So he'd dashed home to clean up after spending the night at Jules' home. The Lustful Lords had all mentioned receiving looks as they came and went at all hours, but the situation was unavoidable for the moment. He hoped this meeting with his man of inquiry would release the group from their guard duty.

Refreshed, he'd just settled behind his desk when his butler, Gordon—husband to the ever-efficient Mrs. Gordon—knocked and entered.

"My lord, there is a gentleman here to see you."

"Send him in, please."

Wolf refrained from rushing out to meet the man, despite the urge to hurry things along. Not only did he want to know what he had discovered, but he couldn't stifle the need to return to Jules so he could ensure she was safe. It seemed without her where he could see her, he constantly worried about her wellbeing.

The nondescript man shook his hand, and then they sat down. Getting right down to business, he handed over a folio. "The report contains all the details of the Marquess of Wallthorpe's current financial situation. You will see that he is deeply in debt. In fact, he is in jeopardy of losing his family seat."

The man paused, giving Wolf a moment to peruse the specifics.

"While that would not strip him of his title, as I am sure you are aware, there is a certain amount of embarrassment that would accompany such an event. In fact, I would think he might find it nearly impossible to marry well if his situation was discovered. He has gone to great lengths to hide the state of his affairs. I am also concerned about a letter I came across from his father."

Wolf frowned. "Go on."

"It seems that part of the reason his aged father took his bride off on a world tour was because his son had an unhealthy fixation with her. The father feared his son might attempt to lure his new wife astray—or worse." The man shook his head. "You fancy types are an odd lot."

Wolf sighed. Wonderful. Wallthorpe was desperate *and* obsessed. Not a comforting combination. "And what have you found out about the sheik?"

"He was certainly more difficult to trace, but I did find that he will be departing London in three days' time. His traveling party is in an uproar, since his first wife—another strange lot, I might add—seems to have acquired some Western habits. She has taken to wearing ladies' gowns and fancying herself up, much to the man's consternation. According to the maids, he has been steaming mad and is dragging her home by her hair. By all accounts, she is fighting him every step of the way."

That bit of news made Wolf smile. The sheikh was clearly far too occupied to be attempting to abduct Julia now. "Anything else of interest? Any more visits to Lucifer's by Lady Wallthorpe, or other men who may be of concern?"

"No, my lord. It seems she has not been back to Lucifer's, nor are there other admirers lurking in the background."

Wolf nodded, satisfied. "Thank you. You've done excellent work."

"Always a pleasure, my lord. You can find my bill for services under the report." The man stood. "I'll bid you a good day."

Wolf stood as well. "Good day to you."

And then the man departed, leaving Wolf to sort out his next steps. He knew that the only way to protect Jules was to marry her. Wallthorpe was many things, but as of yet, he'd not proven to be a killer. If she was married, the man would find another solution to his problem...or not.

For once, Wolf wished he could go to his father for assistance. With his help, he could have easily offered Wallthorpe enough money to simply go away. But that was not a practical plan, as he was painfully aware of his father's stance on helping him in any capacity. Upon graduation from school, he'd received a courtesy title to offer legitimacy and three thousand pounds. His father then informed him that he was to make do on his own. His obligation had been fulfilled.

It had been a decade since he and his father had said more than a polite hello when they met unexpectedly in public. Other than that, he ensured he visited his mother when he knew his father would be unavailable or out of the house. The arrangement seemed to work well for everyone.

That said, he was still left with his original problem. How did he convince Jules that marrying him was not just the better option, but the *only* option? He was too practical to rely on love to sway her. That was too risky a proposition. No, he supposed he'd have to lay the facts out for her, and let her see that marriage was the only way to ensure her safety.

He shuffled through the papers included in the report, and was pleased to find a handwritten copy of the letter the investigator had mentioned. He read through it once himself.

Herbert,

Considering the circumstances I so recently ascertained, in particular your unhealthy fixation with my new bride, I have decided to extend my honeymoon.

You should know I have sealed up the entrances to the hidey-holes you discovered, so there will be no further opportunities to spy on her. I can also assure you that the letter you recently sent professing your undying love has not been delivered, and is, in fact, a pile of ashes in my fireplace as I write this letter. It is for your own good that I have married this woman. She was not suitable to bear the future of our line. She is a wild girl with wild ways, and it will be all that I can manage at this late hour of life to bring her to heel.

It is my great hope that while we are away, you will find your interests drawn to new quarters. I am an aging man. You will one day be the Marquess of Wallthorpe and you will require a poised and elegant wife at your side to bear our next generation. It is your duty to the family name to carry on the line, and I shall brook no more of this business with my wife.

—Wallthorpe

It took every ounce of self-control Wolf possessed not to burn the offensive missive. It explained much of the insanity that had occurred a decade ago, and some of the more current activity. But knowing Julia would need to see the words for herself, he tucked the page back into the report and shuffled through the remainder of the notes. Most of them documented a series of poor decisions on the younger Wallthorpe's part, since his father had passed.

The man had invested in some harebrained scheme to mine gold from the Americas. It would seem the man who had convinced Wallthorpe to give him a large sum of money had disappeared en route. Whether that was due to an unfortunate accident or a carefully laid plan didn't really matter, as the result was the same in the end. Wallthorpe was out nearly one hundred thousand pounds. Wolf's stomach lurched at the exorbitant sum.

Without further delay, he knew it was time to discuss his findings with Jules and get her to see reason. They must marry immediately, in order to ensure her safety.

Julia stared out the window of the hackney, watching as London's denizens spilled into the gaslit streets. Wallthorpe was becoming a rather greater pain in her backside than she had anticipated. Nothing she'd tried so far had worked to deter him, which worried her. Soon she would have only one option left, and while there were parts of the solution she wouldn't mind, she struggled with the notion of shackling herself to another man—even one so handsome as Wolf. Even one she called a friend.

With a sigh, she clenched the note in her hand tighter and prayed the summons would lead to good news. After all, how often did one receive a note, however tersely worded, from the notorious Frank Lucifer?

I have news of your unwanted suitor.

—Lucifer

With a kernel of hope lodged in her chest, and a healthy dose of dread, she had slipped down the back stairs and out into the night without alerting either Ros or one of their ever-present guards. This time it was Flint. If she weren't so busy with her own concerns, she would have sworn that those two were falling in love. But she refused to label whatever was occurring between them until she had some unfettered time to observe them more closely. For the moment, she had other things on her mind.

The cab stopped before the well-lit gambling hell, letting her clamber out onto the street and pay her fare.

The driver took the money, tipped his hat, and hesitated. "Ma'am, are ye sure this is a place you ought to be?"

She cast him a soft smile. He might be a rough man, but he clearly had a gentleman's heart. "Quite sure. I have business inside, and friends who will ensure my safety."

"Very well."

He tipped his hat once more and gave a shake of the reins. The cab pulled slowly away, leaving her to walk into Lucifer's all on her own. It was certainly not the first time she'd done so, though tonight she'd come in slightly more discreet garb. After all, she wasn't looking to stir up scandal any longer.

Too bad fate and the wagging tongues of London hadn't quite caught on yet.

Stepping inside the building, she nodded at the big brute who seemed to always lurk near the door. She thought his name was Gordie, but couldn't be sure. "Excuse me, could you please tell Mr. Lucifer that Lady Wallthorpe is here to see him."

"Come."

The staccato, single-word command prompted her to do as directed. She followed him up the stairs and along the open gallery that sat above the frenzied action below. It was a long—rather brisk—walk to the double doors at the far end.

Then the giant with the long legs stopped and opened the doors, admitting her to what she assumed was Mr. Lucifer's inner sanctum.

She took a few steps inside, and then the doors closed behind her, leaving her to face the darkly handsome man who currently lounged behind his desk. A gentleman would have stood as soon as she entered, but she needed to remember that he was no gentleman, even if he could put on airs.

He slowly rose and came around the desk. "Thank you for coming, Lady Wallthorpe."

"Yes, well, you did have a rather intriguing hook. Though you could have simply sent the information in the missive."

She eyed him warily. It was obvious he wanted something in exchange for the tidbit he'd offered, but the question was what? Money? Her body? She couldn't imagine what else he might desire, and so she braced herself for the coming conversation.

He smiled as he bowed over her hand. Then he led her to one of the empty chairs facing his desk. "You are an intelligent woman, Lady Wallthorpe. Surely you can puzzle out why I did not do that."

"Quite so, Mr. Lucifer. Shall we get down to business then?" She kept her tone formal. She knew the man had found her attractive during her one and only previous visit to his establishment, so she opted to not be overly familiar. The last thing she needed was a *third* man who had it in his head to marry her.

"Very well. I have information about your stepson that might be of interest to you." He paused. "And for the right enticement, I am willing to provide the information to you."

Julia tamped down the growl that had steadily grown as the man spoke, despite her suspicion the conversation might take this kind of turn. Had she found him charming when she'd previously met him?

"Mr. Lucifer, name your price, and I shall write a draft on my bank before I leave. I'd prefer not to sit here all night, bartering back and forth."

"Negotiating is half the fun of these transactions, my lady." He grinned unrepentantly. "What if money is not what I seek in exchange for the information?"

"My body is not for sale. I may not be a prude, but I do not use my desire as currency." She glared at him, furious that he would ask such a thing...or at least intimate it.

What is wrong with the men of London? Are they so deprived of sexual attention?

"As intriguing as the idea of a night with you in my bed is, that is not what I seek." He leaned forward. "I would like some information in return for mine."

Relief and confusion swirled through her. This was not at all what she had expected. "What could I possibly know that would be of value to *you*?"

"I wish to know more of Lord Flintshire. If you'd answer a few questions for me, I shall gladly provide you the promised information."

If she weren't mistaken, the man looked nervous. While seemingly lounging behind his desk, indifferent to her decision, there was still a tension to his body. A small tick near the back of his jaw was difficult to notice beneath his beard, but it was there. Whatever it was he wished to know was important to him—*personally.*

"I am only newly acquainted with him, and I doubt I have much to share. But I shall share whatever I know."

Lucifer nodded, a crisp movement that revealed far more than she thought he'd prefer. "How would you describe his demeanor?"

She paused for a moment, considering her recent interactions with the man. "He is a bit dark, and quite irreverent at times. But he is steady and dependable, and his sense of honor is stronger than most peers of the realm."

Lucifer smiled. "Do you like him?"

She blinked. "Do I like him?"

"Yes, do you like having him around, meeting him, chatting with him?"

His dark eyes bore into her, as though seeking out every last detail he could unearth.

"I don't really speak to him, in particular. But I shall say my sister Ros seems to have a fondness for him. I often walk into a room and find them engaged in quiet conversation, though it usually ceases once they realize I am there."

Lucifer sat a moment and considered her response. "One last question. Do you trust him?"

Julia answered without hesitation. "Implicitly."

Lucifer cocked his head. "Why?"

"You said one last question."

She tried to hide her smile. It amused her that a simple, one-word answer did not satisfy him.

He waved his hand in the air, as though swatting a fly. "The why was inherent in the original question. Your terse answer left me little choice but to articulate it."

She considered his question a moment. The truth of her answer rang through her in an unexpected peal, and had she not been sitting, it might have sent her to her knees. "I trust him because the two people I care most about in this world do. And in a moment when most men would have stepped back, he stepped forward and offered my sister the protection she needed. And he continues to provide her that shelter, even now. He may not embody the commonly accepted vision of a British hero, but somehow, he serves as my sister's."

A strange look danced through Lucifer's gaze as he stared at her. She might have labeled it jealousy, but he was far too practical a man to bother himself with such an emotion. As quickly as it appeared, it was gone.

A knock on the office door shattered the moment.

"Come in." Lucifer beckoned, though he remained where he was.

Curious about who might be joining them, she turned in her seat, peeking around the wingback-style chair. She gasped in surprise. "Wolf!"

Her voice caught his attention immediately, though from the frown marring his handsome face, she gathered he was not as pleased to see her as she was to see him.

"What are you doing here?" His demand was laced with surprise, fear, and quite a bit of anger.

Julia knew instantly what Lucifer had been about. "I imagine the same thing you are."

Wolf's right brow lifted. "You came here alone, to meet with him?"

He pointed at Lucifer, who sat smugly in his chair.

Annoyed with his overly imperious tone, Julia harrumphed. "Oh, do come and sit down. All this craning around the chair to look at you is giving my neck a spasm."

Wolf grunted, but joined their little group, taking a seat in the empty chair. "I assume you sent her the same note I received?"

Lucifer offered a devious grin. "Indeed. It seems I timed the deliveries well. Now that I have received payment, I shall provide the information promised."

Julia cast a glance at Wolf and noticed that his frown had gotten worse, the expression seeming to carve into his face where his brows drew together. And she imagined this was all part of Lucifer's plan.

But why? Why have this little drama play out in such a fashion?

"I believe you were about to share the information *we* were summoned here to receive?"

"Of course." Lucifer paused a moment, looked at a paper on his desk, and then back up at her. "Lord Wallthorpe has been here and a number of other establishments over the last few weeks. He has been playing deep and losing. With few exceptions, I've seen this type of behavior enough times," he cast a speculative glance at her, "to know what the cause of it is. Considering he owes me one hundred thousand pounds, and that he owes Callaghan sixty thousand, I can only imagine his total debt is monstrous. I dug around after realizing the magnitude of his potential problems to see if he is as solvent as his gambling suggests."

"He's not," Wolf replied, cutting in and causing her head to swivel in his direction.

Julia stared at him, waiting for more information.

Wolf lifted one shoulder at her unspoken question. "I was on my way over to tell you. Wallthorpe is in debt up to his ears, and on the verge of losing everything, including his family seat."

"Just so," Lucifer chimed back in. "I learned that the bank is close to coming for his property to satisfy the debt he currently owes. It seems he borrowed a large part of the stake he put into a shipping deal that fell apart when the ship went down."

"You certainly seem to have better resources than even I do. I had not discovered the loan from the bank."

Wolf tipped his head toward Lucifer.

"Yes, well, I discovered long ago that information could be as valuable as money. Sometimes more so." He smiled a moment. "Well, I believe that satisfies our agreed-upon exchange, Lady Wallthorpe."

"It certainly does. Thank you, Mr. Lucifer. I appreciate your awareness of the value I might place on this information." She rose a heartbeat before both men. "Wolf, could I drop you somewhere on my way?"

As they turned to leave the spacious office, he turned to her. "I have my carriage, but thank you for the offer."

"Ah, perhaps then you could drive me home, as I came via hackney. Having to elude my sister and her guard did not allow me to use my own vehicle." She offered a conspiratorial smile to Mr. Lucifer.

"I imagine. Though we should discuss this new propensity for eluding your protectors." Wolf's reply suggested a reprisal was coming.

Chapter Twenty-Three

Together, Julia and Wolf stepped outside of Lucifer's club onto a much busier street than when she'd entered. All around them, people moved in various directions, creating a motion that resembled the heave and flow of the ocean. Curious, she watched as some split off from the steady stream to slip into one establishment or another. Then she noticed that Wolf was staring at a particular business.

"What is it?" she asked.

He remained silent while he watched two men stumble down the sidewalk on the opposite side of the road. As they drew abreast of them, Julia got a closer look and recognized Wolf's friend, Arthur. His associate appeared to have an arm slung over his shoulders, as though they were close friends. Or maybe just inebriated friends. She moved to lift her arm to wave at him, but Wolf stopped her by grabbing her hand and dragging her down the sidewalk behind him.

"Hold on a moment!" He shushed her and kept moving until his carriage appeared.

Once inside, she looked at him in surprise. "What was that about?"

Wolf's brows drew together as he pressed his lips tight. "A private matter amongst friends, and I'll ask you to not say anything about seeing him."

He acted strangely, but she trusted him more than she trusted anyone, so she simply nodded her acquiescence. In the end, she was grateful for the silence that enveloped them between Lucifer's establishment and her home. While seeing his friend had distracted Wolf, she suspected it was merely a delay in the inevitable conversation they would have about her slipping out of the house.

On the one hand, she was well aware that Wolf and his friends were there to protect her. On the other, she had spent the last decade of her life taking care of herself more often than not.

Old habits were hard to break.

The carriage plodded along as Wolf sat staring out the window. Despite his silence, she could not miss the tension radiating from him. She shifted her skirts about in an effort to settle back against the squabs. His head snapped around to watch her until she ceased moving, and then he slowly returned to staring at the city that slipped past.

She repressed the sigh that welled up within and instead, held her tongue. All would come out when they arrived at her home. She doubted he could stay silent forever.

Not bothering to slip in the rear entrance since her escape had been well and truly discovered, they walked in the front door. She had only hesitated a moment when he dismissed his driver for the evening. One part of her was pleased to have him close, to know he would sleep beside her through the night. The other part railed against the fact that he *assumed* he would be staying the night, and that he felt at liberty to simply do as he wished.

Unfortunately, she seemed to be at war with herself quite a lot lately. She did not appreciate the inner quarrel.

Flint and Ros both stood up as they walked into the front salon.

Her sister rushed forward. "Julia! You're home safe!"

"Of course I am. You should never have doubted it." Julia hugged her sister, even as she accepted the disgruntled look from Flint, who hovered nearby. "I did leave you a note so you wouldn't worry."

Ros released her. "That did not equate with your remaining safe. It merely let us know you had left on your own, and were not somehow abducted from the premises."

Then Ros shot her a look that Julia thought of as her sister's mother-hen look. It was sternly affectionate, with a raised brow and a partial smile.

"Duly noted. I apologize if I distressed you, but we have learned quite a lot this evening." She glanced back at Wolf, who stood stiff and unsmiling.

"Indeed, we have learned that your sister could always turn to burglary if her fortune was lost," Wolf said, as he moved closer to her. "We also learned that Lucifer seems to have an affinity for Julia."

She could not have missed the note of anger—or was it jealousy?—that laced his words. "An affinity for *information* perhaps. I was merely a source."

He stilled and looked at her, questions in his eyes. "Information?"

"Yes." She rolled her eyes at the overbearing man beside her and turned back toward her sister to watch the dark-haired, sharp-eyed man hovering next to Ros. "He was more than a little curious about *you*, Lord Flintshire."

Flint blinked as his mouth opened slightly, as though he wished to say something, but nothing came out.

Shooting a pointed look at Wolf, Julia continued on. "*That* was how I paid for the information on Wallthorpe."

"It was?" Relief danced in Wolf's gaze, which only sparked her fury.

She rounded on him, her body alive with outrage. "Just so. But clearly you had it in your mind that I had tendered some *other* form of payment."

He winced. "Not tendered, but I would not have doubted that Lucifer would have asked. I assumed you would say no and offer him money instead. My fear was that you would overpay for information I had already acquired."

She wasn't sure she entirely believed him, but chose not to pursue the matter further—at least for the moment. Turning back to the still-shocked Flint, Julia asked him the question they all were mulling over internally. "Do you have any notion as to why he might've been asking about you?"

"I am at a loss. I've never even set foot in his establishment. Maybe he is planning to..." Flint let his thought trail off, but something seemed to be rattling about in his head.

Ros placed a soft hand on his arm. "What could it be? What might he be planning?"

Flint startled as he looked at Ros' delicate features. Her big green eyes glittered with concern as she looked up at him. Something in his gaze shifted and shuttered in a way Julia had not noticed before, and it clearly caused her sister no end of distress.

Ros pulled her hand from his arm, took a step away from him, and refocused her gaze on Julia. "Yes, well, what did you learn of Wallthorpe?"

Finding it difficult to move on from the unspoken byplay, Julia tried to set her concern for her sister aside and gather her thoughts.

Wolf stepped into the breach. "Wallthorpe is in dire financial straits. In fact, he may be penniless."

Julia filled them in from there. "It seems he has been gambling heavily, and the bank is about to foreclose on his family seat, which he put up as collateral for a loan to fund a shipping venture. The ship sank, and everything was lost."

Flint's upper lip curled in disgust. "So the man is desperate, and his only way out of hock is to marry."

"Yes, he is the worst kind of fortune hunter. Add to that his long-held fixation with Julia, who now has a significant portion of what was his father's money. And the only way to access those funds is to marry her."

Wolf's brow creased to the point that Julia worried it might turn into a permanent furrow.

She sighed. It was becoming more and more evident that the only way to thwart her stepson was to either give away her fortune, or to marry someone. What worried her was that she couldn't be certain that giving the money away would solve the problem entirely. The man seemed inordinately focused on her, to the point he'd pursued her sister as leverage. If she were being forthcoming, she would acknowledge that he'd always seemed overly interested in her, even when she'd been a young debutante. Her stomach churned.

Wolf looked at her, concerned determination lurking in his dark gaze. "Jules, perhaps we should speak in private?"

"I see no reason to hide the nature of this discussion. Ros and Flint are both adults, and they're aware of the situation I find myself in."

For a moment, she was certain she would cast up her accounts, but then she looked at Wolf and allowed flashes of their time together to comfort her. The way he touched her, the pleasure he shared with her, and the way he looked at her all comforted her. Even now, the softness in his gaze made her heart stutter.

He drew a breath and jerked down on his vest. "Very well, Jules." He stepped over to the chair nearest the door and produced a folio she'd not seen before. Then he pulled a sheet from the book and held it out to her. "You should read this."

Warily, she walked over and took the document. The words on the page ran together until she adjusted to the handwriting, but then they jumped off the page. Reading the letter from her dead husband to his son took mere moments, and then she had to reread it.

All the blood drained from her face. "He'll never stop, will he?"

Ros rushed to her side. "What are you talking about?"

Julia waved the correspondence in the air. "Wallthorpe. He's been obsessed with me for years. It's his fault his father married me."

She shook with fear and an utter sadness that opened a great gaping hole in her chest. All her suffering and her year of misery had ensued because a father sought to keep his son from pursuing her. Because she was too lowbrow to bear the next generation. She'd been treated contemptibly by much of London's upper crust during her coming out. She'd been reminded regularly that she was not one of them, but she could not have fathomed that she would be considered so inconsequential that a man might marry her in order to prevent his son from doing so.

And here she was, because of that same man, being forced into a second marriage. Her gut twisted as she realized that the tactic had worked once, and would likely work again. She'd all but made up her mind before Wolf had produced this letter, but now she knew there was no other choice. There would be no dissuading Wallthorpe with more scandalous behavior. Nothing short of murder or marriage would convince him that she was unavailable.

Wolf cleared his throat. "We must marry, and right away. The sooner you are my wife, the sooner you will be protected from him." He paused then, a slight hesitation. "I know you've stated you do not want—"

"Yes." She blurted the word before she could change her mind. Before the truth of what she'd read could sink in any further, and bring any more grief to the forefront of her thoughts. "I'll marry you."

He continued. "No, I'm serious. It's the—"

She stepped up to him and placed her fingers to his lips. "I've agreed to marry you. You're correct, it's the only solution."

Having said it a second time, a strange sense of relief and sadness swept over her. The constant, gnawing worry eased even as doubts about marrying him replaced them. But at least she and her sister would be safe. Or at least she hoped they would be.

Now she need only worry about protecting her heart.

Chapter Twenty-Four

W olf paced his library as he waited for the most important moment of his life to occur. Another hour should not have mattered when he'd waited three days—no, a lifetime—for her. Unbelievably, she had said yes...*finally*.

Not that he could fault her for her logic, and he certainly would have preferred that she marry him for love. But that simply wasn't possible under the circumstances.

His heart squeezed.

They were friends. They were lovers. But they were not *in* love.

Or at least, she wasn't. But now he had time—the rest of his life—to make her fall in love with him. To show her that he was worthy of her trust, and wouldn't desert her again when she needed him most. That was something he could work with.

A knock on the door preceded Flint's entrance. "The guests have all arrived."

"Considering how small the affair is, that's not hard to imagine." Wolf grimaced.

He'd thought about delaying the ceremony in favor of a large wedding with all the pomp and circumstance to publicly solidify his claim on Julia. But she had argued—quite vociferously—in favor of an intimate gathering. One with just their friends and families. He'd finally conceded the point.

"How is the bride fairing?"

Flint's smile was big, bordering on overbright. "She is just smashing, I hear."

Wolf recognized the sardonic humor lurking behind Flint's dark gaze. He knew Jules would be nervous, and possibly even having second thoughts about their union. He also knew she'd go through with it if for no other reason than to protect Ros. After all, once he and Jules were married, Ros would have his protection as well.

He ignored the feeling of having swallowed glass shards and tried to focus on the fact that he loved her. It would be enough for the moment. It simply had to be.

"How are you doing?" Flint's inquiry was casual, too casual.

If Wolf weren't so wrapped up in his own issues, he'd have noticed that his friend was on edge. "I'm as well as can be expected. How are you? I've been rather absorbed by my own issues of late."

Flint made an obvious effort to remain relaxed, and even tried to smile. "Oh, not great, but not terrible. I could really use a trip down to the docks."

He knew his friend visited the seedy underbelly of London regularly to let off whatever anger it was that continually built up inside of him. At times, he seemed like a powder keg about to blow, although there had been a few weeks there where he'd spent so much time with Ros that he had been more like the young man Wolf had once known. But it seemed whatever reprieve that had been granted had since faded.

"Well, I imagine after today, you shall find yourself with all sorts of free time."

"Indeed," Flint agreed, though he did not look as pleased about that prospect as he should.

Another knock at the door ended the conversation. Ros looked in the room. Her gaze sought Flint out unerringly. The two stared at each other for a moment, and then she looked over to Wolf. "We're ready to start."

Wondering what was going on between the two of them, but needing to take his place for the wedding, Wolf vowed to follow up with Flint as soon as possible. Maybe he could find a moment during the breakfast to have a few more words with his friend. Something more than the perfunctory conversation they'd just had.

With a nod, he made his way to where he had been in-structed to wait for his bride. Excitement warred with his certainty that she did not love him, but regardless, this wedding would occur. So, he pushed the latter—unwanted—thought aside, and focused on the excitement, and the fact that he loved her. That was all that mattered.

Julia waited upstairs in Wolf's town house. Well...*their* town-house now. Or it would be shortly. The swirling in her gut reminded her of the time she'd eaten a bad egg as a girl. Shoving the unsavory thought aside, she focused on getting through the next several hours. She had vowed to never be so reliant on a man again, but here she was once more, shackling herself to one. Except she reminded herself that he was no ordinary man. He was her friend. Her lover. She had once been in love with him. *Ugh.* It was the same conversation—slightly varied—that she'd been having for the last three days as they'd planned their wedding.

To her surprise, once she'd agreed, he'd tried to push for a grand affair. Terrified she would balk before such a production could occur, she had insisted on a small, private ceremony. She needed the wedding to happen quickly, before she could do something foolish, like change her mind.

Her palms had grown sweaty and her face felt hot, as though her cheeks were flushed, and her body was covered in chills.

It was nerves.

Normal bridal jitters.

Ros walked up the stairs and found her heading the wrong direction. "Julia!"

Her sister whispering her name stopped her cold. She turned to face her. "I was just going to make sure I didn't forget my handkerchief."

Ros stood there, one eyebrow lifted. "The one crumpled in your hand?"

She sighed. "Very well. But this is a mistake. I cannot do this."

He will change the moment I say I do.

Her sister snorted. "And why not? You managed to go through with marrying that doddering old fool Wallthorpe."

"I was angry and hurt then. Devastated when Wolf deserted me. So numb from it all I didn't care what happened at that point."

Julia hated reliving the hopelessness she'd felt in the days after Wolf had left her standing on a dark London street corner alone. That moment had killed every romantic notion she'd ever harbored. And here she was relying on the very same man to save her from yet another Wallthorpe.

Or more accurately, from the very same one who had wreaked havoc on her life once before.

Her breath stalled in her chest as her body tensed and her thoughts raced. She kept telling herself to calm down, but it was as if her mind was on a runaway locomotive with no emergency brake.

"Julia, he's your best friend."

Sometimes it was hard to remember that Ros was her younger sister.

"*Was.* Once, long ago." Her breathing came in harsh pants as her stomach twisted in knots.

What am I doing?

"You have been lovers for weeks now. Clearly there is some spark left between the pair of you."

Pink blossomed high on Ros' cheeks.

Julia couldn't hide her surprise. "You know?"

"Only a blind man would miss the obvious attraction between you."

"I don't trust him." Her heart ached at the words, but she said them loudly and clearly, as though they weren't a lie.

Take a deep breath. Remember, it is Wolf you are marrying, not Wallthorpe.

Ros shook her head. "You *do* trust him. You simply must let yourself do so."

Panic set in then. The ache in her heart turned into a painful squeezing that robbed the air from her chest. She drew a breath, but could barely collect a lungful, and tried to draw another. The heat in her face seemed to grow hotter.

What if marrying him ruins everything? What if I lose my best friend?

Finally, unnerved by the continued standoff between heart and mind, she yelled at Ros, "I don't love him!"

The silence was deafening in the wake of her roared declaration.

A low growl sounded below, and she peered over the balustrade to see the man she was about to marry standing there with his best man. Without a word, he turned and marched into the salon where the ceremony was to take place.

"Oh, God! What have I done?" Julia wobbled on unsteady legs until Ros guided her to a nearby bench.

"Calm down," her sister cooed as she rubbed her lace-covered back.

How can I possibly go through with the wedding now? There has to be another way!

"Julia, you're breathing too fast. You need to calm down," Ros urged her again.

"I-I-" Fear had set in, and now she was left with nowhere to turn. There was only Wolf.

There had only ever been Wolf.

"Listen to me." Ros cupped Julia's face in her delicate hands and forced her to look in her eyes. "That is a good man down there. He is marrying you despite knowing you don't want this. He is doing so only to protect you. He is *not* like Wallthorpe. He is not going to desert you again. And truth be told, you do not have another choice. There is no other way to protect yourself from Wallthorpe."

Inspiration struck. "I could give him all the money!"

Ros shook her head. "The man is obsessed with *you*. He would simply use the wealth you gave him to trap you somehow. You know marriage is the only way. It worked once before. Stop and consider who else you would rather marry."

Julia tamped down the buzzing sound in her head and tried to think through all the men she knew. There wasn't a single one she would consider marrying outside of Wolf. Not even the sexy Mr. Lucifer. "You're right."

"I am. Now, you must pull yourself together and go down there and get married. Everyone is waiting, but most importantly, Wolf is waiting."

"How can I face him when I just shouted that I don't love him?" Jules felt awful, mostly because she was terrified it wasn't true, and that she was in denial about how she felt about him.

"You don't *have* another choice. Now, chin up, and go down there and get married. The rest will work itself out."

Ros helped her stand, and then together, they walked downstairs. At the bottom, her sister separated from her and the music started as she walked inside.

Then it was her turn.

On aspic-filled legs, she made her way into the salon and faced her less-than-pleased groom.

Wolf watched Jules come towards him, but in truth, all he could hear was her voice shouting *I don't love him*! He'd suspected it, known it even, but it still hurt to hear her say it. Hurt to know it unequivocally. The ring of a heated conversation had given him pause as he'd walked from the library. Concern for Jules had him turning to verify if it was her voice he'd heard.

And then there had been no doubt as she'd peeked over the bannister.

And still, he knew with every fiber of his being that he would not walk away from her in this moment. Not when she needed him so desperately. Not again.

So he sucked up his own pain. Pushed it down deep inside, and waited for her. A violinist played Mendelssohn's Wedding March as Jules slowly made her way up the small aisle. Sans veil, her glorious red hair glowed in the morning light that streamed in through the windows of his front parlor. His heart skipped a beat as she made her way toward him.

Her gaze was trained downward, either on her bouquet, or even the floor. What mattered was that she would not look up at him. That made his chest ache, made him hate that she did not want this marriage. And while it seemed selfish that he had finally got what he wanted, even at the expense of her desires, he refused to stop the wedding. Not when it was the only way he could ensure she remained safe.

As she reached him at the altar, she finally looked up at him. Her beautiful green eyes were dark with some emotion. *Regret? Anger?* He couldn't be sure, but it cut him to the quick and savaged an already deep wound. Resolved that she may well hate him once it was all over, he took her hand and faced the parson with her at his side.

By the time their vows had been exchanged—hers in a quivering voice that rang with all the doubt she'd shared in the foyer—he was focused on reminding her that he was her friend. Not her enemy.

Breakfast was an interminable parade of dishes. How Jules had coordinated the preparation of so many courses in such a short amount of time was amazing. But then, he already knew she was an uncommon woman. He refused to be a lovesick fool, so he tried to focus on eating the pheasant, eggs, and savory patties loaded on his plate.

Jules leaned close to him. "Are you doing well?"

Wolf refrained from snorting at his new wife. He shoved a forkful of eggs in his mouth to avoid having to respond.

A few moments passed, and then she leaned close once more. "May I offer my apologies?"

He was between bites, so he looked at her and sought a calm response. "We are not the first bride and groom to be in a similar position. However, we should delay this conversation until we are in more private surroundings."

Her soft sigh and the sadness in her green eyes was answer enough. He did not mean to be cruel; he merely preferred to spare both of them any further embarrassment than they'd already suffered.

"You look lovely today." He offered the compliment both because it was true, and he wished to ease her very obvious distress.

She blushed a bit. "Thank you. But you don't—"

"I wouldn't say it if it were not the truth," he grumbled, and then refocused on his plate.

Yes, it seemed they still had much to discuss later. The question was, now that he knew she did not love him, could he still win her heart?

Did he still wish to?

Chapter Twenty-Five

J ulia walked through the home that was now partly hers. All the guests had long since departed, and her things had been put away. In the three days since she'd agreed to marry Wolf, they obviously had not had time to discuss a honeymoon. The truth was, she could happily skip that tradition. Her last one had left much to be desired.

Guilt and regret ate at her as she wandered aimlessly. *How could I have been so thoughtlessly cruel to my friend?* She hadn't meant to shout that she didn't love him. The worst part was that it wasn't even true. Fear had simply taken a stranglehold on her in that moment, and had caused her to panic and lash out instinctively. A tear slipped down her cheek as she remembered the look on Wolf's face when she'd looked over the railing. The hurt and devastation she'd glimpsed before he'd turned and walked into the salon would forever be stamped on her memory.

She wandered into the salon where the ceremony had been held and tried to remember how the room had been arranged. Wolf's efficient staff already had everything set to rights, leaving her nothing to do. At loose ends, she sighed.

A masculine throat cleared behind her. "Could I have a word with you in the library?"

She turned as soon as he made the sound behind her, surreptitiously wiping the stray tear from her face, and followed him into his domain. Considering the awful thing he'd heard her say earlier, she couldn't blame him for wanting to have this conversation from a place of power.

He sat behind his desk, and she took one of the chairs sitting across from him.

"I imagine you'd like to address what you heard just before the wedding."

"Not at all." He drew a breath. "Look, Jules. I am well aware you did not want to get married ever again. This was an unavoidable situation. I certainly have no illusions about the state of our relationship."

She hated that he'd been forced to articulate such truths. If she were honest, it gutted her.

He continued. "But we've been friends for a long time, and more recently, lovers. That is more than many *ton* marriages have been built on."

She couldn't dispute his statement. "It is."

His hands fisted on the desk and then flattened out. "So I am hoping that we can move past this morning's less than ideal start and continue down the path we've been on for the last few weeks."

Was he nervous? She looked down at her hands clutched tightly in her lap in order to hide her amusement. That she even felt such a thing after their morning was like a ray of sunshine on a bleak day. After she quickly gathered herself, she looked back up at him again. "I would like that. The notion of marrying again, of being so vulnerable to anyone, had me on edge this morning. Keeping things more or less as they've been would be wonderful."

He apparently had refrained from breathing, because upon her agreement, he released a deep breath. "Excellent. However, as my wife, I would like to cover your day-to-day expenses. New gowns, pin money, whatever you need."

She bit her lip, concern flaring within. "I can't allow you to do that. I have plenty of my own money to address those needs."

He frowned. "Use your fortune for other things, then. Spoil your sister and your family, give it to charity, or maybe invest it. But as your husband, it is my job to take care of you and all your needs."

She shook her head. She refused to be so dependent on him. "I can't allow myself to become..."

Her words trailed off as she saw the spark of frustration in his eyes. For some reason, this was important to him.

With deep reservations, she tried for a compromise. "Might I suggest we share the cost of any new gowns?"

"Have all bills sent to me. I shall tally up your portion and let you know the total on a quarterly basis. Will that work?" He looked about as pleased with the arrangement as she was.

"Very well, though do not think you can fool me with some token amount. I am quite aware of my spending habits." She resisted the urge to fist her hands in her silk skirts. She was *not* a lavish spender, but there were certain luxuries she had come to enjoy. Fine fabrics, such as the softest lawn, silks, velvets, and of course, the gowns that resulted. While she did not frequent Society, she relished the feel of silk against her skin, and a finely made dress was greatly appreciated.

"Noted." He seemed to gather himself for a moment. "I believe we should also discuss the agreement we made previously with regard to sex."

"Do go on."

Her earlier distress and upset forgotten, she let one brow rise as she smirked. She didn't think he could ask for her to be more adventurous than she'd already been.

"Yes, well. I should mostly like to leave things as they are, with a few exceptions. You are my wife, so I'd prefer it if you were available most nights. It is not as though either of us needs to make arrangements to attend The Market any longer."

"Agreed."

While she was certain he was merely trying to put her at ease about their marriage, she did find his attention to detail amusing.

"And while I believe it goes without saying, just to be clear, fidelity is expected on both our parts. I shall no more attend sexually-oriented gatherings at The Market than I would expect you to take other lovers." Something hard glinted in his gaze, a possessive gleam that made her heart flutter and her core pulse. "Any sexual needs you have will be met by myself alone, and vice versa."

Clearly, he was attempting to balance his desire to lay claim to her with her obvious need for freedom. She'd initially agreed to have only one lover, so the reminder was unnecessary, but not particularly worth arguing about. "I believe nothing has changed on that topic. You are, and will remain, my only lover for the duration of this marriage."

He stared at her with a peevish look that suggested something about what she'd said was unwelcome. But since she had merely acknowledged the fact she would remain faithful, that left her comment about the duration of the marriage. She cringed. It was indeed a qualifying statement, but based on his reaction, she had to assume he did not see their arrangement ending once Wallthorpe was dealt with.

While they had not discussed how or when their marriage would end—clearly an oversight on her part—it seemed logical that it would in fact come to a natural conclusion. *Wouldn't it?* Yet something inside her squeezed uncomfortably at the notion. The practical side of her, however, the side that sought to protect her from greater heartache, still argued that falling in love with the same man a second time was foolish—and a path bound for unhappiness.

"Good."

Wolf's single-word answer sounded as though it had been forced past his lips. He took a moment more, fiddling with some papers on his desk, and then looked back at her. "Is there anything you wish to add?"

She considered for a moment, but shook her head. "No, I think we've covered everything. I think I shall retire and prepare for bed."

"I shall be up shortly."

She stood and strode to the door. All the while, the weight of his gaze rested on her. It felt as though he caressed her with his very eyes. It was both unsettling and exciting. With a flutter in her belly at the night to come, she closed the study door behind her. Hesitating a moment, she heard a soft curse and the tinkle of the crystal decanter as he poured himself a drink.

He seemed as unsettled as she was, but she suspected it was for altogether different reasons. Determined not to worry about things like dissolving their marriage until the time came, she headed upstairs to prepare for her wedding night.

It was maybe an hour later, while she reclined on the chaise lounge by the fire, trying to appear calm, that she heard Wolf enter his chamber next door. She glanced down at the pale pink negligee that cupped her breasts before falling to her feet in a cascade of silk. With the fire blazing she was plenty warm, yet a chill swept over her as she waited.

Would sex between them change somehow? He'd indicated that it wouldn't earlier, but men could be fickle creatures. Often, what a man might deem acceptable with a lover might be considered too vulgar for a wife.

After what seemed an eternity, the door between their chambers swung open. Wolf stood still, illuminated by the firelight. His shirt hung loose over his trousers, his necktie and vest discarded, along with his shoes and socks. He was a sexy, yet domestic picture.

"Good evening, wife."

She bit her lip, taken with the moment. Finally, she managed to reply. "Good evening, husband. Would you care to join me by the fire?"

He stalked across the room slowly. A predator on the prowl, if ever she saw one.

"Stand up. Let me see what it is you are wearing."

With no small amount of trepidation—good God, it wasn't as though she were a virgin—she rose up and faced the man who now owned her body and soul. Well, her body, she reminded herself. But her heart whispered that he had her soul as well. Ignoring the never-ending internal struggle, she instead focused on the pleasure she knew this man could deliver.

The silk swept the tops of her feet as she waited for him to comment. Saying nothing, he simply stepped close to her and reached out to trace the scooped neckline of the bodice where it dipped so low it barely contained her nipples.

"What a lovely little creation." Something dark and a little dangerous glinted in his blue eyes. "But not as lovely as the woman it adorns."

Her cheeks heated, even as she trembled with need. Despite her doubts about marrying him, she knew she wanted to feel his hands and mouth on her body. Knew he could bring her all manner of pleasure when she trusted him, and she did trust him with that—if nothing else.

"Thank you."

He leaned forward and dropped a kiss on her collarbone, just beside the fabric that covered her shoulder. With a gentle tug on the sheer sleeve, the garment slipped down her arm and exposed one breast. Then he repeated the kiss and the tug on the other side.

A low, soft growl escaped him as he then kissed each puckered tip of her breasts. "So beautiful, and all mine."

Arms trapped in her gown, she could do nothing save stand there and tremble as he slid his arms around her waist and arched her backwards. He continued to feast on her breasts, nibbling, biting, and suckling her nipples until her core ached with the need to be filled. And still he refused to stop. Her knees grew weak to the point she reached up and grabbed onto his shirt, where she could find some purchase.

Subsequently, he pulled her up against his chest and claimed her lips. His tongue slid past her teeth to explore deep within. She met every stroke, every slide of his tongue, seeking to claim him in whatever way she could. Lost in the heady kiss and the sharp tang of whisky in his mouth, she was surprised when she found her legs suddenly pressed against the bed.

When had they moved?

Wolf broke the kiss, drew back from her, and looked down at the wanton picture she presented: nightgown half off, breasts exposed, hair streaming around her shoulders, and her lips swollen from their frenzied kisses.

His dark eyes sought out her green ones, and then he grinned, a feral possessive baring of teeth. "You're mine, Jules, and I'm never giving you up. *Never* letting you go."

His guttural declaration sent shivers cascading down her spine. She should have been frightened, scared of both the ferocious look in his eyes and the implication that he'd not release her from their marriage.

But all she could think was that she'd always been his. *Only* ever his.

Wolf wanted to howl into the air and beat his chest as Jules stared at him, her deep green eyes wide with some emotion he couldn't identify. Or *wouldn't*. The base need to claim, to dominate her and ensure she understood who she belonged to pushed him past all bounds of reason.

Before he could consider his actions too closely, he reached down and yanked the ribbon from her waist. Then he dragged the sagging nightgown down her body until it fell away from her hands and pooled at her feet. His cock throbbed behind the flap of his trousers, intense need robbing him of the little finesse he could normally claim.

With a grunt, he spun her around and used the tie he still held to bind her hands together behind her back. She was his captive now. His wife. His *forever*.

With the curve of her arse pressed against his aching cock, he tried to reassure her. "I'm going to bend you over and fuck you, wife. I'm going to sink so deep inside you that you won't remember what it feels like without me there. And then I am going to make you scream with pleasure."

Her breathing had grown choppy, her chest heaving with each inhale. Her nipples were hard little pebbles that he wished he could lick and suck on more, but he couldn't be everywhere at once. So he settled for reaching around and tweaking each engorged tip before he bent her over.

Once her face and chest were on the mattress, he spread her legs open. Kneeling down behind her, he spread the cheeks of her backside wide so he could see all of her. See how pretty and pink and wet she was for him. He groaned and then leaned in to swipe his tongue over her sweet flesh. She moaned as her legs quivered. Drawn by her taste, he drove his tongue deep inside her, fucking her with it as he reached up and stroked a fingertip over her clit.

"Oh God. That feels..."

Whatever she'd planned to say was lost in another moan as she canted her hips back to allow him even more access. To let her rub her pussy against his face as he switched from plunging inside her to licking from her clit to her spasming hole.

He had every intention of sliding deep inside her pussy, but then he saw the tight knot of her rear entrance open and close just a bit. Need burned through his plans like a spark set to dry brush. He rose up behind her and quickly shed his clothes before reaching into his nightstand to pull out a jar of salve.

His cock strained up to his stomach, the head dark and mottled with desire. He pushed two fingers into her pussy, working them in and out until they were coated in her juices. Then he dragged them back to her tight pucker and pressed. She gasped, but quickly relaxed into his intrusion. With his fingers lodged in her arse, he aligned his cock to her pussy and sank in slowly.

Heat and wetness engulfed him in the most mind-spinning ways. His cock sheathed in her channel, wrapped in heat and wonderful wetness, while his fingers were gripped by her even hotter rear opening, her body clamping down without mercy. He pumped in and out of her, sinking his cock until the base of his shaft and balls slapped against her clit, and the webbing of his fingers bit against her sphincter. When he deemed she was stretched enough to take him, he withdrew from both holes. Grabbing a bit of the salve to ease his way, he coated his shaft. Then he placed the tip of his erection against the slightly opened hole and pressed against the tight ring of muscle.

"Open to me, Jules. Let me in."

She pressed backward and relaxed against his entry. The tight heat of her rear channel enveloped him, grabbed hold of his shaft and squeezed with a blinding intensity that had his balls drawing up tight. But he refused to blow so quickly. He slid until his hips melded against the globes of her arse, and then stilled.

Mentally, he focused on his last round of correspondence and the long columns of accounting they contained. He thought about standing in a ballroom and making small talk with his peers, and he unsuccessfully tried to replay the last cricket match he'd watched.

Below him, Jules' hands wriggled at the small of her back, still bound, and she shimmied her hips a bit. "Please, Wolf. I need you to move."

He groaned, determined to keep his climax at bay. "Hold on—"

"*Now*, Wolf. I need you to fuck me *now*," she demanded, as she tried to slide forward on his length.

He slapped her backside with a resounding crack. "Hold still, woman."

She whimpered.

For a moment, his breath seized in his chest.

He'd struck her, but would she discern the difference between this moment and her first wedding night? Guilt sliced into him until she squirmed again.

"Wolf, fuck me. Please." And she let the last word drag out in a plea.

Assured she was still with him, he gathered his will and drew out of her back passage and completely out of her body. Her hole sat there open and waiting for him to plunge back inside, and he did, slamming into her arse with a long, hard thrust. He repeated the motion again and again, pulling out completely and then slamming deep inside her. He wanted her to feel him every time she sat down the next day. Wanted her to remember who she belonged to now. Each collision of his hips and her bottom pushed her chest against the mattress, and he was certain the coverlet abraded her nipples, because she yipped and moaned in pleasure again and again.

He climbed toward his peak once more, and so shifted to a shorter stroke, remaining buried in her tight heat. Reaching around her hip, he found her soaked slit and swollen clit. Timing his touch with the slide of his cock filling her arse, he worked her hard. Her moans and groans only got louder when he added his finger to her swollen nub. And then her backside clamped down on his shaft like a vise.

He could barely move inside her as she exploded around him, his name a chant on her lips as she bucked against him. Her entire body shook with her release, a vibration that carried into his own frame and made him desperate to join her. As her tight grip eased, he resumed shuttling in and out of her backside, fucking her hard now that he merely had to focus on his own release.

Three strokes later, his balls tightened, a tingling sensation his only warning before he came, pouring himself deep inside her. He continued to pump his hips, letting the extra lubrication add to the pleasant jolts that still fired through his system. Then everything settled down as he hung over her, careful of her bound hands.

After catching his breath, he straightened up, but found himself reluctant to move yet. Concerned about her arms, he released the ribbon that held her hands tied and curved over her back as he rubbed her arms. "Are you well?"

She chuckled, sending a ripple over his softening shaft that ultimately dislodged him from her warmth. He slid free, and with no reason to remain in place, collapsed onto the bed and pulled her with him.

"Thank you."

She smiled. "I feel as though I am the one who should be saying those words."

"No, Jules, it is most certainly me." He smiled and then yawned mightily. Sleep was coming for him, so he moved from the bed before he would be incapable. After quickly cleaning himself up and then Jules, he crawled under the covers. "Come sleep with me."

She bit her lip but nodded and followed him under the covers. "Good night, husband."

"Sleep well, wife."

He smiled, pleasure stealing through his limbs and dragging him into oblivion.

Chapter Twenty-Six

J ulia and Ros sat in Lady Stonemere's—well, Theo's, because the woman didn't have a formal bone in her body—drawing room. Surrounded by both familiar faces and a few new ones, Julia smiled and nodded even as worry ate at her. She'd been married for two weeks. Two wonderfully, delightfully naughty weeks. And still, she had concerns.

Not about Wolf. The man was proving himself to be a kind and caring husband. He was everything she once thought a husband would be, and certainly nothing like her first husband. If she were honest, a small part of her had worried that once the wedding guests had departed, the man would somehow turn into a monster, too. Perhaps she needed to change up her reading preferences from gothic horror novels to something more soothing—though she doubted she could stand a book of poetry.

No, her lingering concerns were about herself. She'd been an independent woman for so long, and had been so determined to stay that way, that she didn't think she could change. It was part of her internal fabric, but now that she was truly wed to a peer of the realm who was certainly an indulgent husband, he would expect obedience from her. She was doomed to fail at this, and leave both Wolf and herself heartbroken in the process.

A small sigh escaped her. She didn't want her marriage to fail. She wanted to change somehow, if that meant she could have him in her life forever.

Laughter rang out around her, and she realized her sister was enjoying the female company immensely. There was another front of concern for Julia. Ros was well and truly alone now, living in their house despite their parents' insistence she move home. Of course, they didn't understand that living with them could never be home—probably never had been to be honest. Julia also worried that Ros would be lonely, that she might find herself at loose ends without a close companion at hand. She had gone from her parents' home to her husband's home, to her sister's home, never once having spent time living alone.

Julia still remembered her first year after her husband's death. Though some would have considered a houseful of servants to be company, the truth was, they weren't. She had been very much alone then, and it took a while for her to adjust to that. At first it was a relief, a great weight off her shoulders. But then, with so much time on her hands, all she could do was think about the things that had gone wrong in her life, picking apart each decision she'd made or allowed others to make for her. The first six months were the loneliest she'd ever been.

But loneliness wasn't an issue any longer. No, she had a much bigger and more dangerous issue now. If she came to depend on Wolf—or any man, really—could she survive being on her own again when it inevitably occurred?

A gentle touch drew her attention.

Theo smiled brightly and leaned toward her. "You look as though you've brought weighty thoughts with you today."

Julia tried to smile back, but couldn't dissemble in the face of such honest, heartfelt concern. She let her gaze drop to her clenched hands. "Mayhap I did. My apologies for being such a poor guest."

"Do not apologize. If you have weighty thoughts, you have come to the right place. This is my marriage cabal." She grinned wickedly. "While the husbands would be—and have been—dismayed to learn of the plots we devise here, there is no group of ladies better suited to help solve a marital issue."

Julia glanced about the room, seeing Emily, who she'd met through Wolf, and of course her sister and Theo. But Lady Heartfield was new to her, as was Theo's sister, Lady Carlisle.

Theo squeezed her hand. "Trustworthy to a woman. No secrets shall be exposed by anyone in this room. We've all been in the position to have doubts about our marriages, to worry about our futures. If we can aid you in any manner, you must know we will do so without question."

Conversation ebbed and flowed around Julia. The others were clearly otherwise engaged. The earnestness in Theo's steady gaze reassured her, and gave her the courage to reach out. "I'm worried I cannot stay married to Wolf."

The room had gone quiet then, and all eyes turned to her. Cheeks hot, she looked around to see a strange array of looks. Most held sympathy, one woman—Lady Heartfield—looked amused, but Ros appeared quite angry.

Her sister broke the awkward silence first. "Do not be ridiculous, Jules. You love him. He loves you. Why can't you stay married to him?"

"I've lived as my own woman for a decade. I come and go as I please. I have my own funds and my own way of doing things. But most importantly, I have long refused to ever find myself at a man's mercy again. This was only ever intended to be a temporary arrangement."

A lump formed in her throat, making it hard to push the words out.

Theo squeezed her hand, a soft look on her face.

But it was Lady Heartfield who spoke up. "I was like you, possibly worse under the circumstances. I had been on my own for more than twenty years. I was the Madame of The Market"—Julia gasped at that surprise bit of news—"and I had only ever known how to survive on my own. It was a bit of a shock when Heart stormed into my life and wanted to rescue me from it. You see, I didn't *need* rescuing."

The sadness grew within her. She had, in fact, *needed* saving.

Lady Heartfield continued on. "Or at least I thought I didn't. It turns out that I did need just a little. Once Heart battered down all my defenses and I let him in, I realized that I was a stronger woman *with* him than without. Not that I could not have survived...but I wasn't *living*."

Julia inhaled sharply, the older woman's words hitting a bit too close to home. Was that possibly her issue? She considered the last ten years of her life.

"But I have lived. I've lived abroad, taken a sheik as a lover—among others—and I have come and gone as I've pleased. I've also seen many sights and places most women will never have the chance to go."

"Certainly, you have made a good show of living," Ros replied. "But to *truly* live, one must have genuine emotion in their life. Lady Heartfield—"

The blond woman smiled. "Marie, please."

"Marie is right. You've tucked away all your emotions since your marriage to Wallthorpe. Since Wolf left you on that street corner, waiting for him. Even with Tariq, you never allowed him close enough to breach your defenses—not that I think that was a bad choice. But I suspect Wolf has blasted through your walls and has your heart surrounded. And it would seem he is taking no prisoners."

Of course, her sister fell back on a military description. If she had been a man, she would have been a military man—a field marshal, most likely. Julia bit her lower lip in consternation. Her first impulse was to deny her sister's and Marie's words, but the truth was...they weren't incorrect.

She closed her eyes and felt the room sway around her. "I *want* to change, to let him in, but I'm terrified he'll only hurt me again."

"When one has been deserted by love," Marie offered with a gentle, yet knowing smile, "it can be difficult to trust it the second time around. But you *must* find a way to open yourself to him."

"I feel closest to him when we are intimate," Jules whispered.

Theo nodded. "That was how I learned to trust Stone. You must study his desires, learn his needs—"

Julia chuckled. "Those things I know. I need no primer in how to please Wolf. What I need is help in figuring out how to get past my fear of making myself vulnerable to him."

Theo frowned. "Well, then I suppose there is no need to sneak you into The Market for a lesson."

Emily and Theo giggled, sharing a smile. Marie shook her head.

Curious, Julia asked, "What is it?"

With a shake of her head, Theo answered. "A story for another time. We must focus on the issue at hand. Marie, do you have any further guidance from your experience?"

The woman sat lost in thought for a moment as everyone waited for her to speak. "I am afraid physical intimacy is not the solution this time. Or, I should say, not the heart of it. The next time you lay with your husband, afterwards, as you are still entwined, try speaking to him of your past. Of how your marriage and subsequent life have changed you and made you guarded. Do it while in his arms, so you still feel connected. I fear the only solution lies in opening the old wounds and excising the infection."

Julia's brows drew together. "I've already told him of the mistreatment I experienced at Wallthorpe's hands. And he is well aware I took a sheik as a lover. What more need I say?"

"Ah, but have you told him how all that has happened made you *feel*?" A blond brow arched up.

Once more, Julia could feel her cheeks heat. "No. I merely relayed the events."

Theo nodded. "I see where you are going with this, Marie. It wasn't until I acknowledged my fears and truly opened myself up to Stone that we conquered our differences."

Ros leaned over and squeezed Julia's hand. "At least consider what they are suggesting."

Julia nodded. "I shall take it under advisement."

Having reflected on the times she had spent with Wolf in bed, Julia realized her most vulnerable moments came when he tied her up and spanked her. When he left her no choice but to surrender to him, both physically and mentally. So she decided to ask him for what she needed tonight.

Standing in a silky negligée, she pulled the ties from her other robes to give him as bindings. Determined to bridge the gap between them, and to reach for what she wanted, she waited until she heard his valet depart his room. Then she crossed to the connecting door and knocked once before opening it.

He looked up and offered her a tired but pleasant smile.

Suddenly doubting her plan, she tucked her hand behind her back and halted where she was, across the room. He had settled into a chair by a small fire with a snifter of brandy. She knew he preferred that to whisky just before bed.

"I thought I'd just check in before retiring."

She tried to hide her consternation at finding him so relaxed and unguarded. Tired, even.

He stared at her a moment. "Check in?"

Her cheeks heated. "Yes, well, to see if you needed anything."

She wanted to curse herself for feeling and acting so awkward. She was a woman of experience, and yet seeing him looking so worn out yet still pleased to see her had her tied in knots. She'd been about to ask him to tie her up, spank her, and then fuck her, but seeing him like this stopped her.

She didn't wish to impose on him.

Dear God, she was a mess. Didn't wish to impose on him? This was her *husband*.

She wasn't asking him to tea; she was asking him to pleasure her. To do so to the point she had no walls left to hide behind. Disgusted with herself, she huffed out a breath, which only appeared to pique his interest.

Wolf sat up and set his drink down on the table next to him. "No, I can't say there is anything I need at the moment."

She started to turn and retreat.

"However, if you'd like to join me by the fire, your company is always welcome."

He watched her, studying her like a specimen he was trying to learn and understand.

She tilted her head. "No, I'll just head to bed."

She turned, keeping her hand with the robe belts hidden in her skirts. She'd just reached the door once more when he stopped her.

"Jules, what's in your hand?"

She closed her eyes and cursed under her breath as her stomach summersaulted. "Nothing."

As though he had materialized out of thin air, his breath caressed her neck as he spoke from just behind her. "Do not lie to me, Jules."

And then he pulled the silk ties from her clenched fist.

Her face burned. Not merely her cheeks, but her whole face flushed with the heat of her embarrassment.

He shifted around to lean against the wall by the doorway where she stood. "My, my, my. What have we here?" He ran the silk belts through his hands. Over and over again. "I wonder what my wife had in mind as she carried these about?"

Her body quivered. The problem was, now she wasn't sure if it was from fear or anticipation. Possibly a little of both. Without a doubt, there was no turning back now. She bit her lip and waited to see what would happen.

"Nothing to say?" He no longer looked tired as he stood there holding the ties. "Conceivably she intended to tie me up and have her wicked way with me?"

She closed her eyes. "No."

"I see. Then perhaps she wished for me to tie *her* up?"

His voice had grown husky, thick with arousal.

A strangled noise escaped her throat as her eyes flew open. "Do not torture me. You know very well what I intended."

She glared at him balefully.

He reached up and swept a stray hair from her face with a tenderness that stalled her breathing. "Why are you leaving without asking for what you need?"

"You looked tired. I didn't wish to impose."

"Pleasuring you is never an imposition. Now, tell me what you came to ask for."

He snared her gaze with his and refused to look away.

Her nipples beaded, pressed against the silky fabric of her robe. "I wanted you to tie me up and..."

He pushed up off the wall and stepped into her. She trembled and stared down at his chest, trying to come to grips with her doubts. Then he reached up and tucked a finger beneath her chin, tilting her head up until she looked at him.

"And?"

"Spank me."

Determined to see this through now, she held his gaze and tried to gauge his reaction. It wasn't as though she expected him to balk. After all, he'd done that to her before, but she had not specifically asked for it, and had not participated in it with the express intent to break down her walls and open herself up to him.

He licked his lips, desire darkening his gaze. "Why?"

"What do you mean, why? Because I enjoy it."

She blustered in hopes he wouldn't delve too deep. She still wasn't completely sure she could do as Marie suggested, but she thought this was her best chance.

He shook his head. "No, my dear. If all you wanted was a little slap and tickle, you would have no issue with demanding I tie you up and spank you. There is something more at play here. Tell me what you are after."

His command made her knees weak and her breathing shallow. How could he be so perceptive, so aware of what was happening even as his cock stood hard and demanding against his trousers? "I- I-"

He took her hand and led her over to the fireplace. Then he sat down and pulled her into his lap. Once they were settled, he stroked her neck and pulled the pins from her hair. With the mass of her tresses down, he ran his fingers through it in the most soothing fashion. Slowly, he lulled her into a trance-like state. Her heartbeat slowed, and a sense of lethargy stole over her. Long minutes passed—maybe even hours—and then he asked again. "What were you after, love?"

She sighed as he continued petting her with a soothing touch. "I wanted to bridge the gap between us. To make myself trust you with all of my past. With *our* past."

He grunted softly. "Do you trust me now? In this moment?"

She tensed up, fear stealing in to rob her of her resolve. "I- I- I want to."

"You've told me of your time with Wallthorpe. And I am aware of how my desertion hurt you as deeply as your parents' betrayal. Is there more you need to tell me?"

There was a note of worry in his voice.

She nodded. "Yes. I hated you back then. Hated you for leaving me to my fate. But then, while I lived with Tariq, I came to realize that had you come for me that night, I would have become a different person."

He snarled at the mention of her lover, but she ignored his jealous display and continued.

"Granted, I am closed off from everyone, but I am strong. Independent in a way I would not have been had you rescued me from my fate. Which means while I hated you for a time, I know I am who I am now because of you, and I am grateful for that. But I am also scared. Scared that if I rely on you now, make myself vulnerable to you, I shall turn back into that woman I was. The one who allowed her parents to bully her into a marriage she didn't want. And I *cannot* be that woman ever again."

He laced his fingers through her hair and pulled her closer, then placed a kiss on her head. "Thank you for telling me how you feel. I do not want you to be dependent on me. I adore the woman you have become, and while I am sad to know how deeply I hurt you, and how long the damage has lasted, I wouldn't change who you are today. I have no need of a simpering, dependent woman in my life. I have always wanted a *partner*. Someone to share my life with, not merely my name and my bed. You, Jules, are an amazing partner: strong, intelligent, and brazen, when required." He sighed softly against her hair. "And I owe you an explanation for what happened that night so many years ago."

"Wolf, no."

She tried to sit up, but he pinned her against his chest.

"Stay here."

He returned to stroking her hair.

Worry settled in her chest. Fear that he might say something that changed this moment of accord into something else. Did she truly want to hear what he had to say?

Chapter Twenty-Seven

Fear slammed against Wolf's ribs as he held Jules tight in his lap. She had made herself vulnerable, had opened herself up to him. He owed her the truth now. Taking a deep breath, he said the words he'd feared her hearing since she'd come back. Perhaps, if he were honest, the words he'd feared her hearing for over a decade.

"I'm a bastard."

She jerked in his arms. "You shouldn't say such things. You were not *that* bad."

He sighed and held on to her, unwilling to see the moment the truth dawned on her. "Lord Wolfington is not my father. My mother had a lover who sired me upon her."

With a strength he'd not have credited her, Jules sat up from his embrace, though she did not scramble from where she sat. "You are not your father's heir?"

"Oh, I am his heir, as he has not publicly denied me as such. But it is the dark family secret that I am not in fact his natural born son." He closed his eyes and let his head tilt back against the chair. "I learned this fact the night we were to run away. Wallthorpe sent me a letter laying all the sordid details out. How he knew, I do not know, but when I confronted my mother about it, she broke down in tears and acknowledged the truth.

"I was devastated, reeling from the news, but I was still determined to marry you. I went to my father and told him that Wallthorpe had threatened to expose the truth of my birth if I married you. I told him it mattered little to me as long as he would not deny us. But he refused. He told me if the family name was exposed in such a fashion, that he would not acknowledge me as his heir any longer. He would deny me—and you—by extension.

"We would have been penniless and nameless. Christ, I didn't even know the name of the man who sired me. All I knew was that I couldn't protect you without my father's help. Without his acknowledgement, I was a pauper with no true skills other than being a gentleman. Whether I came to you or not, you were doomed. But I had no idea Wallthorpe would be violent with you. Had I known that, I would have damned the consequences and taken you away that night."

A gentle touch swept away the moisture that streamed down one of his cheeks. Then soft lips kissed away the matching track. He opened his eyes as she drew back from the kiss. To his shock, tenderness and forgiveness shone in her gaze. He would have liked to believe he saw love there, as well, but he refused to delude himself.

"Wolf, I am so sorry my life brought such misery to your doorstep. Had you not been tangled up with me, that family secret would have remained a secret."

"No. I am glad it came out. The truth in many ways has set me free. Until then, I had spent years trying to win my father's approval. I had long since given up on love from him, but approval, I believed, was still achievable. Once I learned he was not my father, I let go of that small glimmer of hope. I stopped trying to please him with all my decisions.

"He and I came to an understanding that night. If I kept the family secret buried as it belonged, he would, as well. There was no hope of my having a brother, as proof she was not barren. They had tried for years after I came along. I think they both believed he was the one who could not produce an heir. Since the fault was no longer hers, and to save face, he simply claimed me as his."

Silence stretched between them for long moments.

He looked at her through a half-lidded gaze. She didn't appear disgusted by his revelation, but he couldn't be sure. "If you find the reality of my birth repulsive, I shall release you from your vows. I would never want to shackle you to me if it made you unhappy."

A small cry of dismay escaped her as she clasped his face in her hands. "Never! I cannot imagine my life without you now that you are in it once again. I admit, I have had my doubts and worries"–she pressed her hand to her breast—"but here, in my heart, I know I cannot walk away from you again."

Wolf inhaled sharply. It was not a declaration of love, but it was so close, he was willing to take it. "If you agree to stay, you will be mine. I shall never let you go. If you leave, I shall come for you. I shall hunt you to the ends of the earth before I allow you to disappear from my life again."

"I am not going anywhere," she mumbled, and then planted her lips on his.

Immediately, her tongue pushed past his lips and teeth, demanding entrance to his mouth. Willing to let her have the lead for the moment, he opened to her. Their tongues crashed together, slipping and sliding over each other as they tangled and twisted. The small fire suddenly felt like a towering inferno as his body heated up.

His cock had flagged as he told her of his past, but once her mouth claimed his, the blood had returned to his shaft. The way she squirmed and fidgeted on his lap was driving him mad, even as he relished the need clearly pumping through her.

Cradling his wife in his arms with the robe belts in one hand, he stood and walked to the bed as they kissed. There, he set her down, letting her body slide along his as her feet found the ground. Far enough away from the fire to allow their skin to cool a bit, he still felt the heat from within. The passion he felt for Jules far outpaced both the evening chill and the small fire he'd lit. He could not deny the love he felt for her; nor did he wish to. But he was aware she needed a bit more time to grow comfortable with her own revelations.

Knowing what he did now, he could give her that time.

Setting aside the quagmire of emotion in his heart, he focused on pleasing her. With a gentle touch, he slipped her negligee from her shoulders, exposing the expanse of her pale skin. The longer she remained in England, the paler her skin had grown. Maybe he should take her to his country home, where they could make love naked in the outdoors...under the sun. The naughty thought made him smile as he imagined her rolling about in a field like a fairy or sprite.

Her breath caught then, drawing his focus back to the task at hand, a truly pleasurable one he had not anticipated tonight. She had been right, he *had* been tired when she'd come in. In fact, he'd had every intention of not taking her to bed, since she'd spent every one of the last fourteen nights since their wedding in his arms and in his bed. But then she'd walked in, and his cock had stirred immediately upon seeing her.

And when he'd noticed the robe ties in her hand? All good intentions had been lost.

The evening chill combined with her desire had her nipples puckering into tight little buds. He had to lick them, to roll the hard tips over his tongue. The need pushed him until he bent over and captured one. As he sucked hard, nipping and teasing her, she gasped and arched into his mouth.

So responsive.

He shifted to her other breast and repeated the action until she whimpered with need. Then he released her rosy tip and stood looming over her. A fierce need to possess her rode him, but he tempered it, knowing that soon she would be bound and unable to escape his bed. Taking her hands, he gathered her wrists together and used one of the ties to loop around them.

Her breathing grew jagged with excitement as she realized he had every intention of fulfilling her earlier request.

Once he tied the silk band off, he prowled around behind her. With his chest pressed to her back, he commanded in a soft, but unrelenting tone, "Bend over the mattress, love."

She moaned softly, but did as directed, without argument. With her bound hands in front of her, she lowered to her elbows, leaving her backside raised high in the air for him to do with as he pleased. He loved her submission, the way she willingly gave up control to him. It was heady stuff for this strong and independent woman to bow to his will in such a fashion.

Positioning himself behind her, he cupped the rounded cheek of her backside, stroking the delicate skin with a gentle touch. Then he raised his hand and crashed it back down against her bottom. The slap of his palm hitting her flesh sent more blood rushing to his already engorged cock. He repeated the process on her other cheek, noting how her breath caught and then continued in shallower rasps than before the smack.

Next, he returned his attention to the first side, but sent his hand crashing with a firmer strike. She moaned softly as he rubbed her pinkening skin. He picked up his pace from there, spending less time between spanks as she lifted her arse to meet each blow. When her backside had turned a rosy red he knew would match the flush on her face when she was turned on, he dropped to his knees behind her. With careful attention to the placement of his hands, he gripped her bottom, digging his fingers into the reddened skin and dragged his tongue along her soaked slit.

The salty-sweet taste of her burst over his tongue and drove his need even higher. But he only had one goal tonight: to see Jules lose all control. To watch her come apart around his cock as she fully surrendered to him. With determination riding him, he focused on taking her up and over the precipice of pleasure. He kept his hands where they could rub and tweak her burning backside while he licked and laved her sweet pussy. As her legs trembled and her cries grew desperate, he knew he would tip her over the edge soon. So he tugged her clit into his mouth and sucked hard on the swollen nub. She exploded with a cry of his name, pushing back into his hands and face as she came hard.

Satisfaction settled in his chest and made him feel ten feet tall, but still he *wanted* more from her. *Needed* more from her. So he rose behind her and pressed his aching cock against her drenched core for a moment. He still had the other robe belt, and now he knew what he wanted to do with it.

He grabbed a bolster pillow and lodged it under her hips, then took the strip of fabric and looped it around the bindings between her hands and tied it off, leaving the other end long and free. Briefly moving around the side of the bed so he could tie the belt off on the headboard, he took a moment to appreciate how it forced Jules to stretch forward over the edge of the bed until her toes left the floor. With her backside canted even higher, he could fuck her while he kept up her spankings, as needed, to ensure her bliss.

Pleased with how stretched out she was, he returned to the foot of the bed and leaned over her stretched-out torso. Carefully, he placed a series of kisses between her shoulders and down her spine, until he reached the point where her reddened cheeks met. There he took a firm hold of both warm globes, spreading her open until her rear entrance appeared. He slid his tongue down and over the tight whorl, swirling around it a few times before he dipped lower to her sodden entrance.

She gasped. Then his name slipped from her lips. A moan. A plea. Possibly a benediction.

Standing up straight, he notched his cock against her pussy and pressed in...nice and slow. With every bit he fed into her, stretched her, she shifted restlessly. Biting down on his own lip to fight the need to shove his cock inside her in one swift stroke, he appreciated his handiwork, both on her backside, and the fact that she currently could not push backward into his shaft, since she was so stretched out.

She was well and truly at his mercy now.

Of course, it didn't stop Jules from trying. She started to shift her feet back a bit, but he promptly landed a spank on each side of her arse. "Do not move, my love."

A low wail of need escaped her. "Please, I need you. Inside me."

"And you shall have me," he growled, his own control tremulous at best. "At my pace."

With a grunt, he continued sliding into her, drawing out their pleasure to the point of near pain as he filled her up.

The minutes ticked by, a slow marking of his entrance, and a reminder of how blessed he was to have this woman bound and eager for his attentions after so many years of separation.

In that moment, his vow to always come for her resonated in his head and in his soul, because he knew he could never again be a whole man without his wife.

At last, his hips met her thighs as she engulfed his erection. The heat of her wrapped around him, making him light-headed with the sheer pleasure of it.

"Yes, yes, yes! Now fuck me," she demanded, as she wriggled beneath him.

Two more smacks put paid to her notion that she had any say in the matter. She moaned and bucked against him. Finally taking pity on both of them, he slid back in one firm move until just the tip remained nestled inside her heat.

"You want me to fuck you, wife?"

"Please!"

She sobbed the single word, and his control snapped.

He slammed into her hard as she lay there stretched out before him. One hand on her hip and the other on her shoulder, he pumped in and out of her body, setting a furious pace. Pounding into her over and over, he heard himself snarl as he edged closer and closer to climax. Yet somehow, he registered that she still needed a slight nudge. Shifting his hand from her hip to her mound, he dipped his fingertips into her slit and found the distended nub he'd already teased and tortured. He stroked over it once, and her pussy clamped down on him. With stars dancing before his eyes, he kept his thrusting up as he rubbed her clit, swirling the pad of his finger over it.

Her hips bucked and she cried out, "Wolf, I'm going to come!"

With a savage satisfaction he had never experienced, he dragged his finger over the sensitive nub as he slammed into her, and she exploded around him. The strong rhythmic pulsing of her release threw him over the edge. The stars behind his eyes turned black as he continued working in and out of her body. Pleasure shot from his tailbone across his torso and to all four of his extremities as he came inside her.

Light-headed from the intense orgasm, he slumped to the side of her as his cock slipped free. He lay there, his breath heaving in and out of his chest, as exhaustion, or maybe it was sheer bliss, made it impossible to focus on anything.

Then Jules moaned softly and shifted.

Awareness surged inside of him. He had her bound, and had had her that way for quite a while. Moving quicker than he might have expected, he released her from the bed, then worked her wrists free until she was able to drag her arms down to her sides.

"Are you well?"

He reached down and massaged her arms as she lay there as limp as a rag.

She whimpered softly.

Worried, he rolled her over and found her eyes closed and a huge grin on her luscious lips.

"Oh, I'm quite lovely, thank you."

His pang of worry slipped away as he let loose an unexpected chuckle and found he couldn't stop. The sheer joy of having this woman as his burst free from him in a long hearty laugh that seemed to never end.

Chapter Twenty-Eight

J ulia enjoyed a good spectacle. Watching the actors prance around, singing and dancing during the intermissions, and the bawdy tone of many of the exchanges, delighted her. Wolf, Emily, and Cooper all seemed equally as entertained. Cooper's box at the Adelphi Theater had proven to be a fine entertainment.

Once the program came to its inevitable conclusion, the four of them remained seated. It seemed silly to clamber from the box with all the other patrons doing the same. If they waited a few minutes, the worst of the crowd would dissipate.

As the others chatted about the play, Julia marveled that just the night before, Wolf had stretched her out across his bed and fucked her until she had nearly passed out. In her post-orgasmic haze, the man had coddled her until she'd roused enough to satisfy his concern. He'd wrapped her in the blanket from the bed and held her as little shivers and aftershocks of pleasure had continued to zip through her body. Then he'd produced a glass of water for her, and insisted she drink some before he'd allowed her to tuck in under the covers and drift off to sleep.

"Shall we?"

Cooper stood and offered his hand to Emily, who smiled at him. Julia envied them a bit. They were head-over-heels in love with each other. Certainly, she was aware that Wolf cared for her a great deal, and was willing to go to great lengths to protect her. But while she'd never intended to fall in love with him again, she had. She'd known it the night he'd tied her to the bed, and she knew it now. What she didn't know was if he felt the same about her. And she was tired of the not knowing. It was past time she told him how she felt. Her stomach flip-flopped in her belly, but her resolve grew stronger with every heartbeat.

He offered her his arm, and together they followed Cooper and Emily out of the theater. The crowd had lingered some, so a throng of people still loitered, making it difficult for carriages to draw up to the curb. They spotted Wolf's carriage across the street and decided to cross, in lieu of making the vehicle traverse the busy road.

They dashed out into traffic, but Julia stepped on a loose cobblestone. With a painful jolt, her ankle twisted and she stumbled, losing her hold on Wolf's arm. He stopped and turned back to see what had happened when a carriage pulled up behind her and halted. The door opened as two hulking men leaned out and snatched her up. She was hauled backward into the cab of the vehicle on a scream fueled by fear and anger.

Wolf lurched toward her, his brows drawn down in fury as she was jerked deeper into the conveyance. "Stop! Julia! Julia's been snatched!"

She fought the strong hands that held her, desperate to get back to the door before they moved. Despite her bunched skirts and injured ankle, she used the edge of the bench seat and the coat of one of the villains to drag herself toward the still-open door. She was close, could even see Wolf clinging to the door while he fought with one of the men.

Then the man she'd grabbed onto drew a gun and pointed it at Wolf. The strong hands that had held her before returned. Fisting his hand in her hair, the man yanked on her head—hard. Ignoring the burning pain of her hair being torn from her scalp at the roots, she continued to strain toward freedom and Wolf.

To her utter horror, a shot rang out. Her gut twisted as she saw him crumple to the ground. "Wolf!"

The fist in her hair jerked harder, and yet she refused to give in. But with Wolf now dispatched—Oh, God! He couldn't be dead!—and the carriage moving, the two thugs at the door closed the opening. Then the one who'd shot Wolf turned around, ripping her hand free of his clothing.

"Stupid meddling bitch," he snarled, spittle flying from his lips to land on her face.

Still struggling to get free of the third man, it was a shock when the snarling man's hand quickly followed his spit. Pain bloomed over her cheek and made her eye throb as she found herself huddled on the floor of the carriage. Her heart shattered as she watched Wolf struggle and then crumple over and over again behind her closed eyelids.

Tears streamed down her face as she realized that the man she loved had just been taken from her in the most vicious twist of fate that life had dealt her yet. Her body shook with pulsing anger and despair.

Then a cacophony of sound filled the carriage, an asynchronous mix of the ragged breath of one of the thugs and her own sniffling, punctuated by the steady clop of hooves.

The ragged breather slowly recovered, and the snarly man turned his fury on his companions. "Your fancy bloke had best pay up when we get there. No one said anything about me have'n to kill one of them puffed-up dandies. I ain't signed on for that kind'a trouble."

Julia gasped. This wasn't random, though if she stopped and considered her recent past, that realization shouldn't have come as a surprise. Sitting up, she gathered her wits and blocked out the throbbing across her cheek and eye, as well as the growing pain in her ankle.

"If money is all you three are after, I can offer you plenty of ready cash. How much is this man paying you?"

One of the other men snorted. "More than you likely have, even as fancy a piece as you may be."

Julia considered who would have resorted to this kind of nefarious action, and only one man came to mind. Granted, she couldn't be sure until he showed himself, but she had little doubt he would eventually reveal his role in this drama. "I am far richer than the man I suspect hired you lot." She hesitated, but decided she had nothing to lose but her life at the moment. "I'll double whatever he's paying you."

Snarly growled as he reached down and grabbed ahold of her bodice. He jerked her toward him until his fetid, gin-soaked breath slammed into her. She considered that there might be permanent damage to her ability to appreciate anything more delicate than smelling salts in the future. *If* she escaped alive.

"How do we know you've got that kind of blunt?"

Her head spun at the stench, but she managed to keep her wits about her. It seemed she'd piqued his interest. "Stop and consider my attire. I am wearing a gown made of the finest Indian silk, and my earbobs and matching necklace are real rubies, not paste copies, I assure you."

Her hand trembled as she directed his glare to the necklace circling her throat.

It was a risk. They could simply rip the baubles from her person and then demand more, but she had little ground to stand on under the circumstances. As they passed a gas streetlamp, the interior of the carriage glowed dimly, but enough so that she could see the greed in the man's beady eyes.

Just as a spark of hope flamed to life, it was snuffed out.

"Hold on there. This ain't just about money, you know. That fancy bloke has my Sarah. If we don't do as he says, he'll hurt her."

The third man then ripped Julia away from Snarly, tearing some of her hair out when Snarly didn't let go quickly enough.

Snarly grunted, clearly not happy with letting the extra payment go. "Fine." Then he reached down and ripped the rubies from her neck. "But I'm taking these, and neither of you will say a thing."

The other two mumbled acquiescence as the carriage continued down the lane. Feeling trapped and utterly alone, Julia sagged to the floor. Her body ached from the struggle, and with the burst of adrenaline that had allowed her to fight earlier now depleted, exhaustion swept over her. Clearly these three were taking her somewhere, and she doubted much else would occur until such time as they reached their destination.

Then Wolf flitted to the forefront of her thoughts. She pictured the smile he'd offered her as they exited the theater. One that spoke of caring and emotion—*love*—that she would never know. Not now. Not ever again. Her tears returned, a silent mourning for all that she'd lost in the blink of an eye.

Blinding rage thrummed through Wolf. If Cooper's wife, Emily, had not been present, he might have resorted to venting his fury on the furniture in his study. Instead, he sat calmly, sipping a brandy as the poor woman tried to steady her hands long enough to stitch up his shoulder.

"Wolf, a doctor should be doing this," she said, for possibly the tenth time in as many minutes.

He stilled. "Absolutely not. I have neither the time nor the inclination to deal with some pompous blowhard telling me I should be in bed resting."

She bit her lower lip, then sighed. "I do understand that, and I certainly would not expect you to do any such thing when poor Julia is out there somewhere in those men's clutches. However, alcohol and your housekeeper's needle and thread are not precisely how a bullet wound should be cared for, I am quite certain."

"Nevertheless, this is how I am choosing to handle mine. I wish I did not have to sit here and wait for Cooper to return. I am sure that Wallthorpe lies at the heart of this plot, and I should be making haste to his house."

Wolf tightened his grip on the ball of the armrest as Emily stabbed the needle through his flesh once more.

One of the villains who'd taken Julia had shot at him as they struggled. He'd seen her there, hovering just behind the blackguard when the gun had fired. Lucky for him, the carriage had hit a pothole right at that moment, or he might have been dealing with a whole different level of bullet wound. Possibly the fatal kind.

As it was, the bullet had grazed his left shoulder, causing him to let go of the vehicle and fall to the cobblestones. His luck had held as the trailing carriage had been far enough behind the villains that he had time to roll out of the way before another team of horses trampled him.

Cooper had been working his way to the top of the roof when Wolf was shot and the conveyance took off. Wolf cursed again as he remembered laying there in the street, watching as Julia was driven away. But then he'd seen his friend clinging to the back of the carriage, and he knew as soon as Cooper had ascertained where they were taking her, he would let Wolf know.

Somehow.

So here he sat, with his friend's wife, who had insisted on sending for a doctor. Failing in that, she had opted to at least treat the wound herself. So, with a splash of brandy both in the wound and in his glass, he waited. And seethed.

He'd seen the fear and anger in Julia's eyes as she'd fought hard to free herself. And he'd have to live with his failure to protect her yet again when she'd needed him the most. He knew that whatever chance he'd had to make her fall in love with him had been lost when he'd failed to rescue her from the carriage.

What woman would want a man who continually proved unable to safeguard her? And with the knowledge of his bastard state to boot? Doubt assailed him even as a fierce need to be the man Jules needed swept in.

Emily finally finished setting the last of the neat stitches in his arm.

He glanced down, surprised at how tidy her work was. "Thank you."

"It's not my best needlework, but then I am not accustomed to my sewing being alive."

She smiled, but then clenched her teeth together as though biting back her words.

Wolf noticed her restraint as well as the worry that clouded her normally merry hazel eyes. Yet another woman he'd put in jeopardy by his deficiencies. "I know words are not nearly enough, but my apologies for the fact your husband is currently at risk as a result of my actions."

She snorted. "Don't be ridiculous. I put Cooper in jeopardy to a far greater extent when he courted me. I'm merely worried for your wife. While she is an independent woman, I am not certain this kind of adventure is something she would appreciate."

Despair threatened his composure. "What woman would?"

Emily laughed. Not a delicate, mincing tinkle, but a full belly laugh. "Oh, I imagine Theo and I would find the whole thing rather exciting, once it was over."

He eyed Lady Brougham in a new light as he swallowed another gulp of brandy. Regardless, she was right. Julia would not appreciate the experience of being snatched from a London street and hauled off to parts unknown. Before he could respond, the door of the study opened and all the Lustful Lords walked in.

Stone, as usual, led the group. Behind him came Linc and Flint, as well as their newest member, Emily's brother, Arthur.

Stone didn't waste time on pleasantries. "Any word from Cooper?"

"Not as yet."

Wolf resisted the urge to growl when he knew his friend was risking his neck for him.

The others ranged out around the room, Arthur immediately checking on his sister.

Stone sat next to him in a wing chair. "We'll get her back."

Wolf nodded, unable to reply. Because while he knew he would free her no matter the cost to himself, he wasn't sure if he would make it in time to prevent something unforgiveable from occurring. Not to mention, he didn't know if she would even want him still under the circumstances.

He had long since grown accustomed to being discarded by those he cared about. His father did not want him, for obvious reasons, and his mother could barely stand to look at him. Knowing what he did of his past, he wondered how much he looked like the man who sired him. So many worries swirled in his head, that he felt nauseated as he sat and waited.

After what seemed like days, though in truth it had been less than a couple of hours, Cooper finally walked into Wolf's study. With his shirt tail untucked and his bow tie dangling around his neck, he appeared the epitome of a lord who'd been out rabble-rousing all night.

Wolf was on his feet in an instant. "Where did they take her?"

"Seven Dials. It took a while to walk out far enough so I could hail a cab."

Cooper sank into a nearby chair and picked up a partially filled tumbler of spirits someone had abandoned on a side table.

Wolf tried to be patient with his friend, but it was killing him to stand there while Julia was in danger. "Address?"

Cooper nodded and rose once more. "Let's go."

The six of them departed in two carriages, so they would have room for Jules when they returned. And they *would* bring her home. What happened after that, though, was anybody's guess.

Chapter Twenty-Nine

Julia had no idea where she was, though it was quite obvious she was still in London, mostly because they hadn't driven long enough for the scenery to change from city to country. But she was not foolish enough to believe that just because she was still in the city, she would necessarily be found. London was a large city with a maze of back alleys and city streets that a person could easily become lost in.

Wolf was dead as far as she knew, so even if there was someone who cared enough to look for her, they would have no way of tracking her down quickly or easily. Just in case, she knew her job was to find as many ways as she could to make herself discoverable, while holding off whatever outcome the man pulling everyone's strings intended. Of course, she had her suspicions on who that man was, but she saw no value in sharing her suspicions with her captors.

Not that they had stuck around to chat.

They had arrived at their current location in the dead of night. Then she'd been dragged upstairs to an attic room, pushed inside, and the door had been promptly locked behind her. Being an attic, it had a musty smell that seemed to permeate everything. What all that entailed she couldn't tell, since the space was pitch black, and she did not have the benefit of light beyond the shimmer of moonlight peeping in.

Deciding to avail herself of the little bit of light offered by the moon, she shuffled over to the small, high window near the roofline and huddled below it. It was the only area she could clearly see that was unoccupied, either by boxes or other, more livelier occupants.

As she sat on the floor, she tried to focus on the present and not think about Wolf or his demise. If she did that, she'd cease being functional, and be of absolutely no use to anyone. So she ignored the heavy weight pressing on her chest and tried to close her eyes for a few minutes. Perhaps with a bit of rest she would have a different outlook in the morning. To her dismay, the scrabbling noises of her "roommates" made it impossible to sleep, which left her mostly awake as the first rays of dawn pierced her tiny window.

Fortunately, that also meant that she heard the footsteps on the stairs long before the door opened.

A woman entered bearing a tray of food, as one of the villains from earlier stood in the doorway. The woman looked dispassionate as she set the tray down on a nearby chair. "I suggest you eat this before the rats get to it."

Feeling mulish and angry once more, Julia glared at the woman. Her hair hung lank around her sallow face, and her brown eyes appeared dull and flat, with poor nutrition and fatigue, but to Julia, none of that excused her participation in this outrageous act.

The woman shrugged. "Suit yourself."

Then she and the glaring man left, and the lock was turned in the door once more. Angry, but not stupid, Julia realized she would need her strength for whatever lay ahead. Scooting closer to the tray, she grimaced at the crust of two-day-old bread and bowl of watery gruel. With a sigh, she set about eating the meager sustenance and reminded herself that she had curves to spare. A reduction in food quantity, as well as quality, would not hurt her in the short term.

Shoveling the fare into her mouth, her mind wandered once more to Wolf. Her heart ached once more as she thought of his death. Sitting there, she forced herself to survive, praying to whatever deity might be listening. *Please, let me live. Don't let him die in vain.* A tear slipped down her cheek. *He was a good man who deserved to live and find happiness. I love him so much... If only I'd had the sense to tell him...*

No longer able to eat, she set her food aside and curled up on her side. It seemed unfair that she should only now accept how much she loved him, just when she'd lost him. Crying softly into her arms, she huddled there in her misery.

Sometime later, more steps sounded on the stairs. Julia had lost track of time, though the sun still seemed weak, as though it were morning. Assuming it was the woman returning for the crockery, she barely looked up when the door swung open.

"My, my... How the haughty have been brought down a peg or two," Wallthorpe remarked, sneering at her from across the room.

Fury sparked to life within her, as though someone had lit a match near a gas lamp. The anger sizzled and popped in her veins, zipping along her limbs until she felt she could barrel right through the vile little man who believed he'd won. "You will *never* succeed."

"But I already have, Julia. You don't mind if I drop all the formality, do you? After all, with your husband so neatly dispatched last night, the way is now clear for me to marry the grieving widow."

"*Never.*"

She spat the word at him and turned away, as though she couldn't be bothered with entertaining him.

Then a hand sank into her hair and jerked her head back until she looked up into an all-too-familiar pair of dark eyes that held a malicious glint. Like a specter from her past, the burning gaze of her dead husband seared into her miserable soul.

"That debauched bastard is finally dead—as he should have been years ago. Now there is *nothing* keeping us apart. You're all mine Julia. *Mine.*"

The last word came out a snarl as he slammed his lips down on hers.

Repulsed by everything the man said and was, she waited for him to jam his tongue into her mouth, and then she bit down. Hard. The coppery tang of blood satisfied a little of the rage that burned within, but her victory was short lived.

"Bith!" Wallthorpe drew back and backhanded her across the cheek with a brutal force that whipped her head around.

Pain burst through her face for the second time in less than twenty-four hours. With a cry of outrage, she sprang at him, her fingers curled into claws as she reached for his face. The evil man deserved to look as hideous on the outside as he was on the inside. When her nails found flesh, she dug in and then raked her arms in a downward motion.

Wallthorpe slapped her hands aside, but left her free to try and run as he pressed his hands to his bleeding face. With fierce determination, she picked up her ragged skirts and shouldered him out of the way as she ran toward the door, ignoring the searing pain in her ankle as freedom teased her from the other side of the door.

Just as she was about to throw the portal open, a hand snagged her dress and yanked her back into the attic room. Wallthorpe had abandoned his scratched face in favor of keeping her contained in the attic. He then wrapped a hand around her wrist and dragged her toward a tattered old mattress she hadn't seen tucked in the corner.

With a strength she'd never have credited him with, he threw her on the pallet and crashed down on top of her, pinning her with his hips and legs. Fear choked the breath from her lungs as she realized his intent. With her wrist once again manacled by him, there was little she could do to fight him off. Free to do as he wished, he reached down and ripped the front of her bodice until her corset was exposed.

"Bloody undergarments are a fucking nuisance," he cursed, and then shifted tactics.

His free hand reached down and yanked on her skirts, hauling them free of both their legs. Desperate to escape as her nightmare became a reality, she attempted to jam her knee up into his family jewels with no success. He was too close for her to do more than bruise her own thigh.

With a shriek of fury, she balled up her free hand and swung at his face. To her surprise, she connected with his cheekbone, though her blow did little more than infuriate him further.

"You stupid little hellcat. I bet *you* killed my father that night! He probably keeled over with a heart attack, from fighting you as he tried to fuck you."

The thin gruel she'd eaten curdled in her belly as she remembered the night her first husband had died. The apoplectic anger that had washed over his face as he raised his arm to beat her with the riding crop he'd held high. And Julia realized that his son shared the exact same look as he loomed over her prone body.

For the first time, she considered she might not survive what was to come.

Wolf stood outside the ramshackle building in Seven Dials as dawn forced the night back where it had come from. Linc, Flint, and Arthur were making their way around the back of the building, while he, Cooper, and Stone waited in the front.

Then a feminine shriek pierced the morning stillness, and his barely harnessed agitation snapped free of its reins. With a growl, he unleashed his rage and kicked the door in. As he barreled into the rickety house, he slammed into one of the thugs he'd grappled with the night before. He punched the man square in the jaw, sending him reeling into the wall. Then he turned and made for the stairs, as Stone and Cooper swept in behind him to clean up the riffraff.

Fear and fury propelled him up the stairs, where he met the man who'd shot him. With a low growl, he powered into him, causing him to stumble backward on the stairs. More of a match for him, the thug landed a solid punch to Wolf's gut that took the wind out of his sails a bit. Gasping for breath, he threw himself down on top of the shooter. As they wrestled on the stairs, thuds came from behind them. The next thing he knew, Flint had pulled him off the brute.

"Stop wasting time with the hired help. Get the hell upstairs."

Then Flint reached up, grabbed the thug, and jerked him forward until he fell down the stairs. With his path cleared, Wolf continued up until he came to a door that sat ajar. The unmistakable sounds of a struggle sounded from inside as he pushed the entry open.

What he saw nearly undid him. Wallthorpe had Julia pinned to a putrid excuse for a mattress as he tried to rape her.

With a roar that was as animalistic as a jungle cat's, he lurched forward and ripped the bastard from her body. Wallthorpe stumbled backward against a wall. Wolf's gaze swept over the weasel as he noted his pants remained fastened.

Relief swamped him. He hadn't been too late. And yet, despite the balm that the knowledge brought, it was not enough to calm his rage. Wallthorpe *had* to pay. He had to pay for his sins and his father's, since Wolf would never have the opportunity to right that earlier wrong. He'd not have considered punishing the son for the father's behavior had he not proven to be as bad, if not worse.

"You rotten bastard. I'll kill you for this."

Wallthorpe paled, but did not cower. "Not if I finally kill you, once and for all."

Then the man pulled a knife from some hidden sheath and brandished the weapon.

Wolf grinned. The stubby weapon required close contact, and Wallthorpe wouldn't be holding it for long.

With a cry of anger, Wallthorpe launched himself at Wolf. Prepared for the attack, Wolf easily batted the weaker man aside. Again, Wallthorpe ran at him. Again, Wolf socked the man and sent him reeling. With each attempt, Wallthorpe grew weaker, and more tired. Eventually his adrenaline would desert him, and then Wolf would take the knife from him and gut the conniving bastard.

Once more, Wallthorpe ran at him, and this time Wolf grabbed him, swung him around, and slammed him into the wall. The exhausted man ricocheted off of it and landed facedown on his stomach, with one arm awkwardly twisted beneath him. Disgusted with the weak showing, Wolf took a step near him, intending to pick him up off the ground and punch him again.

But then he noticed the growing pool of blood that had formed on the floor. Somehow the fool had fallen on his own weapon.

Using the toe of his boot, Wolf nudged the body and found him unresponsive. A soft whimper behind him reminded him that Jules was also still in the room. With a silent curse, he spun around and found her curled into a ball on the sorry excuse for a mattress, holding her bodice up as tears streaked down her filthy face.

His heart shattered as he took in the broken picture before him. Wide green eyes stared at him and drank him in, as though he might disappear at any moment. He dropped to his knees on the pallet, scared to touch her, but desperate to, all at the same time. Her whole body shuddered, racked by a sob as she reached out toward him. Then her trembling fingers made contact with his face, and suddenly she launched herself into his arms.

Chapter Thirty

H^{e is alive!}

Her heart thundered in her chest as her fingers collided with his skin and confirmed that he was real, and not a figment of her overwrought imagination. She'd launched herself into his arms because she'd thought she would never have that chance again. Tears streamed down her face, uncontrolled, from a mix of joy, solace, and love.

Wolf clutched her against his heaving chest, as safety and warmth chased away all her fears. Then his chest rumbled as he spoke. It took her a moment to tamp down her sobs so she could understand him, but by the time she did, he'd said the most important words.

"...I love you."

After experiencing a brief glimpse of life without Wolf in it, she was no longer willing to live in fear or worry that she might lose him. Rising up on her knees so she could look him in his eyes, she cupped his sharply carved cheekbones in her hands and locked her gaze with his. "I love *you*, Grayson Powell, Viscount Wolfington, and I never want to live without you ever again."

In that moment, she watched his fear and sorrow be replaced by all the feelings that currently overwhelmed her. Then he captured her lips with his and seared her very soul with a kiss. Eventually their heartbeats slowed until they fell into sync. All the while, they tasted and touched each other, savoring the knowledge that not only were they both alive, but they were *in love*.

At some point the authorities arrived, a blanket was procured to cover Julia, and questions were answered. After nearly an hour of such treatment, Wolf put a stop to the interrogation. In a few days, the officer in charge of the newly opened investigation could come by to speak with them both. For now, she was just grateful when Wolf swept her up into his arms, carried her to his carriage, and took her home.

That night, having soaked in a bath, she ate a hearty meal shared with her husband when he refused to allow her to come downstairs. Later, she lay next to him in bed unable to sleep. She could hear him breathing, light and shallow, but not the deep, sonorous tones of sleep.

"Thank you for rescuing me."

He rolled onto his side. "You have nothing to thank me for. It was my arrogant assumption that you were safe with me that allowed this to happen in the first place. I figured that after the failed attack in the gardens, and our subsequent wedding, Wallthorpe would give up. I greatly underestimated him, and as a result, you were taken."

Flags of red colored his cheeks as he spoke. It was obvious he felt responsible, but she refused to allow him to bear that responsibility alone. "I was just as sure as you were that I was safe. Once we'd married, it never crossed my mind that either of us might be in danger. Who expects to be abducted once they are no longer viable to be coerced into marriage?"

"Regardless, it was my responsibility to protect you, and once again, I failed you." He looked down at the mattress for a moment. "If you wanted to divorce me, now that the threat is over, I would understand."

Julia's heart squeezed, a sharp pain slamming through her chest. She sat up, shifting to her knees. "Are you saying you don't want me?"

He sat up, and looked at her from beneath his long blond lashes. They should have been feminine, but somehow, they weren't. They merely softened all his hard edges.

"I'm saying that I would understand if you didn't want me."

She frowned at him. "Do you remember what I said to you this morning, after you rescued me?"

He looked up at her, his eyes glowing a golden brown. "I remember every word. I shall never forget hearing you say you love me. But it was a moment fraught with emotion. You'd just been rescued from a life-threatening situation and discovered I was alive. I shall not hold you to that declaration, now that things have calmed down and you are no longer so caught up in the moment."

Dismay and anger flared to life within her. "Caught up in the moment?" She leapt from the bed. "You cannot be serious! You cannot mean to say that you think I said that in a moment of gratefulness?"

Wolf looked cautious, wary even. "Not gratefulness, exactly, but caught up in the emotions of being saved."

"Why, you insufferable jackass! How dare you assume I would toss my love at you like some trinket for saving me?"

She started pacing the room, mumbling to herself about fool-headed men and their inability to reason effectively. She'd never been so angry and insulted in her life. She'd just told the man she loved him, and he assumed that she had lost all her wits.

"Jules." He had climbed from the bed, and now stood wearing just his nightshirt, his hairy legs exposed by the short garment. "Jules, listen to me."

"I've heard enough. Now *you* listen to *me*, and listen well, *Lord Wolfington*." She spun on him and crowded into his space. Then she poked her long, thin finger into his chest. "I. Love. You." She punctuated each word with a poke, causing him to step back toward the bed. "I would love you if you had died. I would love you if you hadn't saved me." She took more steps toward him, driving him back further. "I would love you if you were plain old Grayson Powell. I would love you if you had no arms. I would love you if you had no legs." She poked him one last time, and he finally collapsed back onto the bed. "I would love you if your spectacular cock ceased to work."

"Easy now, love," he rumbled, as a smile stretched his full lips.

She pulled her long nightgown up and straddled his lap on the bed. "I shall always love you." Then she sighed as the truth spewed out of her, no matter how much she wished to hide it. "I've *always* loved you, you foolish man."

Then she leaned over and captured his lips with hers. Her tongue slid past all his barriers and stroked over his. She tasted him, the faint hint of spiced meat and brandy.

And she also tasted desire.

As their tongues tangled, sensuously twining around each other, her heart pounded. She'd never felt so free, and yet so exposed. Knowing he would bring their kiss to a halt if she didn't make it impossible, she reached down and hauled her nightgown up her body.

Breaking their kiss, she jerked the fabric monstrosity—the one *he* had insisted she wear—up over her head. "I love you, Wolf. And I plan to prove it to you over and over again tonight."

A low groan rumbled from him as he took in her naked form. Beneath her heated core, she could feel his cock growing hard. She knew he wanted her as much as she wanted him, but still, he hesitated.

"You've had a traumatic—"

She lifted her breast up and presented it to him. "Suck my nipple."

He growled. "I'm trying to be chivalrous here. A gentleman."

She reached up and fisted her hand in his hair, tipping his head back, so he had to look her in the eye. "I asked you to suck on my nipple. I've bared my body to you in blatant invitation. Nobody here requested a gentleman."

He scowled at her as his gaze lit with an intensity that promised epic delights. "Then I'll stop pretending I am one, and simply fuck you as I've wanted to since I found you in that ramshackle attic. I'm going to claim you in the most elemental way."

And then he wrenched free of her grasp, latched on to her breast, and sucked. She gasped, as first pain and then pure pleasure spiked through her body, arrowing right to her core. Her pussy grew hot and wet and needy as he pulled on her hardening tip.

Then he switched to the other one.

Wrapping her arms around his shoulders, she hung on for dear life as he played with her breasts like a man starved. Lifting them up and together, he took both nipples in his mouth at once and drew on them. Shivers of pure ecstasy pulsed through her body as he drove her close to climax.

"Please," she whimpered.

He released them and looked up at her. "Come for me."

Then he returned to playing with one pebbled tip before switching to the other. Meanwhile, he slipped his other hand down to the juncture of her thighs and stroked. With a firm, sure-handed swipe over her clit timed with the sucking pulse of his mouth on her breast, she exploded.

"Wolf! Oh, God!"

As she writhed on his hand, letting the tug of his mouth draw out her pleasure, she floated. And then she found herself whipped around, lying flat on her back on the bed. When he spread her thighs wide and slipped to his knees, she bit her lip and waited to see what would come next. While always an attentive lover, she didn't suspect that he would have the patience for more foreplay.

To her surprised delight, she sucked in a breath at the first stroke of his tongue over her sensitive tissues.

"Mmmm..." he moaned between her thighs. "So sweet."

She whimpered as he licked all around her, pushing her past her recent orgasm and driving her toward a new peak. Sweat beaded on her chest as she lay there writhing on the bed, pushing her pussy into her husband's face. "More," she demanded, and slid her hands into his hair.

He lapped at her entrance, drove his tongue inside her, and then withdrew to repeat the invasion with his fingers. The familiar tingle that promised another climax teased her core. She dug her heels into the mattress and ground up into the pleasurable assault. Her love for this man blossomed in her chest and made every swipe of his tongue more intense.

And then her orgasm slammed into her. Her body clenched around his fingers as bliss radiated out along her limbs. He continued to lap at her, easing her down from her high until she was barreling toward yet another release.

"Wolf, I need you. Inside me this time."

She all but keened the demand as he continued working her core.

He lifted his head, his mouth shiny with her pleasure. "I could eat you all night."

A soft whimper escaped her. "I don't think I could survive that. Please..."

He rose up and pulled his own nightshirt off as she reached for him. "Scoot back on the bed."

His glittering gaze tracked her movement. The moment she hit the center of the big mattress, he crawled on the bed. All predator, he moved up her body until he spread her thighs. Then he took his cock in hand and rubbed the tip along her swollen folds.

"I don't think I can be gentle tonight."

"Not required. I want to feel you in me tomorrow, even when we are apart."

She couldn't explain such a strong need for him after two incredible orgasms, but there it was. She wanted to feel him battering into her until nothing but the two of them remained.

With a grunt, he slammed into her with one hard stroke.

"Yes!" she cried out, the feeling of him filling her an incredible sensation.

Then he balanced on his arms and started pistoning in and out of her hot core. She wrapped her legs around his hips and thrust up to meet him on each downstroke.

"Amazing. You are the most incredible woman."

His rumbled praise sent a spike of warmth through her.

Then he threw one of her legs up over his shoulder, changing the angle of his entry. Suddenly, he was hitting that sensitive spot inside her that made her scream. And with each successive strike, she felt another climax gathering like a pending storm.

Over and over, he thrust inside of her, binding them in an irrevocable act of love. Her orgasm built slowly, rumbling low in her pelvis as he shuttled in and out of her body. Finally, he plunged inside her again and the storm broke. She screamed his name as she shattered and flew apart. Little bits of herself exploded outward, expanding to fill the room and the space around them.

For a moment, it seemed she hovered there, all the little bits of her, only to reform as she regained awareness of the room around her and her rutting husband. Looking up into his glittering blue gaze, she knew what he needed.

"Come for me, Wolf. Fill me with your seed, and make me yours." The words rasped from her parched throat, and she swallowed, trying to moisten her mouth. "I love you."

And then, with a roar, he slammed deep inside her and came. His whole body tensed up, one taught string of agonized pleasure as he shook above her. When he finally returned to her, he looked down as he lowered her leg and shifted to cup her face. "I love you Jules, and I'll love you for eternity, no matter how scandalous it may be."

The End

Start Reading His Not-So-Sweet Marchioness

Chapter 1 - June, 1862

Lord Flintshire's, cheek exploded in a flash of pain that quickly morphed into pleasure so intense it made his cock stiffen. He smiled at the man squared up across from him in a dark, slightly fishy, corner of London's wharf. The area was as rough and seedy as his five-foot ten-inch opponent whose shoulders seemed to span as wide as the man was tall. With his tattered clothing, tobacco-stained teeth, and the permanently swollen appearance of his ears, his challenger was a sight to behold.

Considering the man's rather ragged appearance, Matthew Derby, Marquess of Flintshire wasn't the least bit intimidated. In fact, just the opposite. "Come now, surely you can hit harder than that?"

The man's eyes widened in surprise. "That's a mighty smart mouth ye' have there. Perhaps I'll pop you in it next?" Flint's pulse spiked with anticipation. He wouldn't be kissing anyone later, but a split lip was a ten-fold gift—until it healed. All around him, the ring of voices acted like a shield, blocking out not only the late-night sounds of London. But the echoes of his dead brother's screams, the disappointed tones of his father's voice, and the throaty demands of his grandmother that he take a wife and continue the family line. Loudest of all was the shame that always accompanied his hunger for pain. All of them melded into a cacophony that trailed him wherever he went. One that he desperately sought to escape any way he could—even through violence.

He circled around to his left, leading with his non-dominant hand for now. Eventually, when his opponent had provided enough pain to satisfy the ugly hunger inside him, he would switch up to his right and end the fight. But for the next little while, he relished what was to come. It was too bad that he couldn't follow the evening's activity up with a rousing good fuck, but such was the life of a courting man.

Even a fiancée in name only wouldn't tolerate such poor form. And though Mrs. Rosalind Smith would only be engaged to him for a short while more, he felt bound to protect her. Damned if that same sense of honor wasn't what had driven him to act as her suitor to begin with when her sister's unwanted beau turned his sights on Ros. The whole situation was all confoundingly odd, considering he had never met her before that night.

Then he stumbled over a loose cobblestone, which jerked him out of his thoughts and back to the fight he was currently engaged in. That was when the hapless chap across from him dipped his right hand—a clear indication he was about to punch—and Flint reached in with a left jab, just catching the man's cheek. The hulk of a man stumbled back a step. While not as stout as his opponent, Flint was easily two inches taller and still roped with muscle. He trained with former bare-knuckle champion Jem Langston, the erstwhile leader of the Lustful Lords, Lord Stonemere. They trained together at the same boxing club. So, there could be no doubt that he kept himself in top physical form.

His opponent regrouped and leaned in with another solid punch to his left eye. The swelling set in quickly, limiting his vision, but not as quick as the man's follow-up body blows. After taking a combination of punches to his ribs and stomach, he decided it was time to make the switch.

The moment he shifted his stance, the stout man hesitated. "Here now, what's this?"

Flint offered up a bloody grin. "Just settling in."

Wary, but clearly still under the misapprehension that he had the upper hand, the man circled around a bit and then stepped in to drive a solid punch to Flint's gut. Except, with his shorter reach, the water hydrant of a man never made it. Instead, he stumbled backward in confusion after Flint's right fist connected with his face in a solid jab. Blood spewed from his opponent's bulbous nose spilling down his chin and onto his shirt. There was a decided nip in the air, making it too cool to be fighting shirtless.

Still on his feet and willing to continue, the man kept moving. Flint stepped in to land another punch, and the goon swung around, slipped in behind him, and landed a rabbit punch to his lower back right over a kidney. Pain lanced through Flint, sending another wave of ecstasy through his body. His cock was half-hard as his knees hit the ground.

Unable to take a moment to relish the feeling, he quickly popped back up to his feet and whipped around in time to catch the stout man with another solid jab to his already broken nose. The man bent over, screaming and clutching his face. At that point, his manager, more aptly his chum, stepped in to stop the fight. "That's it. The man's gotta be able to fight again."

Disappointment crowded out the pleasure and adrenaline coursing through Flint's veins. With a studied casualness he did not feel in the least, he dropped his hands and headed over to where the man holding the wagers stood. The money man growled, low and menacing. "This fight ain't over. Not until a body drops to the stones."

Flint considered the cobblestones beneath his feet and cast a glance back at his opponent. The man shook his head and walked away, clearly prepared to forfeit his money for the cessation of the fight. Flint looked back to the money man and shrugged. "Ain't my fault, the chap refuses to continue. I won, I suggest you pay up what you owe me."

It wasn't that he needed the blunt *per se*; it was the principle of the thing. Also, he used the money for a very specific purpose. With a fierce glare at the money man, he stepped closer. The man looked at him, perused his fine lawn shirt and the tailored trousers he wore. It was obvious, even in the dim lighting of a wharf-side alley, that the moneyman was considering stiffing him on his payout.

"Ah. Ah. Ah. I wouldn't do that if I were you." Flint shook his head.

"Do what?" the man demanded, though, with his thick cockney accent, it was all slammed together into more of a blur of syllables than words. The guy seemed to consider the mauling he'd just witnessed in addition to the fine clothing on Flint's back.

"Take my blunt and run. Appearances can be deceiving, none so much as mine." Where most men looking to intimidate another man would have crossed their arms at that point, Flint was not most men. He was a fighter, through and through. And he was all too aware of the fact that crossing his arms over his chest would only hobble his ability to react in the event the tosser decided to attack or—as he suspected—run.

Suddenly the man's shoulders slumped. "You're a nasty blighter despite all the spit and shine."

Flint grinned and held out his hand. "Just so."

The moneyman handed over Flint's winnings with a grimace.

"If you consider how the fight had turned, I was about to drop him to the stones at any rate. So, technically, you were going to lose whether he fought on or not." Flint tucked the wad of bills away and shrugged.

The moneyman merely grumbled about hoity-toity lords and their highfalutin ways as he melted into the shadows and disappeared. Most of the crowd had dispersed during their little exchange, so Flint grabbed his coat from the boy hovering nearby who held it. At the flip of a half-sovereign, the kid grinned, caught the metal disc, bit it, and then melted into the back-alley shadows.

The Market was unusually quiet when Flint strolled through the front door. In contrast, his body still hummed with the residual pleasure, pain, and adrenaline cocktail from his fight. Normally, he would have happily headed upstairs to work off his excess energy with one of the women who either frequented or worked at the notorious London brothel. But now, he had Ros to consider. He was many things, but one of them was not a cad.

Hoping to find Linc and Arthur having a drink, as opposed to other less suitable activities, he made his way up the grand staircase and down the hall to the blue room. His injuries were beginning to make themselves known. In fact, he was sure he had some bruised ribs, and his eye was quite swollen, which made the stairs a bit of a welcome challenge. Happily, he found his friends sans any female company. Pouring himself a whisky, he sat down with the duo.

Linc whistled as he looked him over. "Holy shite! You took a walloping tonight."

"I needed one." Flint snorted. "Besides, I think it probably looks worse than it really is."

"I don't know. You look pretty worse for wear." Both of Arthur's brows rose in punctuation. Then he took a great gulp of his drink and slammed the empty glass down. "Why do you do it, Flint?"

Linc grew quiet as Arthur's question lingered in the silence. Flint groaned internally. There was no good answer to that question—certainly none he wished to discuss—and though he knew what his friend was asking about, he decided to play stupid. "Do what?"

"Come on, chap, you know what I'm asking. Why do you fight?" Arthur stood up and sauntered over to the sideboard where the bottles of liquor were ranged. He poured himself another drink and then returned to the table.

Flint considered how best to answer that question. Stone and Cooper had never asked him why. They'd merely accepted that this was part of who he was. It was possible they simply understood what drove him a bit more than the others. As for Linc and Wolf, perhaps they never asked because the others hadn't? But Arthur was new to their group, and so clearly, curiosity had gotten the best of him.

"Why not?" Flint tossed out the flip response in hopes it would suffice. There were no words to fully explain why he fought. Why he needed the pain. Why it felt so damn good. So he'd long ago quit trying to find them.

Arthur sighed. "Bloody hell. If you don't want to talk about it, simply tell me to shut up. No need to be an arsehole about it."

"Then shut up." Flint tried not to glare, but between being denied the release of sexual pleasure after a good beating and the uncomfortable brush with an inner truth he'd long avoided, he wasn't feeling very chipper at the moment. His faux engagement to Ros had utterly disrupted his usual routine. He was fairly certain that any woman would take exception to her fiancé—even a decoy fiancé—having sex with another woman. But his current limitations were soon to be removed now that Lady Julia Wolfington, Ros' sister, was happily and safely married to one of his best friends. Ros simply had to break off with him at one of the upcoming balls. With his reputation already blackened of his own doing, the plan was for her to break off their association.

Now, he just had to keep his hands to himself long enough to allow her to do what needed to be done. Unfortunately, that small task was proving harder and harder to accomplish. Despite being more than aware of how inappropriate he was for a woman as sweet as Ros, something deep inside him wanted to possess her, to strip her naked, and show her all the ways he could pleasure a woman. After all, he was one of the notorious Lustful Lords.

Linc leaned over and slapped the back of Arthur's head. "Don't be a nosy nit. He doesn't hurt anyone who doesn't willingly sign up for it. Besides, watching Flint fight is a thing of beauty. The man is poetry in motion."

Flint rolled his eyes at his silver-tongued friend, who had a flare for the dramatic. A ruckus down the hall saved him from responding. The noise proved loud enough to draw the three of them out of their private retreat.

He was the first to the door and opened it, but Linc and Arthur were right beside him. Two doors down, a half-naked man stood in front of a cloaked woman. He leaned forward and then away before listing to the right. He was so obviously inebriated, it was laughable. But the woman was still clearly in distress, what with the way she was pressed against the wall.

With his cock hanging out of his trousers and no shirt to cover the gentle swell of his stomach, the drunken man lurched toward the woman. "Come on, luv. Come join us."

"I told you no. Now, take yourself back into your room this minute." The woman's voice carried down the hall and all but punched Flint in the face.

Ros? What the devil is she doing in The Market?

His gut twisted. Who the bloody hell was she here to see? Not him, since she was not aware he had planned to visit this evening. As far as she was concerned, he had plans with Linc and Arthur. And he had not indicated *where* those plans were to take place. But he would have thought that her assumptions on the matter would have leaned more toward White's than a house of ill repute.

With a growl, he stepped free of the doorway. He recognized the man as Lord Calhoun, a harmless drunk, really, but he did tend toward a bit of exhibitionism when the drink was on him. "My lord, I believe one of your companions is calling for you."

Surprised by his interference, Lord Calhoun looked at him in confusion for a moment, then turned and walked back into his room and shut the door. Whether the man retreated as a result of Flint's suggestion or Calhoun's recognition of him made little difference, though his penchant for violence was well known. Flint's goal had been achieved.

Ros turned to face him. "There you are. I've been looking for you for nearly a quarter of an hour!"

Can't wait to read the rest of the book?

About the Author

Sorcha Mowbray is a mild mannered office worker by day...okay, so she is actually a mouthy, opinionated, take charge kind of gal who bosses everyone around; but she definitely works in an office. At night she writes romance so hot she sets the sheets on fire! Just ask her slightly singed husband.

She is a longtime lover of historical romance, having grown up reading Johanna Lindsey and Judith McNaught. Then she discovered Thea Devine and Susan Johnson. Holy cow! Heroes and heroines could do THAT? From there, things devolved into trying her hand at writing a little smexy. Needless to say, she liked it and she hopes you do too!

Find all of Sorcha's social media links at
link.sorchamowbray.com/bio
~
or scan the QR Code

Read the Whole Series

His Wanton Marchioness
A Lustful Lords Novella

She waited her entire life to be married, and she refuses to let anyone interfere with her happiness...not even her new husband.

Elizabeth Grafton, the Marchioness of Carlisle just married the man of her dreams. Or he was. Now, he barely spends time with her. But most disturbing, he comes to her bed under the cloak of darkness—the man won't even light a candle!—and insists she keep her nightgown on until he leaves.

Alexander Grafton, the Marquess of Carlisle is deeply, madly in love with his wife. But, he wants to do things to her that a man could only do to his mistress. He's struggling to keep his baser instincts in check, and that was before his wife decided to seduce him. If she knew what he really wanted...she'd run away.

Armed with "professional" advice, Elizabeth sets out to thwart all of her husband's best intentions and show him just how shameless she can be. Can her wanton nature tempt her husband, or will he win their battle of wills?

His Hand-Me-Down Countess
Lustful Lords, Book 1

His brother's untimely death leaves him with an Earldom and a fiancée. Too bad he wants neither of them...

Theodora Lawton has no need of a husband. As an independent woman, she wants to own property, make investments and be the master of her destiny. Unfortunately, her father signed her life away in a marriage contract to the future Earl of Stonemere. But then the cad upped and died, leaving her fate in the hands of his brother, one of the renowned Lustful Lords.

Achilles Denton, the Earl of Stonemere, is far more prepared to be a soldier than a peer. Deeply scarred by his last tour of duty, he knows he will never be a proper, upstanding pillar of the empire. Balanced on the edge of madness, he finds respite by keeping a tight rein on his life, both in and out of the bedroom. His brother's death has left him with responsibilities he never wanted and isn't prepared to handle in the respectable manner expected of a peer.

Further complicating his new life is an unwanted fiancée who comes with his equally unwanted title. Saddled with a hand-me-down countess, he soon discovers the woman is a force unto herself. As he grapples with the burden of his new responsibilities, he discovers someone wants him dead. The question is, can he stay alive long enough to figure out who's trying to kill him while he tries to tame his headstrong wife?

His Hellion Countess
Lustful Lords, Book 2

A duty bound earl and a jewel thief might find forever if he can steal her heart...

Robert Cooper, the Earl of Brougham must marry in order to fulfill his duty to the title. He's decided on a rather mild mannered, biddable woman who most considered firmly on the shelf. But, her family is on solid financial ground and has no scandals attached to their name.

Lady Emily Winterburn, sister of the Earl of Dunmere, is not what she seems. With a heart as big as her wild streak she finds herself prepared to protect her brother from his bad choices, even if it means committing highway robbery. But marrying their way out of trouble is simply out of the question. What woman in her right mind would shackle herself to a man, let alone one of the notorious Lustful Lords?

Cooper's carefully laid plans are ruined once he must decide between courting his unwilling bride-to-be and taming the wild woman who tried to rob him—until he discovers they are one and the same. And when love sinks its relentless talons into his heart? He'll do anything to possess the wanton who fires his blood and touches his soul.

His Scandalous Viscountess
Lustful Lords, Book 3

Once upon a time, a boy and a girl fell in love…but prestige, power, and a shameful secret drove them apart.

Julia fled abroad after the death of her husband, Lord Wallthorpe. She has finally returned to England, but little has changed.

Except for her.

As a dowager marchioness, Julia lives and loves where she pleases. And the obnoxious son of her dead husband does not please. But what can an independent woman do? Why, create a scandal, of course!

Viscount Wolfington is no stranger to the wagging tongues of the ton. Between being a Lustful Lord and the scandal of his birth, he learned long ago that society had little use for him. So when he walks into The Market and finds the woman who once stole his heart being auctioned for a night of debauchery, he jumps at another chance to hold her—even for just a single night.

As Julia and Wolf unravel their pasts, will villainy win again, or will love finally conquer all?

His Not-So-Sweet Marchioness
Lustful Lords, Book 4

He's shrouded in shame, fighting with his demons in the shadows. Until she sets her sights on him…

Mrs. Rosalind Smith once followed her heart and love to the battlefield and left a widow. Spending the remainder of her life alone is enough... until she meets a man who's need for pain sparks an answering flame deep within her soul.

Matthew Derby, the Marquess of Flintshire is a fighter, it is all he's known since childhood. Throwing his fists is the only way to keep his need for pain at bay, and a certain gentle woman off his mind. She deserves a better man than him—Lord or not. Though when faced with the prospect of losing Ros, Flint realizes he has found something to fight for...something to live for.

To Ros' dismay, everyone around her believes her demeanor too sweet for someone like Flint. When his world begins to unravel and his dockside violence bleeds into the drawing room, a shocking family secret won't be the key to all the answers. Questions remain, can he solve the mystery, tame his dark needs, and still win Ros' heart?

His Reluctant Marchioness
Lustful Lords, Book 5

A notorious woman must rely on the devil himself for help. Too bad she learned long ago never to trust anyone...

Frank Lucifer is having one hell of a week. His gambling hell is short staffed after firing his floor manager, and his half-brother has offered him a title—one he doesn't need or want. Then the woman he's obsessed with dismisses him from her bed, and the problem is he doesn't know who the hell she is.

Mistress Lash has her hands full. Her apprentice is missing under sinister circumstances, and Scotland Yard refuses to lift a finger. A liaison with Frank Lucifer—however attractive she finds him—is something she no longer has time for. Besides, someone should take the arrogant rake down a peg or two.

She sets out to find her apprentice on her own, but everywhere she turns, up pops Lucifer. He's following her, and she's growing suspicious about why that is. When he suggests they join forces, she reluctantly agrees. After all, one should keep their friends close and their enemies closer... she's just not sure which he is. Yet.

Working together to find her missing apprentice, she worries about her ability to protect both her heart and her own secrets from the perceptive man. And as events play out, she must decide if Lucifer is the villain she is searching for... or just the devil who haunts her scorching hot dreams?

Other Books by Sorcha

The Market Series
Discover the series that started it all...

In this sizzling series The Market becomes the setting for Londoners of all walks of life to discover pleasure, lust, and even love. But can they do what is required to claim the ones they've fallen for?

Love Revealed (The Market, Book 1)

Love Redeemed (The Market, Book 2)

Love Reclaimed (The Market, Book 3)

The Market Series Books 1-3 (Boxed Set)

Love Requited (The Market, A Short Story)

One Night With A Cowboy

The One Night With A Cowboy series is a set of short stories linked by cowboys and Soul Mates Dating Service, a dating service with an uncanny ability to match up soul mates. These sizzling little treats are perfect for a quick hot read.

Claiming His Cowgirl (Book 1)

Taking Her Chance (Book 2)

A Cowboy's Christmas Wish (Book 3)

Roping His Cowboy (Book 4)

One Night With A Cowboy Books 1-4 (Boxed Set)

Stealing His Cowgirl's Heart (Book 5)